KICK THE DUST

After three tours of duty in Afghanistan, Liam Andrews is home safe in Queensland. His weekly life drawing class, full of colourful local artists, helps him manage his post-traumatic stress disorder. But he's struggling to open up about a past that still haunts him. Belourine 'Billy' is an Afghan refugee who lost everything before arriving in Australia as a child. She finds joy in her daily swims in the lake. After years of upheaval, she's still searching for a place to call home. But her past makes it hard to trust people. When Liam and Billy meet, they form an instant connection. But will they ever overcome the past? And will it be together?

RHONDA FORREST

---◆---

KICK THE DUST

Complete and Unabridged

AURORA
Leicester

First published in 2019

First Aurora Edition
published 2021

A catalogue record for this book is available
from the British Library.

ISBN 978–1–78782–657–1

Published by
Ulverscroft Limited
Anstey, Leicestershire

Printed and bound in Great Britain by
TJ Books Ltd., Padstow, Cornwall

This book is printed on acid-free paper

To Lauren
Nicole
& Natalie

1

Liam Andrews held one hand over his eyes, shielding the brightness of the sun as he watched a brightly-coloured kite flutter and weave. He squinted anxiously, aware of the rising tension, the quickening of his heartbeat and a clammy sensation on his skin. It had been a long time since he had seen a kite fly and he stared transfixed as the twirling colours flashed above him.

Now that he was back in the safety of his home in Queensland, his morning swim routine, along with his art, were supposed to help him deal with his anxiety. He'd made the changes needed; a mowing and handyman business had taken some of the pressure away and the new property he had bought, which was only a short walk to the beach and lake, had provided a tranquil sea-change. Everything was in place for him to simplify his lifestyle and improve his well-being.

This morning however, familiar waves of fear rolled in and he wrestled with the conflicting notion of where he was. He took short sharp breaths, inhaling the salty air of the lake that lay behind the dunes of Cotter Beach, a tucked away coastal area south of Brisbane. He wanted the spinning in his head to stop, the blurry visions to focus.

A weight crushed his chest and waves of fear washed over him as he closed his eyes. Distorted sounds filled the air and the sand on which he stood moved and swayed, rising up to meet him.

He imagined the sand engulfing him, suffocating and covering his body. Under the sand there would be no pinholes to breathe through and the granules would eventually fill his nose and mouth, finding their way into his lungs that were throbbing with the imagined heaviness. It would be like drowning, except instead of water, a fine dust would cover him and infiltrate his body.

Feeling unbalanced and resisting the desire to run, to sprint over the dunes and escape as far away as possible, he forced himself to sit down. He ran his hands through his thick wavy hair, staring transfixed at the dark strands that stayed on his fingers when he placed them back on the sand. The thoughts he had been trained to put into place were blocked by the images in his mind and a sticky sweat tingled across his skin.

Take deep breaths, think about what you're really looking at. You're home safe in Queensland.

Liam sucked air in through his mouth and pushed it out steadily through his nose. He concentrated on controlling the choking feeling in his throat and clenched his hands together to stop the escalating panic.

Earlier he had enjoyed watching the family who were now flying the kite. A young woman and two small children had sat together and eaten their lunch, their chatter and laughter drifting across the water to where he was warming up for his swim. The young woman usually arrived at the lake alone, and like him, had a regular routine that saw them both swimming numerous laps of the lake around the same time each morning. Sometimes she had her children with her and on those days, she would not swim but instead play on the sand with the young boy and girl.

Liam was amused by her unusual style of swimming and in his mind had nicknamed her the 'butterfly girl'.

Today she was not swimming but had instead taken a kite from her backpack, helping the children assemble the pieces ready for its flight into the sky. The conversation between the woman and the children was inaudible, the wind taking their words in a different direction to where he was further around the shore of the lake. The two children jumped around excitedly, the smallest one, a young boy, indignantly placing his hands on his hips and stamping his foot when she placed the spool into the hands of the older child, a girl around seven, or eight-years-old. The woman bent down and talked to the small boy, who reluctantly clasped her hand, walking with her over to where the kite was being prepared for take-off.

The palpitations in Liam's chest had started then, as the young woman bent down and talked to the children. Her laughter and words lilted on the wind, a sweet sound mixed with the excited chatter of the children, transporting him back to another place, another time. He watched transfixed as she threw a handful of sand into the air, letting it go with the wind. His lips moved but no sound came out, instead the familiar words — 'kick the dust, kick the dust,' resonated, echoed, bouncing around in his mind. A painful tightness overcame his body and he held his head with both hands.

3

The words did not come from those he watched, here today on the sands of Lake Cotter, but were instead echoes from an earlier life, one that no longer belonged to him, but would not let him go. A previous life that had left permanent scars, with repercussions that had to be contested on home ground; tussles in his mind, anxiety, dread, sleepless nights and the depression waiting around every corner for him.

★　★　★

It was seven years since Liam had returned to Australia and it was only recently — perhaps in the last twelve months — that he had truly turned a corner, regaining some of his former self. He had come back looking stronger, more mature and seemingly full of bravado and confidence. However, below the surface of the tough exterior was a damaged, eroded shell of his former self.

His family had rallied around him and luckily been quick to jump on the warning signs that had presented not long after his return. They had stopped him from taking off and roaming the world by himself, removed the bottle from his hand and done everything they could think of to stop his spiral of self-destruction. Instead they formed a tight group around him, making sure he kept every medical appointment, picking him up and connecting him with the support groups nearby and even living with him when it was needed. They had taken turns to ensure he survived, watching over him as he clawed his way out of a deep hole of despair.

The year after his return was the lowest period in his life, but eventually he made progress. Step by step, one foot after the other, he moved through one day at a time, aiming for a distant light that he occasionally glimpsed. Life smoothed out a little, his mind balanced and he even managed to maintain a relationship with a woman he met after his return. After many years he reached the end of what had been a long, dark and twisted tunnel. Looking back now, he knew that his devoted family had saved his life, stopping him from going down a self-destructive path like so many others.

Today was the first relapse in a very long time and waves of nausea wracked his body as the familiar grip tightened around his heart, his ears aching with a pounding noise that reverberated in his head. He wanted to run; run as far away from reality as he could to get rid of the sights and sounds that punched in his head. He rubbed his eyes, looking down at the granules of sand against his feet, trying to control the moment, to kick the madness from his mind.

2

Some of the turmoil in Liam's mind that morning, was because the butterfly girl and her children were of Middle Eastern appearance. Although the children were dressed in western-style clothes, the girl and the woman both had their arms and legs covered, their head scarves revealing only a few fringe curls of dark hair. The boy wore a plain coloured T-shirt, and long trousers that the woman had rolled up for him when they first arrived at the beach. Later that day he tried to work out if the similarity in ethnic origin had accentuated the issues and flashbacks that he'd experienced when watching the family flying the kite.

The butterfly girl came to the lake around the same time as he did each day. Usually they were in the water at the same time, both intent on their swimming, but not too close to each other as they stayed in their designated areas of the lake. They had never had a long conversation with each other over the last two years, however they always greeted one another as they passed on the sandy track that led to the lake. A few words, a polite nod and a smile as they made their way to their individual spots to prepare for the morning swim.

'Good morning for a swim,' Liam would say with a smile.

'Yes, it's going to be a hot day,' the butterfly girl would reply.

'The water is warm,' Liam would add.

'The sun is heating it,' she'd say.

One day the butterfly girl had called out to Liam from a distance. 'Excuse me. Excuse me.' Her voice had reached him as he began to do his stretches.

A set of dark green eyes stared into his as she passed him his sunglasses. 'Thank you,' Liam said. 'I must have dropped them. I would have been lost without them later, when that sun gets up higher.'

'They were on the path. I hope you enjoy your swim.'

They stood staring at each other, an awkward silence between them.

The butterfly girl finally nodded her head before turning to make her way to her usual spot further up the beach. When she turned around to look back, Liam was still staring after her and she giggled, lifting her hand to wave to him.

A chuckle escaped his lips and he waved a couple of times before turning towards the water.

* * *

Sometimes the butterfly girl would arrive before Liam and he would watch her as she thrashed through the water. Her swimming left a lot to be desired, her arms slapping down on the water's surface, her legs kicking vigorously as she made her way to the other end of the lake. It was her habit to finish with a lap of attempted butterfly stroke. He stifled his laughter. Her arms lifted and flapped in an ungainly fashion around her head, before smashing down erratically into the

7

water. After two years of practising each morning she had never improved, the style, the strokes, it had all remained the same from when he'd first observed her.

★ ★ ★

Liam had always loved swimming and it hadn't taken much persuasion from his counsellor to get him to return to the water on a daily basis. The stillness of the lake provided a perfect lap pool, although today he had to force himself to stand up and walk down to the water's edge. Still trying to control his breathing and shaking legs, he adjusted his goggles and strode into the lake. The water closed around him and he waded out further before diving across the surface, arms and legs moving automatically as he began the first of his laps.

Every part of his body felt rigid and he paced his strokes and kicks with the throbbing painful thoughts in his mind. All six foot of him powered through the water, his arms and legs pounding the water in a robotic manner. The words in his head blurred into a tiny voice, slowly disappearing as he concentrated. The sound of the water blocked everything out and his swimming style returned to a skilful gliding action, as he swam lap after lap across the lake.

By the time he left the water two hours later, his body ached, the pains in his legs and arms a result of the madness that had driven him at the start of the swim. His legs were like jelly; the number of laps he had swum today far more than what he normally completed. But the swimming had worked, the pain and throbbing in his mind, the flashbacks and panicky tension in his body had disappeared. In its place was a feeling of control, a tingling of the cool water on his skin and a calm sense of satisfaction.

He stood tall, looking up at the sun that was high in the sky. The warmth of its rays coated his skin and he enjoyed the prickly sensation of salt as it dried on his shoulders. The rest of the day beckoned, and he picked up his towel, walking back around the edge of the lake, past where the children and woman had been playing. A smattering of footprints on the sand and a tiny sliver of red string from the kite's tail, evidence of the family's activities that morning.

A blue headscarf similar to the one the woman had been wearing was wrapped around a rock at the rear of the beach, the wind pushing it, trying to tear it from where it was snagged. He picked it up, the fabric, silky and smooth on his wrinkled palms, a faint whiff of perfume rising from it.

It was the one thing about the woman that confused him. On the days when she came by herself, she was dressed in typical attire for a woman swimming at the beach. Her one-piece swimmers were modest, and she made no attempt to cover the rest of her body or her head. Often, she would lie on her towel after her swim, sunning herself, her long legs stretched out on her bright towel. When the children were with her she wore long trousers or a skirt, arms covered and a scarf such as the one he now held in his hand, concealing most of her hair. She'd play with the children on

9

the sand, usually throwing a ball or a Frisbee back and forth. Sometimes she took them over the dunes to sit and watch the ocean, or walk along the beach. He had passed her once when he was walking. She had been alone and had not seen him as she stood in the shallows, staring out to sea. Today had been the first time he had seen her with a kite, and now, able to think more rationally, he wondered if she had managed to get it up into the air.

A small dog that raced out from a narrow track behind the lake broke his thoughts. It spun around him in excited leaps, furry paws scratching at his legs as it tried to jump up. When Liam picked it up, a tiny pink tongue tried to lick his face and he laughed and gave the dog a welcoming pat before placing it back down on the sand.

Liam looked up and watched as his ex-girl-friend, Amanda, emerged from the bushes. Tall and blonde, she walked towards him, her hands trying to straighten her wind-blown hair. She stopped at the edge of the sand, frowning as the wind whipped the sand around her legs.

Liam stooped down and picked up the dog again before walking towards where Amanda stood, the look on her face bringing back memories of her often surly disposition.

'God, Liam, I don't know how you stand all the sand blowing around down here. I thought you'd be back up at the house by now. I really didn't want to walk down here. Shit, now I've got sand in my shoes, and —'

'It's nice to see you, Amanda. Did you just want to drop Casso off, or were you going to grace me with your presence for a visit?'

Amanda wrapped her hands around the fluffy dog, taking him from Liam. 'I would prefer it if Picasso doesn't come to the beach and he's definitely not to go in the water. I've paid a fortune over the last year to get his coat just the way I want it and,' she straightened a blue ribbon on the top of the dog's head, 'he's really a house dog now. You're just a cutesy, little city dog aren't you?' She nuzzled her face into the dog's white curly coat, Picasso responding by squirming in her arms.

Liam said nothing, knowing it was no use arguing. He had split from Amanda over a year ago, however they still occasionally spoke on the phone. Her new job often involved long stints overseas and Liam was the only person she trusted with the care of her beloved dog. He had, after all, been the one who had surprised her on her birthday a couple of years ago with the tiny bundle of fur. Even though Liam ignored many of her demands for the care of Picasso, she knew he would take care of him and make sure he was fed and warm at night.

Liam was doubtful if Amanda had ever actually been in love with him or if it had been more of a physical attraction. Often he had agreed with her, just to keep the peace. That was of course when he was thinking rationally. Throughout the two years they were together there had been many times when Liam had been stubborn, unreasonable and had put up a brick wall. An impenetrable barrier that pushed them further apart. Amanda liked things to go the way she wanted and although Liam was sometimes compliant, at different times he completely disagreed and then there was no budging him. Before long, what had once been rational debates escalated into infuriating heated discussions, culminating in huge arguments, often resulting in Liam disappearing for days on end.

Amanda was possessive and Liam had often thought she stayed because she couldn't stand him being with anyone else. Even though they were no longer together, her comments verged on telling him how to live his life and reminding him she was the best thing that had ever come his way. She wasn't in love with him, but he could tell there was some connection or control she liked to think she still had over him.

Liam had taken on a new purpose in life since they parted and although she would still suggest different ideas or enquire into any relationships he may be involved in, she trod warily. He had grown stronger in mind and it wouldn't take much for him to avoid any communication between the two of them.

Amanda remained connected, planning his art exhibitions and ensuring there was no one else who might take her place. Once she had been the central figure in his life. When she posed, and he painted, his total attention focused on her and whatever she wanted or needed at the time, she had received.

Liam's family had found Amanda to be aloof. They had, however, kept their thoughts to themselves, relieved to see him enjoying life and no longer struggling with so many conflicts of the past. Amanda only just tolerated 'his interfering family', and never made a connection with any of them. She showed jealousy to anyone else he was drawn to and went out of her way to avoid family gatherings or social events. She did acknowledge though, that they were more helpful than she was, when the darkness seeped in and wrapped around his mind.

For the first couple of years she ensured everything went the way she wanted. The relationship had been steady sometimes, however as Liam began to recover he started to focus on what he actually wanted in life. Their love of art had brought them together and Amanda had been the one who had pushed his painting career to where it was today. But the lifestyle she wanted was not what he was chasing, and slowly but surely, their lives began to take different paths.

After they separated, Liam purchased a run-down property not far from the beach. Amanda had tried to interfere in the decisions he was making, but Liam had taken on a new lease of life and stood firm on his choices. Eventually Amanda also moved on, although arrangements already made for an exhibition had kept them in contact. Liam looked at her now. No doubt it pleased her that he was still single, and she didn't have to vie with anyone for his attention when they were together.

3

The two of them walked along the path that led to the property, Amanda cuddling Casso as she walked ahead. She stopped when she got to the first small shed, passing the dog to Liam so she could hose the sand from her feet.

'God, I was only down there for a minute and I feel like half the beach is on my clothes and in my hair. Don't dare let Picasso get that sand in his coat. It'll make his skin itch. He has sensitive skin and my goodness,' her eyes widened, 'where did you get that exquisite scarf from?'

She pulled the scarf from between the fold of Liam's towel, the intricate patterns highlighted by the rays of sunlight behind as the breeze caught it, lifting it into the air.

'Oh, I forgot I had it. I found it on the beach, but I know who it belongs to. I'm going to return it when I see them next.'

'Is there something you're not telling me? Do you have a girlfriend? Perhaps you need someone to look after you.'

'No, I don't have a girlfriend. And I look after myself, you can't really say that you did.'

'I tried my best under the circumstances. You're not an easy person to live with.'

'What and you are? C'mon now.' Liam chose his words carefully, aware that Amanda's nonchalant attitude was just for show. During the time he had been with her, he had continually been frustrated and saddened by her jealous nature and prickly manner towards any other females he had been even remotely friendly with. Even after the breakup she had tried to interfere with his life and he was always careful not to let his guard down and offer her even an inkling of where his life or relationships were headed. A few times he had witnessed an extremely nasty streak in her and he knew much of what she said and did in public was just for show and not a true indication of her personality.

Amanda trounced off in front of him, turning around when she reached a small wooden cabin. She was a stunning woman, her bright red lipstick and large round sunglasses sitting perfectly on a face that was always made-up.

Theirs had been a steamy relationship while it lasted, and he had gone along with her whims, the payoff a pleasurable physical relationship that soured once he regained the ability to stand on his own two feet. It had been his decision to end it and even though she had tried to persuade him to give it another go, in the end she had agreed. Although there were some good memories, the only thing they now had in common or agreed on was his artwork. And this, Amanda concluded, was not enough to keep them together.

'Do you have any new work I could look at? I am after a piece for my new apartment. I realise that I would have to pay for it. Money's not a problem.'

Liam followed her along a rocky path through the cottage style garden, towards his studio. 'I don't think I have anything for sale that you wouldn't have already seen. At the moment all of my work is going towards the collection for the exhibition you're organising.'

'I hope you're getting quite a few together. I've promised them a good variety of your work.'

'I have quite a few pieces that I'll put in. They've been getting in some great life models at art classes, so I've had some good options.'

'Right,' she said, her voice taking on the efficient business tone that he knew so well. 'Let me have a look then.'

'I haven't done the final pieces.' His voice was cranky and he knew she would guess that he was stalling. Liam's studio had always been his own space and it was rare for him to let anyone else enter.

'For God's sake Liam. I need to be sure what's coming so I can work out hanging areas and what other pieces we can bring in to complement your work. I can't go any further in arranging anything until you let me see what's coming. Just a quick look.' As had so often been the case in the past, Liam conceded that it was easier to give in and let her have a look, rather than listen to her whining voice. Besides, he had made a commitment to the gallery and he would see the exhibition through. Therefore, she would need to see where everything was going to go. He had to admit she did have a good eye when it came to setting up displays and her forte was organising other people.

'Just quickly then.' He pushed opened the creaky wooden door, shafts of light from the windows that filled the opposite wall, greeting them as they entered.

'God, what a mess! When's the last time you cleaned up in here?'

'I've been too busy working, painting and going to classes. It's okay. Remember, it's a studio. I like it the way it is.'

A large wooden bench took up an entire wall, its top spilling over with paint palettes, brushes, jars, newspapers, rags and an assortment of oddities that one day may just come in handy. Its surface was a colourful kaleidoscope of artist's wares, to be picked up and flung back down again, chosen carefully during the flurries of work that took place in the sunlit room. An ancient velvet lounge chair covered in dark patterned cushions was positioned in the middle of the room. Casso took a flying leap before snuggling into the familiar soft cushions of the chair. Several easels with large boards propped up on them stood in a range of unfinished states, while finished works on canvas hung in no particular order on the walls. The room was awash with colour. Bright lightshades hung over chunky timber tables, joined by wooden chairs, painted in a variety of different colours. The furniture was complemented by the warm golden glow of the well-worn floorboards, splattered with drops of different coloured paint, unintentionally flicked there over the years.

'Can I look please?' Amanda asked, using her sweetest voice. Liam pointed over to the far corner where the latest finished pieces were.

Stacks of framed works leaned against the wall, their colours hidden by cloth that draped across them. During their relationship Liam had asked Amanda not to enter his studio. He was guarded

17

about his work, preferring not to share it with her before it was handed over for sale or hanging in an exhibition or gallery. His desire for privacy had caused many arguments between them, but thank goodness he had kept it that way, he thought, as he watched her pull away the cotton sheet from the canvases.

She stood for a long while in silence. When she spoke, her voice was loud. 'My God, they're amazing. The tones, the shapes — your work has gone from strength to strength.'

Liam had really come into his own with his art once he and Amanda separated. He had been able to focus, discovering and experimenting with new and creative styles. Without her pressure and clingy nature, he had attended as many classes as he wanted. Even though Amanda had been a suitable model for many of his earlier works, he had revelled in the freedom of painting a variety of women. His latest paintings were done at art class, the women who posed, sitting and standing in a variety of seductive and provocative poses.

Now she sounded sulky. 'Your work has changed. I can see a real difference from when you painted me.' She looked closely, appraising each one, peering closely and raising her eyebrows at some of the more risqué positions. 'You must have enjoyed painting these.' She pointed to the last two paintings, both of a voluptuous red-haired woman who posed with her legs spread slightly apart, her large breasts firm and upright, as she sat on a velvet chair in the corner of a room.

'They're just models to me, you know that.'

'They look like they're enjoying it.' She peered

18

at the woman's face. 'After all, it's not every day a good-looking thirty-five-year-old artist wants to stare at your naked body for hours on end.'

'They don't just pose for me, there are other artists painting at those sittings as well. They are well paid, Amanda, and besides you never minded posing for me.'

'That was different, and I never sat for the entire class. You make it sound like I was just another model to you. At least you always hired a private room at the gallery where I could pose, so don't make out I was just one of a number for the classes.' She walked back and forth in front of the paintings. 'You've really captured the curves and shades in these. How many more do you have to do until the collection is complete?'

'I have another ten months, so whatever I get done in that time will go up. I am looking for something special to finish off the collection.'

'Was I once that something special?' she asked. 'I don't see any bodies here as perfect as mine. This one here,' she pointed to one of Liam's favourites, 'I can see lumps on her legs.' She peered closer. 'That is a vein! Honestly, don't you think it's better if those bits are left out?'

'As I've told you many times, it's not about what *you* perceive as the perfect body, it's about the emotion and story in the piece. That's what makes a painting really something.' His words were impatient and clipped; he was annoyed that she just didn't get it. She never really had. Thank goodness the choice of the paintings was his job and hers was the organisation, sales and exhibition part.

19

'Right then, don't forget to let me know when it's all ready to go. I'd love to see them all together under proper lighting.' She walked back over to the couch and picked up Picasso, her tone changing as she swung back into bossy mode. 'I have the dog dinners in the car. God knows, you probably wouldn't buy the right food. His bed and coat are there too and I have a list here of his other requirements.'

Liam covered the paintings before following Amanda through the door and up to the house. He silently counted to ten, holding on to his patience, waiting until she was finished nagging and telling him what he needed to do.

Holding Picasso high in the air, he breathed a sigh of relief, waving a little too excitedly as her red convertible drove slowly out of the driveway, rounded the bend and disappeared from sight.

'No, of course he wouldn't let the dog in the mud, or feed it scraps. No, he knew the dog wasn't allowed at the beach, or down in the bush and no, definitely there would be no paint splattered on him this time and he would stick to the routine and make him sleep with the dog-coat on, in his own designer doggy bed that had cost a fortune.

'Six months of freedom, Casso! Just you and me.' Liam threw the little dog into the air, catching him on the way back down, before setting him gently onto the ground. Casso twirled around chasing his tail before yapping loudly and then running back and forth through the muddy puddles lining the driveway. Leaping like a rabbit, he bounded through the long grass that flanked the edge of the lawn before rolling in the dirt that made up the newly-dug vegetable patch. Liam smiled and turned back along the path, the dog still running wildly around the yard, the blue ribbon left behind, floating in one of the puddles. He whistled once and Casso stopped in his tracks before jumping over a log and racing towards where Liam stood. He wagged his tail nonstop and faithfully trotted behind Liam into the house. 'You and me are going to have a good six months,' Liam said as he shut the door firmly behind them.

4

Even as a small child, Liam had drawn. His school notebooks and pencil cases were a testimony to the fact that wherever there was a flat space he would create a picture to decorate it. At school he had often been in trouble for drawing when he was supposed to be doing something else. Any spare second alone, or whenever he tuned out from the lesson, his hand would move compulsively across paper, creating a picture, a transfer from his mind to the page.

His mother, Jean, had been an artist and Liam's earliest memories were of sitting on the floorboards of the family's seaside cottage, looking at the array of jars filled with different colours of thick paint. He could still remember the feeling when he dipped his brush into the rich oils, his mother showing him how to wipe the excess off, before layering it onto the surface in front of him. He had felt the excitement back then as the colours on the brush formed a picture; a rolling texture on the canvas that he could run his tiny hand over once it had dried.

Her hand had often guided his across the painting area and he recalled the smoothness of her touch when she wiped his hair away from his eyes or stroked his arms when she held him. Her voice had been soft and her nature gentle, always patient when talking to him and his three older brothers. That was before the time that Liam thought of as, 'the sadness'. A time where the once noisy, boisterous home had filled with a heavy gloom; sorrow filling every corner of the house as his father, John, tried to not only cope with the fact that he was now a sole father to four young boys, but also that the love of his life had been taken from him, succumbing to the insidious cancer that had stolen her away from them forever.

Liam had been six when she died and his memories of her had faded over the years. Thank goodness there were boxes of family photographs as well as the stories his older brothers loved to share. The family had knitted together tightly and his dad, who had never remarried, had devoted his life to bringing up the four boys, and as he often liked to remind them all, he'd done a bloody good job.

Although their mother's death had left a gaping hole in their lives and there had been a period of great sorrow, John, following his wife's wishes, made sure there was still plenty of laughter and fun for their young family. With four boys in the house it was never going to be any different and the years had been full of the usual pursuits that went with active and sports keen youngsters. Life continued, and the boys had turned into young men, all with their own different strengths and qualities. Now all of them, apart from Liam, had their own partners and lives, their homes scattered across the country, but all still in constant contact with each other.

The eldest, Chris, was married with three children and lived in Western Australia. His wife, Kath, held a special place in Liam's heart. Chris and Kath had been a couple even at high school and for as long as Liam could remember Kath had been a part of their family. After Jean passed away, John immersed himself in his work, spending long hours as a train driver to keep the family income rolling in.

Liam had often been left to his own devices and when he started to head down the wrong path after high school, Kath stepped in and helped fill the void of not having a mother.

Kath had never been in favour of him joining the army and had tried hard to steer him into a range of different careers. Dragging him to university open days, career expos and organising work experience with a local tradesman, she pointed out some other great opportunities available to him. But Liam's goal was set in his mind and there was no swaying his choice. At nineteen he joined up and by the time he was twenty-eight he had completed three tours of duty.

His other two brothers, Jack and Nate, both lived locally. Although there'd been a few steady relationships over the years and at the moment they both had girlfriends, as yet there had not been any weddings or kids.

His dad was right when he said he'd done a good job raising them all. It had been tough on everyone, but his dad repeatedly said that the one thing Jean had worried about was the effect her death would have on her boys. He'd told the boys right from the start, they would work together and come through alright; they would lead happy lives–it had been her dying wish. She would not die in vain and the four healthy beautiful boys she had given birth to had filled her heart and entire life with happiness. She had been blessed, each day filled with their laughter, tears and cuddles and that was how she wanted it to continue. John would know what to do, she'd said. He'd pull them all through.

Over the years John had shared some of Jean's words with Liam. She had written letters that his dad still kept in the top drawer of his bedside table. The words told how much she loved them all, what a good father and husband John was and how she knew he would find the strength to bring them up to be as decent and loving as he was himself. The letters were worn thin now, the writing in the creases barely able to be read, due to being unfolded and folded throughout the years.

Jean also left behind a legacy of love in her artwork. Kath had been the one who had plucked up the courage to ask John if she could go through Jean's paintings that had lain untouched since she had passed.

She had chosen one of the largest watercolours, painted only a few months before Jean's death. The treasured picture, now framed in a beautiful timber frame, took pride of place in John's house. It hung in the middle of the lounge room wall where everyone who came to the house could see it. When Liam had first returned from duty, he would stand in front of the painting, transfixed by the happiness and family unity depicted in the scene. His mother had captured the closeness of their family and unlike many of the photos she had taken, this time she was in the picture, along with himself, his three brothers and Dad. Even the family dog and a few hens scratching in the grass off to the side were included.

His mother stood tall and elegant in a long flowing dress, one hand holding onto a straw hat as she looked down at the yellow patch of dandelion daisies covering her feet. She looked whimsical, as if contemplating the beauty of the flowers, perhaps thinking about how she could paint them later, one bare slender foot with pointed toes running over the top of the blooms. The side of her face was visible, and she wore a contented, happy look as if everything she cared about was with her, contained in the area that was being used to play a game of cricket.

In the centre of the painting was Liam, with cricket bat in hand. His legs and arms were chubby, and he wore, as did his brothers, cotton shorts with no shoes or shirt. It was a perfect summer day, the sky blue; lush leaves on the trees a dark green against the lightness of the cricket pitch. Off to the side a small table nearly invisible under a tray, held a cut-up watermelon, offering cool refreshment on a hot summer's day.

Nate was in full flight, running hard, his right arm high in the air, ready to unfurl a cricket ball straight down the pitch to where Liam stood ready, bat in front of him, eyes focused. Chris and Jack were the fieldsmen and both were bent over, Chris with his hands on his hips, Jack holding his hands out in front, laughter on both of their faces at the thought that the tiny six-year-old Liam would be able to bat to where they stood. John was the wicketkeeper, and Liam always imagined when looking at the painting, that his dad was talking to him as he prepared for the onslaught of Nate's pitch. It was a typical scene of their backyard at the time. In the background the Hills Hoist clothesline was full of clothes flapping in the wind, surfboards and fishing rods were stacked up against the old fibro shed and a variety of colourful chairs with towels draped over them decorated the lawn.

Jean had captured the moment perfectly. This was their life before the sadness came, and it helped them all to look at it now, to remember how good life had been before she left them. Perhaps she had known when she painted it, that her time was near and she wouldn't be there for those precious years: childhood, adolescence and then adulthood. Instead, John had been there by himself and still was to this day, mother and father all wrapped in one. He had done what Jean asked and brought his sons up to be kind, loving and decent men.

5

Liam never fully discussed with his family what he had experienced. It was only once he started getting help that he opened up to the counsellors and psychologists who Kath had ensured he was regularly booked in with. Now, most of the details were tucked away, dealt with by recognising the warning signs and using strategies to allay what built up in his mind. Sometimes when he was feeling low, the effects could be seen in the pastimes that had played a big part in saving him, his art and his swimming. Yesterday at the lake his reaction to the family flying the kite had shocked him. A sudden attack provoked by sights and sounds that triggered memories and deep sorrows.

Today his body ached due to the vigorous swimming. He stretched out, leaning down to pat Casso, who sat patiently at his feet, wagging his tail. The dog remembered that mornings in this household meant beach and swim time and soon the door would open, and beyond the walls of the house was freedom. Places where a dog could dig in the sand, water where he could chase fish and scratchy thick bush to sniff around in.

Liam had already treated him to the rinds of bacon from his plate, a small piece of toast that he skilfully caught in the air with his mouth and, his favourite, the leftover milky tea with honey when Liam got up from the table. Casso tilted his head to the side and watched Liam, who didn't finish

28

the large cup of tea, instead pouring it into the old china plate kept especially for Casso when he came to stay.

Once their breakfast ritual was finished, they would make their way down to the lake. Today, puffy dark clouds bustled across the sky, throwing shadows across the lake's surface as they rolled forward towards the choppy seas that lay just over the sand dunes to the east. The lake was mostly protected from the winds and although its water moved with the tides—draining in and out through a small creek at the far end—it always had a good depth to it. Even at low tide Liam couldn't stand in the middle, and the sandy banks dropped off steeply once you waded in a short distance.

It was a popular spot on the weekends, particularly for families, as the water was constantly refreshed from the ocean. A large grate near the mouth of the lake stopped any larger fish or sharks from entering, making it safe for swimming all year. Although the nearest town was half an hour's drive away, regular buses serviced the area, allowing the town residents access to a peaceful and secluded area. During the week it was usually quiet and often there was only the butterfly girl and Liam who swam in the refreshing waters. Often after his laps were completed he would throw the ball for Casso or walk to the top of the dunes.

When he returned home he completed the next step of his workout. A gym session took an hour each morning, the equipment and weights set out in a shed behind the studio. His weightlifting workout had become an obsession; the powerful muscles that had developed in his body, a result of disciplined training routines.

The exercise session was usually finished by mid-morning, giving him the rest of the day to run his business. He knew it would have been better to start work in the cooler hours, particularly in summer, but part of his recovery was exercise and he wanted the mornings to be slow and relaxed. Lifestyle was the priority now and the rundown property he'd bought was the perfect place to chill out and do the things he loved.

* * *

Today as Liam swam, his strokes were calm; his breathing even, as his arms pushed up and then glided down into the water. His body propelled rapidly across the surface, the water pushing out behind him as he did lap after lap. Casso bounded out from the bushes as he came out of the water, the scruffy dog as usual barking and jumping up on Liam as if he hadn't seen him for months. He bent down to pat the now filthy dog and out of the corner of his eye glimpsed the butterfly girl, today clad only in her one-piece bathers and a straw hat. She must have been in the water at the same time as he had, because her hair was wet, hanging in long, dark strands down to her waist. He had meant to bring the scarf, to return it to her. He would try to remember it tomorrow.

Walking back towards the pathway that led off through the bush, he went directly past where she sat on her towel, a book open next to her on the sand. She looked deep in thought, only noticing him when he was near. As usual he nodded politely, but today she didn't smile back, only nodding quickly, her forehead furrowed as she stared out across the water. Casso barked a couple of times as he ran past her before tangling himself in Liam's feet as they both made their way back to the house.

6

As usual, the exercise regime left Liam feeling invigorated and motivated to begin his gardening work. The physical toil of yard work and handyman jobs kept his mind and body busy throughout the day and he loved the feeling of finishing the work and looking back over a completed yard. The lawns were mowed, trees trimmed and edges neat and clipped. Today there had also been fences to paint and some steps to fix. He stopped only briefly, relishing the throbbing ache developing in his muscles.

Today he wanted to knock off early. He needed to be cleaned up, finished dinner and be ready to go by six o'clock. Art workshop started just after that and he always enjoyed a few minutes before the start of the lesson, to chat with the others in the class and look over some of the work they'd done.

He had been going to the same studio, aptly named, 'Renoir's', for the last year, and had become friends with quite a few of the other artists, mostly all older than him. The modern studio was in the middle of town and ran three different classes at the same time, two portrait classes and then the one he attended, which was a life drawing class. Although his mother's paintings had both people and scenery in them, Liam had always been inspired and intrigued by the lines and curves of the human body. When he first took up painting it seemed only natural to choose the life classes and today his paintings of nude women in a variety of positions were renowned, both in the local area as well as the larger galleries that displayed his work in Sydney and Melbourne.

He was a natural at drawing the human body and these latest sessions had motivated and improved his style, giving him plenty of opportunities to try the different techniques always bubbling away in his mind. When he painted, time slipped past and he was oblivious to problems that had earlier haunted him, instead focussing on creating a picture on the canvas in front of him.

Creativity that was once stilted now burgeoned, and his new techniques produced high quality artwork containing talent and emotions that had not previously existed. His earlier works showed women reclining in Renoir pose fashion on a chaise longue or daybed, their private areas hidden behind a curvaceous hip or leg positioned just so. More lately though, he had thrown caution to the wind and painted women in all sorts of positions, not worrying about what was or wasn't exposed. The experts and art lovers had commented in reviews and gallery writings that his work, although becoming more provocative and revealing, was not crude, but rather delightful and sensual, revealing the true lines and curves of a variety of women.

Tonight was his favourite class and as usual there were about twenty or so local artists in the room, ready for the life art sessions. It was a popular class and each night a life model was employed to sit nude, the artists choosing to sketch or paint in whatever medium they liked. The diverse group of people were mostly advanced in their genre, and the sessions untutored, the director of the studio simply organising the model and making sure everything ran smoothly.

The models who posed, varied in sizes and body shapes. Occasionally the director at the art school would surprise the artists and the model would be male, however most of the time they filled the positions easily with female university students, who had no inhibitions and enjoyed the good money to be made.

Liam walked towards the back of the room, preferring to be at a distance and not have anyone looking over his shoulder as he worked. Those who attended were mostly regulars and tonight just like other nights, two older ladies began setting up to the left of where he had positioned himself. Lottie and Annika had been regulars at the classes from the beginning, and like him and several others, rarely missed a session.

The two vibrantly-dressed women were born in the same year and only last week Liam had joined them for drinks at the local pub to celebrate their seventieth birthdays. They were both loud, colourful characters who admitted to anyone who would listen that life classes were the highlight of their week and the second-best part of it was that they got to mix with creative people with likeminded interests.

They loved nothing more than to openly flirt with Liam and would loudly proclaim, 'Heaven forbid anyone who dares to take our spots next to the best-looking, most talented, man in the room.'

In between focussing on their art, their jibes and jokes would often leave even the broad-minded Liam blushing or turning away.

'It's the best thing about getting older.' Annika would flutter her eyelashes, 'You can get away with saying exactly what you think.'

Although they liked to joke, once the class started the two ladies would lower their voices, only breaking the silence with an occasional whisper to each other. Both were talented artists with a lifetime of experience and concentrated intensely once the model began his or her pose.

Lottie liked to paint in a style of vivid colours, her brush and paint producing luminous portraits that others often interpreted in much paler colours. Her finished work was photographic in detail, the lines and creases of the body on the canvas depicted in intricate detail.

In contrast, Annika's work employed a bold, cubism style that blended the background into the foreground and showed the body and other features from various angles. At the end of the class when her fellow painters gathered around, she would delight in their admiration of her work; her favourite line to them, 'My work is a point of view. If you pick a piece out, it will float all on its own. Nobody, absolutely no-one, can depict the body as well as I do using this particular method.'

Annika loved to stir the pot a little and throw superior comments in the way of the two older men, Rolande and Pierre, who sat on the other side of Liam.

'It has taken a lifetime of practise and my inherited skills to master this style. It is a pity that you don't have even some of the vision that I do,' she would say.

'Good God, Annika. It's not that good. Anyone can paint squares and shapes. The kids at the kindergarten down the road do similar,' Rolande quipped.

Pierre would also add in, commenting on how it would be nice if just for once Annika could relax and do some natural lines. 'Who wants to see a square arse and triangle tits? Seriously Annika, is that what yours look like?'

Apart from all of the stirring and taunting, the group of painting friends was tight, and the teasing taken in good fun. However, if Annika carried on too much or crossed the line about the supremacy of her work, it wouldn't take long for someone to take her down a peg or two.

'Alright Annika, take your brush out of your fat arse and remember those around you who aren't as fortunate to have your amazing talents,' Rolande would tease. His bushy eyebrows raised as he pretended to scowl at her, before turning to Liam. 'She thinks she's the bloody ant's pants, she does.'

Liam would stay out of the banter. Annika was a bit full of herself but her aim was to stir the older men up. 'Just like reeling in a big fat fish.' Her Dutch accent always made Liam laugh, and he smiled as she put her shoulders back, stuck her nose up in the air and threw one last haughty look towards Pierre and Rolande before resuming her painting.

The group of artists had become good friends and although they painted in very different styles, they had great admiration for each other's work.

Tonight, Lottie and Annika greeted Liam loudly, setting up their own equipment before coming over to give him the customary hug and kiss on the cheek. They reminded Liam of thespians from the forties: their faces made up with just the right amount of blush and lipstick, their nails painted in bright red polish, colourful jewels dangling from their ears and large unusual rings adorning their fingers.

Both had their grey hair twisted and wound in a similar fashion to each other, a coiled flat bun sitting high on their heads, wispy pieces of silver hair that escaped the numerous hair pins springing out around their necks.

'You two look like sisters tonight,' Liam commented as he walked behind them, re-arranging some easels from an earlier session.

'Good evening, Liam. As usual such a pleasure to see you here,' Lottie said, a wide grin stretched across her face. 'It makes me feel young just to see you and you look very handsome. That blue shirt brings out the blue in your eyes.'

'He always looks handsome. Why if only I was younger,' Annika added, sending a playful look his way.

Liam passed them a chair each, accustomed to their remarks. Aside from the light banter that flowed back and forth, there had been many other more serious conversations between the ladies and Liam. He had been able to tell them about some of his problems. 'I don't usually share my thoughts,' he'd said one night, 'but it worries me that I don't have strong feelings for any of the women I've met recently. It's as if the love has been taken from me. Perhaps I'll never experience that strong bond that others talk about.'

'It will come, young man,' Lottie said. 'One day when you least expect it, there it will be.'

'I'm not so sure. I like my own space, but I know how much Mum and Dad meant to each other. I'm not sure I'll ever have that.' His voice betrayed his emotions and his words came out shaky and stilted. 'I'm scared I've lost the ability to feel, to love, to care for someone. For a long time I felt numb, even when I was with Amanda. I was on the outside looking in. It wasn't really me.'

Annika smiled fondly. 'You've come a long way since then. Take each day as it comes and your mind, like your body, will recover. You have a strong base with your family and from what you've said your dad has done a marvellous job and all by himself.'

'He did. He gave us everything we needed in life. Not material items, although we never really wanted for anything. But he gave us a solid grounding and all that Mum wanted for us. Yes, he is amazing. I often tell him that.'

Annika's and Lottie's words often did more good for Liam than his therapist's.

Both of them had experienced their fair share of heartbreak and hardship over the years and their advice was practical and soothing. They spoke eloquently and positioned themselves as extremely ladylike and proper. That was of course when the situation suited them. Other times, when it was just him or a few of the others from class around, they let loose. The rude jokes, foul swear words and hilarious stories of their sexual exploits before they were married joined other tales of wild soireéss and party jaunts of their younger days.

'It's so refreshing to speak to a young man who can talk about his emotions,' Lottie told Liam. 'Back in our day, men weren't allowed to reveal their deeper feelings, well not to outsiders. They were told to be strong, don't show emotion and never cry. What a load of codswallop.'

'Bit like these two over here,' Annika said, inclining her head towards the two men sitting on the other side of Liam. 'Thank God, you sit next to us Liam. Apart from the fact I can feast my eyes on you, if you weren't here we'd only have those boring two old farts, Rolande and Pierre to talk to,' Annika said.

Ignoring Annika's loud voice, the two men who were also both in their mid-seventies kept busy, sorting out their pencils and papers, chatting amicably, their jokes already started about what sort of model they could expect. They weren't much older than the ladies, however they were very different in nature; they tended to grumble quite a bit. If something didn't run as planned or their work didn't go the way they wanted, they'd get cranky and swear loudly, causing the three ladies who sat in front of them to turn around and give them, '*that look*'.

'*That look*', as Pierre called it, informed them that the ladies, who were much younger—probably in their late-forties — were trying to concentrate, and Pierre and Rolande's chatter was disturbing them.

Liam chuckled. It was the diversity of the group

that he loved, the different ages and genders making an interesting group of people to work with. They came from a range of backgrounds and social groups, their styles different, their opinions diverse. There was however one interest that they had in common and that brought them together. They all loved art and particularly the creation of a piece that depicted the human body.

7

Tonight, as Liam sat down behind his easel, the lady who was directly in front of him turned around to greet him. She was the oldest artist in the room and sat upright, eager to begin the night's work.

'Good evening, and how are you tonight?' Her bright blue eyes sparkled and Liam felt the warmth of her smile greet him.

He smiled back, always pleased to see her. She was his favourite out of the group and he had developed a steadfast fondness for her. 'Good thanks, Matilda. I hope you're going to behave yourself.'

'Of course I won't, my love, you know me better than that.'

Matilda was almost ninety. Her birthday was coming up and as she told them every week, they would all be invited to a special banquet to help her celebrate. 'The best champagne will be served, and we will dance until the sun comes up.'

During her twenties Matilda had been an entertainer and loved to reminisce about her dancing days. She had been a Tivoli dancer and showgirl in Sydney, as well as performing in a variety of dance shows and live theatre in Melbourne. These days she preferred the challenge of painting the nudes who posed each week at Renoir's studio. Liam often thought that he would like to paint Matilda, not naked, but a portrait that would be full of her colourful clothes, large jewellery and charismatic personality. He would paint her exactly as she appeared in front of him each week, equipment neatly organised, brush or pencil in hand, ready to begin before anyone else had even arrived.

Her hair was gathered up in a loose bun, strands of dark red breaking free and hanging down onto her shoulders. Large red glasses framed her heavily made-up eyes and bright red lipstick covered her thick lips. She always sat up straight, but as Liam observed from sitting behind her each week, she had a lot of trouble sitting still for any length of time.

Often when the model first stripped off, she would turn around and give Liam a look that let him know whether she approved or disapproved of the studio's choice for the night. If she was not happy with the look of the model, she was known to spend most of the night just roaming around the room, standing next to some of the artists as they worked, or more often than not, standing next to Liam, observing his brush as it was loaded up before moving expertly across the canvas. Only rarely did she comment, instead just taking everything in before returning to her position to continue with her painting.

She never held back from making extremely coarse and rude comments about the models, and Liam would shake his head as she whispered to him about the size of the their breasts, or the rounded hips of some of the older female models.

As an artist, Matilda loved bottoms and many of her paintings would be a very detailed painting only of the model's bottom, leaving out the rest of their body. 'I just love bottoms,' she told Liam. 'Look at the roundness, the shapes, the colour of the softness. No two alike.'

Some nights she could be very naughty, and Liam would laugh when she turned around and pulled a funny face, or made a joke.

It was a wonder any work was done at all during the class. But the different personalities had all learned to work together in the same room and for Liam in particular, the nights at art class took him away to a different world.

Tuesday and Thursday nights were a time and place where there was laughter, friendship and creativity. It was a therapy in itself. The positivity and humour of the older women, the grumblings and conversation of the men beside him, and most importantly the beauty of the human body as an art form positioned on the stage in front of him, drew him into a peaceful place. Art classes had quickly become his favourite nights of the week.

8

The model had already started to position herself on the table at the front of the room. Liam glanced at her as he continued to set up. She sat relaxed, her robe wrapped around her as she messaged on her phone, waiting for the artists to get ready. The director buzzed around, checking they were all in position and had everything they needed. He spoke to the woman and the room quietened as she casually took off her robe, placing it on the table next to her.

Positioning herself towards the front of the table, she rested one foot on a slightly lower table, her other leg hanging over the edge. Her back was straight, her bottom large and rounded, and her face pointed over to the right-hand side of the room. Probably in her mid-thirties, she wore her hair up high in a ponytail, the ends of it flowing down onto her back. Liam assessed the lines that ran from her shoulder to the lovely V-shape formed by the way her lifted leg was positioned. Her breasts were large and hung freely, her stomach flat, curving down to a cluster of curly black hair between her legs.

Matilda turned around, her glasses hanging precariously on the end of her nose and gave Liam the thumbs-up. She would be happy, Liam thought, looking at the model's voluptuous bottom that curved around fully to the underneath of her solid upper leg.

Beside him Annika and Lottie had already begun, their pencils moving quickly across their papers. Pierre stood staring intently, transfixed at the curves and lines, and the perfect pose the woman had quickly moved into. Liam wondered if he was trying to read the tattoo that appeared on the side of the woman's torso. The room became quiet, the only sound was of the artists choosing their materials.

Liam liked to look for quite a while before he began, ensuring he had taken in the full picture of the pose before picking up his pencil to begin. In front of him he could already see Matilda's entire large canvas filled with a huge curvy line that so accurately portrayed the shape of the woman's backside. Calmness descended and he began to draw. His breathing slowed, and his arm moved naturally over the canvas, stopping only to change pencils, or to look more closely at the area he was drawing.

Before he knew it, an hour had passed and the woman stood and stretched, her hands drawn high in the air, her stance on tiptoes revealing the full scope of her body. She pulled a robe on and walked out through the back, leaving them all to finish off the work from this first sitting and to have a stretch themselves.

Rolande stood looking over Liam's shoulder as Liam finished off the underside of the woman's leg. 'You've got that going nicely,' Rolande said. 'She has nice lines. We haven't seen her before.'

'No, she must be new. I like the way they find so many different-aged models and a variety of body shapes. Everyone has something to offer, and I just love the muscle tones in the underside of her legs,' Liam said.

'Time for a break.' Pierre joined them both and they stood back to appraise what Liam had drawn.

'We're going out for a smoke,' Rolande said. 'Hate to leave you with all the ladies but we'd be kicked out if we lit up in here.'

'Liam would rather talk to us anyway.' Lottie stepped to the side to allow for the two men to pass her. They both stopped at Annika's canvas.

'Love it,' Rolande said, shaking his head. 'Just love it Annika, although I think you've got one breast twice as big as the other.'

'Get on with you both. I've got to fix that up yet and besides maybe one of her breasts is bigger than the other.'

'It is,' Liam added. 'Maybe not by that much, but one is definitely bigger than the other.'

'For goodness sakes, it's a human body, it's not going to be perfectly even.' Matilda had joined them, her eyes bright and enquiring as she surveyed the different drawings around her.

Annika stood up and stretched, her long slender fingers playing with the strands of hair that had escaped from her bun. 'Do you see the two new ones that came in late? They've gone out the back for a free cuppa, I'd say. The church group has paid for them and encouraged them to join us. I was talking to Jason, the director, and he was telling me their story.'

Lottie joined the conversation. 'He said they don't speak very good English and they need to mix in, you know, find some sort of hobby to keep them busy. I tell you what if you turned the lights off you'd only see the whites of their eyes.'

Liam scrunched his face up in disapproval at Lottie's comments. 'Well, it's good that the church is supporting them.'

'That's because they don't work. They have plenty of spare time to do what they want. The government will keep them and give them everything for free; you know those types always get everything for nothing,' Lottie said.

'You don't know that for sure,' Liam said.

Lottie frowned. 'Jason told me that they'd walked into the wrong class. They're supposed to be in the fully-clothed life art class down the other end of the building. They'd already set up though, and he didn't want to ask them to leave.'

'Well, I don't think it's right that they're here gawking at our models. Who knows who they are and why should they get everything for free,' Annika said.

'You didn't complain when the large African man posed the other week,' Matilda raised her eyebrows.

'That's different. He was educated and spoke quite good English. These look like boat people. There're so many of them out here now. We can't take them all in you know, we'll be overrun before we know it,' Annika said.

'I wonder what the model thinks about two African men staring at her for hours on end,' Lottie added.

'It didn't look like she was worried and really what's the difference if you're black or white.' Liam couldn't help the exasperation in his voice. He loved the two older ladies and usually agreed

47

with many of the topics they talked about. That was not the case though once they started discussing the intake of refugees to Australian shores over the last several years. On more than one occasion he had needed to remind them that they had both arrived as immigrants, and unless you were Indigenous, at one stage you or your ancestors had come from somewhere across the ocean.

* * *

Liam had noticed the two African men arrive. They had come in late and nervously set up their equipment, which he guessed was the generic resources supplied by the studio. Once the class had begun he had only glanced once more their way, noticing their focus and intent, as they also became engrossed in their work.

Now the model returned and began to disrobe, re-positioning in the exact position she had left. It was another one of the reasons that Liam liked these particular classes. They were more expensive than many other places but the models the studio brought in were always practised, and only on a rare occasion had he been disinterested in the person who posed for them. He knew that they were paid well and many of them were professional life models.

Lottie raised her eyebrows and gave Annika a solid stare as the two African men re-entered the room, taking their positions like the rest of the class.

9

Even after the model had finished for the night, put her robe back on and left the room, Liam continued to work. Rolande and Pierre patted him on the back as they passed, commenting that he had done an excellent job in the shading around the girl's legs. Others around him were already packed up and the ladies chatted, their laughter a background clatter to his still focused mind and hand. Eventually he felt like he had completed what he wanted, and sat back, surveying the canvas in front of him.

Someone was standing behind him and he turned to see the two African men chatting in their own language, pointing and talking about his work. They both nodded and smiled at him as he turned around. Liam stood up and pushed his hand forward, shaking their hands as he introduced himself. The men, who Liam guessed to be about the same age as himself, replied, their speech easy to understand, and contrary to Annika's remark about them not speaking very good English.

'I am Nadir and this is my friend Yared. We ask how you have done that shading there?' Nadir said, pointing to the darkness around the girl's abdomen and under her legs.

Drawing on a discarded piece of paper from his art book, Liam gave them a quick demonstration of how he had completed the work. They nodded and asked more questions about the particular method he had used. Liam's style was different again to those who painted around him and he was well known for the expressions and atmosphere that he managed to capture in his work.

It was always about the light for him, and previous life paintings he had completed had fetched good money, the portrayal of emotions and the way he worked the light into the painting leaving the viewer drawn into the exquisiteness of the human body and the elegance of the poses. It was as if he captured what the model might be thinking, the viewer often contemplating what their story might be.

'You have her feelings on the paper,' Nadir said.

'I try to capture both the body and mind. It is what intrigues me. Have you painted before?' Liam asked.

Yared's voice was deep when he answered. 'We were both artists in our homelands, but because of war there is no need for art. It has been this way for many years.'

Nadir peered closer at Liam's work. 'Our journey has been similar. Both of us had to escape with our families from our home countries and travel a very long way until we come to the biggest refugee camp in the world; Dadaab Camp in Kenya.'

Yared's voice was deep. 'We both lived there for many years, but did not ever meet in the camp. One day United Nations came and gathered our families. They said, you are going to Australia.'

Liam listened intently, intrigued by their story.

The Sudanese-born Nadir, was a tall thin man

with long arms that were covered in a variety of scars. His manner was calm and serious and he kept moving around to view Liam's painting from different perspectives. 'My family is from Sudan and my friend Yared is from Eritrea. Both of us walk, walk and walk across different countries to get to Kenya. Conditions were very bad in the camp, but safer than where we both come from.'

Yared was also tall, a solid build and much the same height and size as Liam. A wide smiled stretched across his round face and his manner was friendly and happy.

Nadir and Yared talked animatedly while Liam packed up his gear, their thick voices and deep-sounding chuckles a pleasant and interesting ending to the class.

Before they left Liam asked if he could see their drawings. Yared carefully unfurled his paper, placing it down on the table like a treasured possession.

'I just drew her face,' Yared said. 'I could not take home a picture of her body. My wife would not be happy with me.' He chuckled, a deep throaty noise, his grin stretching across his face.

Liam was sorry that Annika had left. The work in front of him followed many of the same principles that she used, and the abstract drawing was close to, or even of a higher standard than Annika's.

Nadir's drawing was also only of the model's face, the most description where he had worked obsessively on getting her ponytail correct. Hundreds of tiny pencil strokes made up both her hair and her face and Liam stood in awe, looking at

51

the fine, intricate strokes that formed the model's face.

'Both of these are incredible,' Liam said, his eyes wide as he scrutinised the two very different pieces of work. 'Where did you learn to draw like that?'

Nadir's face finally broke into a smile. 'I spent many years as a child drawing. I use anything I can find. The war came and my family had to leave, but I always draw. Sometimes I draw on the ground, or on books I can find. I came to the camp when I am older. Mostly I learn English and math at school, but there is a teacher who likes me and so he gets me pencils and paper. That teacher shows me art. He teaches me pencil art like this.' He pointed to his drawing. 'The teacher stayed at the camp, but when I left I gave him all my drawings. I only brought the ones I had done of my wife. I like it best to be drawing people.'

Yared laughed. 'We have never seen a naked model. Australia has different art rules.'

Liam's eyes moved onto Yared's work. 'So where did you learn, Yared?'

'Much the same as my good friend here. Always drawing as a small boy. Always in trouble from the teacher. When I went to university in Eritrea I wanted to do art. But I must do science and math. I have two degrees in both. Art, I teach myself. But same as Nadir, once I am at the camp, there is no more art for me. I spend the time teaching the younger students English and math. I was in the camp for five years and then came to Australia.' He straightened himself up. 'I have a wife and four children, the youngest one born last month in Australia.'

'How long have you both been here?' Liam was intrigued.

Yared spoke quietly. 'My family have been here now for six months. Australia is a very good place and we know we are very, very lucky. I have not found work though and the care group, they say Nadir and I need help with the problems of being bored. They asked what we like the most and then they send us here. They even help pay for the art.'

Nadir's smile had disappeared, his face serious, his eyes sad. 'We have seen many bad things, both in our home country and when we are travelling to the camp. Sometimes,' he looked up at Yared for confirmation, 'sometimes we are lost and sad. Our wives worry. Our wives they talk, talk a lot to other women. But the help group said because we are not working we need to be busy. Both of us study also.'

'The help group suggested that we come to art school. Now we do not tell our wives that art school is naked.' Yared laughed again, the three of them packing up and making their way to the door.

They stood on the pavement for a bit longer before Liam realised his car was the only one still parked outside. 'Where are your cars?' he said looking up and down the now empty street.

'We walk here and walk back,' Yared said.

'How far?' Liam asked.

'Probably an hour that way.' They both looked eastward.

'Jump in, fellas.' He gestured towards his car. 'You're not walking. I'll give you a lift home.'

The two men who lived in the same street were

grateful to be driven home and thanked Liam, nodding and waving as he pulled away from their houses. He had told them to make sure they came to the same class next week and that they would soon get used to the models being naked. There were so many more interesting shades and shapes to draw when the body was not disguised in clothes. 'I don't draw or paint anything else any-more,' he'd told them, laughing when they asked what his wife thought of his interest.

Their eyebrows had raised high when he had told them he wasn't married.

As he waved them off he looked around at the houses and streets that he had driven through. It had been many years since he had come over to this side of town and he noticed that not much had changed, the area still housing many of the more vulnerable members of the community.

The men's homes were located in the streets that had recently been allocated for newly-arrived refugees. The older wooden houses with large backyards provided enough space to grow vege-tables and plenty of room to play soccer with the kids. The conversation in the car had been primar-ily about the international soccer matches playing at the moment and Liam loved the fact, that like art, sport easily broke down any barriers between different nationalities.

'All of us love soccer. Sometimes there is not much else to do when we were in the camp,' Yared said. 'But, there is always a soccer ball. Every camp kid is an awesome soccer player.'

Nadir added in, 'All my girls play with the boys. They all love the soccer.'

Now as Liam drove through the streets leading back into town he mulled over the events of the night. He followed the highway a bit out of town, eventually turning off onto the road that headed out towards the beach and his house. His mind was still full of the lines of the woman's body, drawn on the canvas that was now rolled up carefully in the boot of his car. He thought about the styles of the others at the class and his mind turned to his conversation with Yared and Nadir. Their grateful approach to their new life in Australia, and their stories about how they came to live in what they described as the luckiest country in the world, churned over and over in his head. He was pleased he had met them and heard their stories, as well as helping out and saving them a long walk home.

It would be a mixture of personalities if Yared and Nadir became permanent attendees at the classes, and the regulars, particularly Annika and Lottie, would need to learn to accept them. Matilda, of course, was always open-minded, and she had previously informed Liam about the nationalities of the different men who she had fallen in and out of love with over the years. She had proudly announced she was going to buy a map of the world and put a pin on each country, designating the origins of the men she had slept with over her long life. She made sure to add, 'Of course I haven't participated in that sort of romp for many years, Liam. But once, oh yes, when I was a lot younger. I loved and was loved by men from all over the world.'

10

The next morning was one of those perfect summer Queensland days. The sun threw its heat across the beach, the warmth permeating Liam's shirt as he walked towards the lake. Casso raced around in circles, the sand kicking up as he dug deep into it, burying his little pink nose into the wet patches at the bottom of the hole he had dug. Now he lay still, his ears pricked up and head turned as he watched Liam enter the water.

Liam kept thinking about Yared and Nadir. They had only touched on their stories as newly-arrived refugees and he tried to imagine what it must be like to arrive in a country like Australia and learn to adapt to the different culture and landscape you had been thrown into. Hopefully they would continue to come to classes because he had found it refreshing and interesting to talk to them. Their artwork was also stimulating, and he was instantly drawn to them as fellow artists, the style of their art so different to his own but of a high standard and intriguing in the interpretation of the human body. He wondered about the art they might have previously done, in another place and different time, a world so different to where they now lived.

Another swimmer passed close to Liam as his strokes carried him across the lake. The swimmer was going in the opposite direction and he realised he had steered a bit off course. When he reached the end, he was close to where the butterfly girl was swimming. As usual her arms smashed down onto the water's surface, both of them raised high in the air before banging down on the water. Her body twisted as she did one of her final laps of what she attempted to imitate— the butterfly stroke. He watched her for a while, shaking his head, wondering how she eventually made it from one end to the other without stopping, or tiring from the irregular and awkward strokes.

Some things just never change, he thought. How could she not make some improvement with the amount of swimming that she did? She had been swimming here for as long as he had, and often swam for longer periods of time than him, but still the awkward thrashing style only moved her slowly and awkwardly through the water.

He adjusted his goggles and started on his final laps, noticing when he passed her due to the amount of splashing from her side. It wasn't the first time that he wondered if he should say something to her, or even just give her a small hint on how to improve her swimming. The trouble was he loved this time of the morning. Swimming in the lake gave him space, time to think and to appreciate the solidarity afforded to him by living in this tucked away area. If he started talking to her he'd have to give more than a nod each morning. It was better to leave it the way it was. It seemed to suit them both.

★ ★ ★

Liam was delighted to see Nadir and Yared at the Tuesday class the following week. He was later than usual and they were both set up and ready to draw when he arrived. Casso had wandered off and refused to come when he was called. Liam scolded him when he found him. He would need to spend some time washing and combing him tomorrow because he was now a dirty brown colour, his fur matted with small sticks and dried up mud entwined in what should have been a pristine white coat. If only Amanda could see her city dog now.

He nodded a greeting to the two men as he made his way to his usual spot. Matilda was straight onto him. 'We're in store for some fun. I was worried you weren't coming,' she said. He looked across to Lottie and Annika who were sitting up very straight, looking expectantly towards the table at the front of the room. Looking to the right he observed Pierre and Rolande both grumbling to each other and he picked up on their conversation. Liam smiled. It didn't take long judging from the reactions around him, that the model tonight was going to be a male. He wondered how Nadir and Yared would react to the change in gender from last week.

The next time Liam looked, the model was already positioned, the room silent as the artists took in the body that was presented for them. Choosing his pencil carefully he began drawing the outline of the young man's body.

The man was sitting on the edge of the same table the woman had used last week. One leg hung over the edge of the table, the other leg drawn up so that his chin could rest on the bent knee.

Matilda complained to Liam halfway through the lesson. 'Conveniently hiding all the important bits!'

The model's body was robust and his arms that wrapped around the bent leg were lined with muscles, long slender fingers never moving as they rested on his tanned legs. The young man stared straight at his captive audience, his dark curly hair that grew to just below his ears finishing off the picture of a very handsome male model. Luckily for Matilda his left buttock could be seen behind one arm, his positioned body slightly twisted so as to give sight of his upper thigh.

Everyone in the room focused and began working silently, even Rolande and Pierre soon stopped their grumbling and became engrossed in drawing the man.

It didn't matter about the perception of what was good-looking and what wasn't, because in every model there were parts that were beautiful, no matter the age or size of the person. Occasionally though, as was the case tonight, the model was exquisite, the lines defined, the skin flawless and the chiselled facial features a joy to look at. The young man also had the ability to sit still and unfazed, in front of an audience that clearly liked what they saw.

The ladies were quick to approach Liam during the break and wasted no time appraising and rating the ease of painting such a magnificent model. Eventually Matilda also joined them. It had taken her a while to put her pencil down and Liam looked over at her work, which had so skilfully captured for once, the entirety of the man's body. 'I need to make it good,' Matilda said to them. 'I think I'll hang this one in my house.'

'So refreshing,' Annika said. 'A well-lined proportioned male body, with no saggy tummy or lumpy bits on the legs.'

'Well, it's not making us feel very special,' Rolande quipped. 'Christ, the joy of being young. To have all of your bits firm.'

'Please spare us the details,' Lottie said, laughing as they chattered, all of them except Liam ruing the loss of youth, particularly the firmness of body and sometimes mind.

Liam waved to Nadir and Yared, gesturing for them to come and join the small group he stood with. When the men hesitated, he went and got them, telling them to come and meet some of the regulars. Lottie and Annika stood back, only nodding and not putting their hands out to be shaken. Matilda had no such qualms and greeted the men warmly, asking their names and making sure they felt welcome. Rolande and Pierre hesitantly shook hands and stood silently as Liam made conversation.

'How are you going with a male model this week?' he asked them.

Yared, as usual a wide grin on his face, answered. 'This is much easier for us tonight. Better to know where we can look and then we can draw the entire body.' The two newcomers looked at Liam's drawing.

Nadir looked closely, his sharp eyes moving over the page, taking in every aspect that Liam had so far completed. 'This is very, very good. I think you show, what is the word? It is, what your thoughts are.' Nadir spoke to Yared in his own language before coming up with the word he wanted. 'You have a lot of motion in your picture.'

Yared corrected him. 'Emotion. I agree. Perhaps different experiences in your life? There is something to read in your work.'

'Thank you. Perhaps drawing is a release for me also. It calms my mind,' Liam replied.

The two men nodded, not asking any more questions. Both understanding that much had been left unsaid. At that moment Liam felt a special connection to them. They had instantly picked up on the emotion that was hidden behind the colours and lines of his paintings; the turmoil and angst that he could rid himself of, when his brush or pencil moved over the canvas and created the picture that he wanted.

It wasn't always about the finished piece for Liam; it was the process of the painting that evoked his feelings. Different outlines, moods and sensations he connected with, or found within the body of the model, travelled through his mind; to be expressed in the colours and pictures that could be found in his work.

At least he had been afforded some moments of calmness between the madness. These two men from such a different world had constantly lived with fear and anxiety for most of their lives. War, lives and families torn apart, the horror and apprehension of what the next second would bring and the inability to protect your loved ones no matter how hard you tried, was embedded in their souls. But, he dragged his mind back to the present - for tonight, it was all about the model at the front of the room and the transfer of creativity to their canvases.

Vying for his attention, Matilda clicked her fingers in front of Liam's face. 'Come on, young man. Back to work. You are a million miles away.'

Soon all of them settled back into their places, the model resuming his earlier pose, the artists once again fixated with trying to perfect the flawless body in front of them. Liam's hand flew over the page, his mind trying to settle back into the earlier calmness and focus of the class. Soon he had forgotten about the earlier conversations, where he was and who was around him. Instead, the exhilaration of creating a piece of work flooded over him and his mind was immersed in the task at hand, blocking out all exterior influences.

11

Yared and Nadir had again been grateful for a lift home after the class and the three chatted excitedly as Liam's car made its way across town. He was fascinated by how the men coped with their new lives in Australia and listened with interest to their stories. Nadir was in the process of buying a second-hand car and was about to sit for his driver's licence for the second time the next day. 'I did not understand the instructions last time. I don't think my driving is a problem, rather the English the man spoke. He said he was from Scotland. I was not sure about the words and I found it very, very difficult to understand. Maybe this time I will get it. My wife would be happy if that could happen.'

Yared had also been busy and had been trying to get work as a science teacher. He had however been unsuccessful in passing the stringent English test to get his qualifications recognised. It had been the second time he had tried and although he was disappointed not to be working in his regular field of work, his attitude was positive. 'Once I was a science professor at the University of Eritrea, but then there were problems with the government. Now I have to get a different job. We are very lucky to come to such a great country and my children will grow in such a nation of peace that gives them a good education.'

Liam felt humbled listening to their gratitude and appreciation for things that he knew most Australians took for granted. He listened intently as they chatted, the two men appreciative of another man to talk to. Yared had made some contacts at the school where his children attended and the following week he was to begin working as a school cleaner, his hours early morning and late afternoons. He was very excited about the new start and Liam smiled as he listened to the animated ex-university professor, extol the benefits of his new role at the school.

Nadir also was looking for work, having been a carpenter in Africa. 'My father built houses for the government and army people. They had big houses. He was a very clever man and he taught my five brothers and me to build. I can construct anything, but I don't have the proper paper to say that. Each time I go for a job, they say, show me the paper. I don't have it.'

'Where are your family now?' Liam asked.

'Most of them are no longer alive. One of my sisters and her husband, they make it to Europe, but my other sister and brothers were killed. My mother and father both passed away from illness. I walk day and night, day and night for many days, weeks and then months to the camp in Kenya. Across countries where many die. Finally, I make it. I meet my wife and then we have children. One day in the camp they come for us and they say, bring your belongings, you are going. It was the best day of our lives and soon we are on a huge aeroplane, across the sea and here we are now. Best country in the world. All my children, they will be Aussies.'

Liam relaxed in the men's presence and admired their English. Yared explained that when you could find a way to learn English you grabbed it with both your hands. 'When you have nothing, and you have seen the worst, education is like a present. We know and so do our children that to get ahead, to find good job, marry, have children and a good life, there must be education.'

Nadir was also philosophical and forever reminding Liam that they now lived in the best country in the world. 'Here the government is very good to us, they help us settle. We can work hard and bring up our children to be very well educated and get a job, perhaps better than us. This is a very, very good place for us to come.'

Lottie and Annika were not so taken with the two new attendees and at the Thursday art class during the week tried to tell Liam he should be careful when driving the African men home on a Tuesday night, and to that dreadful suburb. 'They've seen all sorts of things in their lives, Liam, plus that's where all the terrorists come from,' Lottie said.

Annika thought the same. 'We should not be letting them all in here. We're going to be overrun by terrorists. Plus, they get everything for free.'

'I think you'll find they'll work as soon as they can get something,' Liam was losing patience with the two women. 'And they'll take any jobs. A lot of the jobs they'll take on, our unemployed won't even look at.' He cut his conversation short, ignoring Annika's and Lottie's last words. Instead he immersed himself in the task at hand, readying his equipment, his easel set up in front of him.

Exterior noises were blocked, and he relaxed, happy to see the male model from Tuesday's class back again, this time in a different pose. He didn't really care about the age, shape or gender of the model, as long as they were unclothed so he could rise to the challenge of getting the curves and shadows where they were supposed to be.

12

Work, exercise, and art classes kept Liam busy each week, as well as finding time to finish many of his life art compositions after the classes were over. Most evenings he spent in his studio at home, completing pieces of work for the exhibition coming up later in the year, as well as experimenting with different ideas that were bouncing around in his head. He also spent some time renovating and cleaning out the two small cabins that were on his property. His father was coming to stay later in the year and he always preferred his own space in the smallest cabin nearest the house. Once the second cabin was cleaned up he could make some extra income and rent it out.

'You know you can stay up in my house,' Liam said one night when his father called.

'No, I'm happy in the cabin. It gives us each our own space. I'm really looking forward to coming up to see you. How are you going?'

'I'm going fine, Dad. I've only had one bad moment in the last year, so that's okay. I keep busy and the swimming and art have been the best therapy for me.'

'I'm looking forward to seeing some of your work when I'm there.'

'I have a few new paintings to show you. There have been some interesting models at the art classes and as usual my friends there keep me in good humour. They're a happy crowd and I'm hoping you'll get to meet some of them when you're here. You'll also have to come and swim with me. The lake is perfect, and those morning swims are my favourite time of the day.'

'I can't wait, son. I'm looking forward to the swimming and walking on the beach. I'll see you when I arrive in a few months.'

'I love you, Dad.'

'Love you too. See you soon.'

Openness and saying your feelings out loud were something Liam's mother had asked John to maintain after she had gone. She'd told him she wanted her sons to be able to talk about their feelings and to be able to say, 'I love you', both to each other and their father.

Saying those three words had been easy for Liam to say before he went away. After he had returned though, he had struggled and for a long while the barrier between him and his family had seemed insurmountable and never-ending. He was lucky to have conquered many of the hurdles that had surfaced and was forever grateful for the tight bond he had regained with his family.

It would be great to have the old man with him for a full month and exciting to think about the time they were going to spend together.

★ ★ ★

Art nights came and went and between the classes and working in his own studio at night, Liam was building up a worthy collection for his exhibition. There had been a continuous round of male and female models at classes and tonight they were due for a different one. The previous model had posed for the last two weeks and he wondered what gender the model would be tonight.

Yared and Nadir who were now in phone contact with him, messaged to say they wouldn't be at class tonight as they both had a school function to attend. Liam messaged back. He had finally convinced them to let him know when they weren't coming so he could let the director know. He also didn't mind how often they needed to ring him for help with other matters, or what questions they wanted to ask. Nothing was too much trouble and he was more than happy to help.

Tonight, it was just the regular old crowd and he was surprised when Lottie asked him where Yared and Nadir were. 'They have school functions to attend. They messaged me to say they'd be here again next week. I'm surprised you're asking. I didn't think you approved of them being here?'

'Well, I'm getting used to them. Besides I saw the tall fellow, not the skinny tall one, the other one, well, I saw his drawing the other night when I walked past him. You didn't tell me he could draw like that.'

'You never asked, Lottie.' Liam's reply was short; he was annoyed that Lottie was now interested in Yared's work, when she had previously made no effort to show any friendliness towards the two men.

'You're cranky,' Annika chimed in.

'I'll be fine. I just need that model to get out here and get started. I really need just one last special painting to add to my work. The exhibition's getting closer and I'm looking for the *pièce de résistance*.' He smiled back at the two ladies, unable to stay angry with them for long.

Matilda turned around. 'I took your advice, Liam. That Nadir is a very handy carpenter and in the last week he's fixed my shed and built me a lovely shelter out the back. He also helped me move in and position my new outdoor setting. I'm more than pleased with his work and I made sure I paid him more than what he asked for. You need to have a chat to him about his prices because he's too cheap.'

'That's great. I'm glad he's got some work,' Liam said.

'I've told some of my friends who I play bridge with about him and they've also booked him in for some work.'

'What's this?' Annika came over to them, listening keenly to their conversation. 'I've been looking for a carpenter to finish off our deck. It's not a big job. Why didn't someone tell me that he takes on work?'

Matilda and Liam looked at each other and raised their eyebrows, neither of them replying to Annika, who continued to ask questions about Nadir's carpentry skills.

Rolande and Pierre both sauntered over, all of them trying to fill in time while they waited around for the model, who was running late. They were now fifteen minutes into the lesson and no one had arrived to pose for them.

'God, if no one comes soon we'll have to put Liam up there. Now wouldn't that be fun.' Matilda winked cheekily at him. It wasn't the first time

70

she had suggested he pose for them.

Rolande muttered impatiently, all of them getting restless as time ticked on.

'Here we go,' Pierre said, most of them quieting as Jason the director stood at the front, waiting for them to stop talking.

Jason cleared his throat to gain their attention, glaring at the three ladies in front of Pierre who continued to talk. He stared hard at them until they were quiet. 'There's been a bit of a mix up and the life model we had organised for tonight won't be coming. We have however managed to procure a model who normally works for the clothed life drawing studio. She's only new to this type of work and a bit nervous. So give her a bit of slack, because she's helping us out.'

'We'll be kind,' Matilda called out, sitting down ready to begin.

Liam also moved back behind his easel, eager to get on with the night.

'Oh,' Jason said. 'One more thing, she will be posing clothed. She's not a life model and she won't pose unless dressed. She will also only pose for an hour.'

'That's me out,' Rolande said as he started packing up his bag.

'It would be great if you could all give her a go,' Jason said as he beckoned to the model to come out from the back room.

Liam had begun to also pack up his bag, sorting out some pencils as he got ready to leave. There was no use staying; he would just have to wait until the next lesson. He'd long ago given up drawing fully-clothed models and the idea of drawing a woman with clothes on did not appeal to him at all. An early night would be good anyway; he still had a lot to do before his dad arrived.

Some of the class had left already and Liam watched the three women who always sat in front of Rolande and Pierre picking up their belongings and passing comment on the lack of organisation as they walked out the door. Liam gathered his brushes, stopping when he noticed that the room had gone silent. He looked up to see that others in the class had started drawing, their focus on the model who had taken her position on the table at the front of the room. The two men next to him had stopped talking and Rolande unpacked his pencils, standing beside his easel, staring out the front.

Liam looked up at the model who Jason helped to settle into position. It was obvious that she was new to the job, as she nervously moved a little each time someone coughed or made a noise. Her back was to the artists and she sat with her legs tucked under her, her bottom resting on her feet. Her arms were stretched out to the side of her body, then bent upwards, creating a straight line across her upper arms and shoulders. Her hands held the straps of her dress on her shoulders, as if she had just thrown the garment on and was about to tie it at the back. The dress was cream and hung down loosely, covering her bottom, her front and the top of her legs. The top part of her back was visible due to the small split that opened up from the shoulders down to the arch in her lower back.

Liam inhaled sharply, the beauty and lines of

her slender back drawing his attention, the curves of her arms, delicate but defined as she held them up, accentuating the tone of her shoulders. Her dark hair was drawn up in a bun high on her head and her face gazed slightly downwards, only her neck and side of her chin visible. The soles of her feet poked out from under the coils of fabric that wrapped under her bottom.

Never before had Liam been so drawn in by the purity of a model's body, the curves that twisted and turned. He stood staring for a long while before picking up his pencils. Slowly and carefully he began to sketch an outline on his paper.

He positioned himself to get the best view, his hand moving across the paper, stopping only momentarily from time to time as he tried to take in and reproduce the beauty and innocence of the pose.

Matilda also had been drawn in by the model's stance, however she had not begun drawing, but instead came to stand behind Liam. There was of course no naked bottom for her to draw, as the woman's lower half was covered by the soft flowing fabric, leaving the observer guessing what the skin below might look like.

'If only you could see the look on your own face.' Matilda whispered to Liam, watching him intently as his sketch started to develop. 'Your eyes have not left the young woman's back and already I see a passion in the lines you've drawn.'

Liam whispered back. 'I hope being a novice, she doesn't get tired or move too much.'

'She's doing well so far, she hasn't moved at all and her posture is delightful!' Matilda stepped back, looking at Liam's work from a distance.

Liam worked quickly, worried that the exquisite pose the woman held would change. He wanted to capture this first moment, the nervousness, naivety and loveliness that flowed from her stance. As he worked he stared harder, his eyes finally moving away from the small part of her back that was visible, up over her shoulders and to the side of her face. There was something familiar about her and he searched his memory, wondering if she had perhaps posed for the classes previously. Something jogged in his mind and then he realised where he had seen her before. The woman with the beautiful back, posing on the table at the front of his art class was the butterfly girl. His hand stopped moving and he looked harder, trying to peer around to get a better look at her face.

Matilda watched him with interest, moving back next to him, intrigued at his reaction. 'What is it, Liam?'

'I know her. Well, I've seen her before. She swims at the same place as me,' he whispered to the older lady.

'Her body is incredible. I feel quite flushed looking at the innocence of her pose. Sometimes it's not what we can see, but that what we cannot see, that brings us to life and stirs the emotions.' Matilda's eyes were wide, and she shook her head, watching also the reactions from Rolande and Pierre. Both of them normally unhappy and quick to complain about any changes in the schedule, were also both absorbed in their drawings, neither taking their eyes away from the model or the picture taking shape on the paper in front of them.

Lottie and Annika both looked over to Matilda, Annika giving the thumbs-up as they also both bent over their work, intent on the task. The entire class who had stayed were absorbed by the beauty of the woman seated on the table at the front. The room remained silent, apart from the scratching of pencil on paper.

Liam had forgotten that there were other people around him as he drew. This was the piece he had been looking for and one of the most pleasing sketches he had done so far. Who knew, that a model had been there in front of him every day for the last two years, and that he had failed to notice. He thought hard about that as he worked, reasoning in his mind that usually the girl was thrashing around in the water, often her arms and body were covered, or if she was in her swimmers, he purposely never let his gaze linger, instead ensuring that the proximity and regularity of them swimming at the same place did not interfere with his purpose of the therapeutic morning swims.

Now, the purpose was different, and he observed her closely, taking in the elegance of her pose, allowing himself time to stare as long as he wanted, aware that she could not see any of the artists working behind her. As the hour came to an end he sketched quicker. The vision in front of him would soon disappear and he wanted as much down on his paper as possible. The butterfly girl had only moved a tiny bit over the last hour and the director spoke to her briefly before announcing that she was happy to go for another ten minutes so that they could all finish their work. Liam thought how he would have loved to have asked if she could just open the dress up a tiny bit more at the back, so as to expose the curve that formed in the small of her back. He held his words though as he finished up his work for the night, aware that this was also the same woman who often covered her arms, legs and head.

Her pose tonight added further confusion to the way that he had seen her present herself in the past. In the mornings at the lake she sometimes covered up and sometimes she didn't. Occasionally she wore the clothes that Islamic women wore and then at other times swam and walked around in a swimming costume, sunbaking and relaxing much like any other Australian beach-loving woman. Now she was posing for life art classes and although fully clothed, was revealing some of her back and shoulders, as well as her arms and legs. *Strange,* he thought, *very strange.*

He sat down behind his canvas watching as Jason helped her from the table, ensuring she didn't fall as she untwisted her legs from what must have become a very uncomfortable pose. Keeping her back to them, she dangled her long copper legs over the far side of the table, rubbing them to get the pins and needles from them. Her back was still visible, and Liam held his breath, unable to draw his eyes away from the movements of her body as she stood up and made her way out of the room. She never turned around, or came back to see any of their work, instead simply disappeared out through the back door. Often the models would throw their robe on at the end of the lesson and take great pleasure in seeing how the artists had portrayed them. But not tonight. Just a quick word with Jason and she was gone.

Everyone around Liam began packing up, many of them stopping to look at his drawing as they left.

Lottie peered closely at the shading Liam had so successfully completed. 'My God, you've nailed the tenderness in her pose. I almost feel like I want to stroke my hand along her back, that is, the one on your paper.'

Liam continued to stare at his drawing.

'Goodnight, Liam.' Annika joined in. 'You will be dreaming about that back. There's something very erotic about that girl, and goodness me, I feel quite hot.' She waved her hand rapidly in front of her face, mimicking actions as if she had a fan in her hand. 'And you've captured it perfectly in your drawing.'

The entire class had gathered around Liam's drawing, all recognising the special qualities that were captured on the paper. Jason also came over, his eyebrows raised high when he saw Liam's work.

'I think that's the best piece of work I've seen you do. Will you make a painting out of it?'

Liam's eyes were still riveted on the drawing. 'When does she come back again?'

'Well, she probably won't. It took me a lot of talking and cajoling with a much larger payment than usual to get her to even walk into this room. There was no way that she would show any more skin than what you saw. Sorry, but that was a one-off.'

'What's her name,' Matilda asked. 'She looks a bit Middle Eastern, like perhaps from Turkey.'

'Her name's Billy,' Jason replied.

Annika and Lottie spoke together. 'Billy?'

'Yes,' Jason said. 'Billy.'

'She'll be Greek for sure with that dark hair and olive skin. Or maybe Italian,' Lottie said.

Matilda had packed up and now begun walking past them. 'Cheerio, see you all on Thursday.'

'Wait for us,' Rolande said. 'We'll make sure you get to your car, Matilda. Don't you walk out there by yourself. See you all Thursday.'

Soon there was only Jason and Liam in the room. Liam had purposely waited until the others had left because he wanted to talk to Jason by himself.

'I'd really like that woman, that is Billy, to do some modelling for me. I've got the exhibition coming up and I think that after tonight I know exactly the piece I want to finish it off. She's great Jason, the lines, the way she holds herself. My God, the beauty just in her back alone. Can you imagine the lines in the rest of her body?'

'She won't pose for life drawing, Liam. She's only just started, and it has to be fully-clothed and covered up. I know the other classes wanted her to wear something flimsy the other week and she just wouldn't be in it. I don't want to scare her off. Beautiful models like her aren't easy to find. She just has that edge of innocence.'

'I need to draw her again. I would like to do a range of paintings. We didn't even get to see her face properly. Do you know anything about her?'

'A friend of mine originally told her to ring me. That was for the other classes though. I didn't really understand the full story, but I know she wasn't keen on the idea of posing but said she'd do it if she didn't have to show too much of her body. My friend knew she was short of cash and told her the sort of money she could make. That's why I thought if I offered her extra she'd do the class for us tonight. She was adamant that she'd be wearing a dress and I wasn't to ask her to show any more skin than that. I figured that at least some of you would be happy with drawing her. She holds a beautiful pose.'

'Maybe if I paid her well she might do some professional private sittings for me. Perhaps she might pose unclothed for me? It would be easier for her in a private room with only one artist than to be in the large studio with a number of people.'

'Listen, I'll be seeing this friend again later this week. I'll see what she thinks and if she'll ask her for me. Billy is her housecleaner, only once a fort-night. She works somewhere else on the other days.'

Liam had packed up his gear and slowly driven home, his mind full of the vision of the woman, Billy. He couldn't wait to continue working on the drawings he'd just done and he visualised the sections of the sketches he wanted to work on. Hopefully Jason would be able to contact her to see if she would consider a well-paid modelling job. He could create an entire series, a number of large paintings with her in a variety of poses. They wouldn't need to be risqué positions. He would take into consideration that she might want to position her pose so that certain areas of her body weren't showing. There were different ways to lie or place your arms and legs that could allow the model to feel more comfortable if they were a bit nervous. He could discuss that with her and talk about the different paintings he had in mind.

He wouldn't be happy until he could paint her again.

13

Liam, along with Casso hot on his heels, made his way slowly down along the beach track. His schedule wasn't running as smoothly as usual this morning, and he already felt out of sorts. Last night he had gone straight to his studio when he got home, drawing and then painting until he noticed the light outside getting brighter, the sun starting to peep up over the horizon. He had in mind the picture he wanted to complete. Now he had several drawings and some uncompleted paintings on canvas that showed a little of what he was aiming for. His usual exercises had been given a miss and he thought that perhaps after swimming he would need to fit some sleep into his schedule.

It had been a long time since he had been so motivated to draw all night. Now as he walked down to the lake he wondered if he would be able to hold back from saying something to the butterfly girl. It would be better to go through the correct channels and get Jason to approach her about the modelling that he wanted her to do.

Liam was a bit later than usual and he thought that this morning she might have already finished her swim. Perhaps she'd gone for a walk along the beach afterwards. He walked briskly through the bush, following the winding path, the sand cool under his bare feet. Casso yapped excitedly, flitting off every now and then to chase lizards that raced nervously through the undergrowth. Warm sunshine filtered through the trees and Liam looked up, appreciative of the freshness in the air and the clarity of the blue summer sky.

When he came to the end of the bush path he stopped and whistled to Casso, who came bounding like a rabbit out of the grass before leaping up into Liam's waiting arms. The bitumen would already be hot for the dog's feet and it had become a habit for him to pick him up before walking across the small car park adjacent to the lake.

Liam hitched Casso under his arm. He tried to lick Liam's face, only stopping when a movement nearby caught his attention. Liam followed the dog's gaze. The car park was usually empty this time of the morning and Casso growled and then yapped loudly at a black car parked near to where they usually walked.

He became even more agitated as they got closer, directing his barking towards a short stocky man standing in front of the car. Liam could see that next to the man stood the butterfly girl, or Billy, as Liam had now begun to think of her.

He held tight to Casso who barked incessantly, his hackles standing on edge. The man near the car was dressed in a suit and probably in his forties. Even from a distance Liam could see that an argument was taking place and he watched as the dark-haired man drew himself up taller, pushing his face closer to Billy's. As she stepped backwards he grabbed one of her arms, his other arm flailing in the air as he tried to get his point across. He spoke in Arabic, the words loud and menacing and Liam tensed as he waited to see Billy's reaction.

She argued back, her words quick and angry. Perhaps she was going to get the last word in, Liam thought, pleased that she had pulled her arm from his grasp, turned her back and was walking away. The man however strode after her and grabbed her arm, roughly turning her body towards him. She pulled her arm away again and began to swear loudly at him in English. The man pushed his body against her, his face right up close to hers.

By now Liam had seen enough and with a firm grip on Casso, he strode calmly but quickly towards where the altercation was taking place. From what he'd observed he assumed that the man was her husband, and this was a domestic dispute between the two of them. He was hesitant to interfere in what was obviously a family argument, however the man's aggression was unacceptable.

The children who were often with Billy were nowhere to be seen, and today she wore thongs on her feet and a short floral dress over her bathers. There was no sign of any scarf or covered clothing that she sometimes wore.

As he came up beside the car he could hear what the argument was about. The man flicked her long hair with one hand, as if in disgust, his other hand once again firmly gripping her arm. His words were clearly audible. 'You will dress as I say in front of the children and my family,' he said. 'You look like a harlot and you now are to do as I say.'

Liam quickened his pace, cautious about the

intrusion on a marital argument but also now aware of the terrified look on Billy's face as the man pushed her up against the bonnet of the car.

'Is everything alright here?' Liam's voice was loud and deep.

The man turned around and looked up at Liam, whose stature was much larger than his own.

Casso growled in Liam's arms and Billy also turned to look at both the dog and the tall man who had been her swimming companion for the last two years. Her eyes pleaded with Liam, a single look from her letting him know that any help would be gratefully received.

'It's nothing, mate.' The man tried to put on his best Australian drawl, the Middle Eastern accent clearly discernible as he tried to placate Liam. 'Just a bit of an argument; no need for you to get involved.'

'It doesn't look like nothing,' Liam scowled and pulled himself up taller. 'You need to let go of her, you're clearly hurting your wife.'

'I'm not his wife.' Billy spoke loudly, her angry words confusing Liam who now stood between the two of them. Nothing was as he expected.

'I only work for him.' Her eyes flashed furiously even though there was fear on her face.

'She is part of my family,' the man said, a false smile on his face making the hairs on Liam's neck stand even more on end. 'She is just being a bit difficult and we are about to drive home. It is nothing, just a misunderstanding.'

Billy pulled her arm out of his grasp and picked up the backpack that she had dropped on the ground. Her voice was shaky but her words resolute. 'I will not be coming back to work. You cannot control me, I'm twenty-seven years old and you cannot tell me what to do. I quit. Now leave me alone. Do not contact me again.'

'You will be sorry you have done this. You have nothing, and we are the only family you have. There is nothing but shame in your life. The way you live, the way you dress. I have looked after you, provided for you and paid you well. We will work it out. You will come back with me. The children will want you to stay.'

'I have always stayed for the children. They are not mine, they are yours. I will not come back. I am never coming back.'

'I am sorry I have become angry. My wife will be lost without you, and the children, you are like their second mother. They need you.'

'I will not come back. I am finished.'

The man spat on the ground next to Billy before moving back to the side of the car.

'You will be sorry. You will not have any money and now no family. You have nothing and no one. Once you leave that will be it. I tell you one last time to get in the car and come back. We will work it out.' The man's voice had taken on a sickly wheedling tone and Liam could see that he was trying hard to get her to reconsider. 'You are our family. My wife and children will not cope if you leave.'

'I am not your family. Leave me alone.'

The man reached forward to try and take her backpack, his voice pleading as he offered her more pay, less hours and the freedom to come and go as she wanted. He played on the fact that the children would suffer if she left.

Liam wanted to make it clear that he was ready to intervene further if needed and by now he was getting tired of the man's persistence and the grip he had on Billy's backpack. He took a step towards him, intimidating the much smaller man. Liam's voice was firm and steady when he spoke. 'I don't know what your problem is, but you need to let go of the bag and leave the young lady alone. It's obvious that she does not want to go in the car with you or continue with this conversation.'

The man let go of the backpack and ran his hands through his hair. By now Liam was standing between the two of them, leaving the man no other option but to stop with the argument. The man's face reddened and scrunched up in anger. 'She will be sorry she has left. I have tried and offered her more than she deserves. This is the line in the sand and she has chosen. Now I will not take her back, no matter how hard she begs.' With that he turned and got into the car. He slammed the car door before starting the engine, his fist shaking high through the car window at Liam.

Liam grabbed Billy's arm, pulling her up onto the footpath and out of the way of the squealing tyres of the car as it sped away from the car park, narrowly missing a vehicle that was approaching. A couple walking past stopped to check if everything was alright, Liam assuring them that it was and that he would stay to make sure everything was okay. He picked up her backpack, watching as she took deep breaths, both of them staring at the black car that now sped out onto the main road.

'I think you should come and sit for a moment,'

Liam said as he put his arm around her shoulders, guiding her over to a bench seat under the trees at the edge of the car park.

'Sit for a minute. Get your breath. You're shaking,' he said, propelling her gently onto the bench. 'It's okay, he's gone. You know me, I'm Liam, I swim near you at the lake most mornings.'

Her voice trembled, her eyes still looking towards where the car had exited. 'Thank you.'

She followed his instructions, taking long sips from the water bottle he offered her. Liam watched closely as she drank, her eyes flitting back and forth, looking around the car park as if she expected the man to return any minute. Her black hair was thick and shiny, reaching down to the middle of her back. Close up, her face was beautiful, her features delicate, and her large dark green eyes peered back at him through the longest eyelashes he had ever seen. Her eyes though were full of tears, threatening to spill over as she struggled to maintain her composure in front of Liam.

'It's okay. I won't leave you here alone. I don't think he'll come back anyway.' Liam tried to calm her. He had never really taken much notice of her before, intent on his purpose of swimming, and focused on himself, rather than anything else around him that might detract from his resolve. She had always been at a distance from where he sat and when he passed her, she usually had large sunglasses on or had only looked quickly at him.

Finally, her breathing evened out and she wiped her eyes with her hands. 'Thank you so much for your help. If you hadn't stopped, he would have probably made me get back into the car.'

'What's the story with him? He appears to be quite a violent man.' Liam said, placing Casso, who was still wriggling in his arms, down on the ground.

'I work for him. I look after his children, his wife and his house. I cook, clean, do the shopping, take the children to school and help them at home. For that he thinks he owns me.'

'No boss can own you.'

'You would not understand.'

'Try me,' Liam said, his eyebrows raised at the anger in her tone.

'It is a long story, but that man is from Iran and he thinks I believe what he says, that a very long time ago he was connected to my family. But it is not true, and I am my own person. I don't have to work for him any longer. And that is why we argued. This morning after I dropped the children at school I told him that I was not coming back to work for him and I wouldn't go and live in the new city where they are going to move to.'

'What does his wife do, if you do all the work?'

'She does nothing, except spend all their money and use all of her time to look the best she can for him.'

'Why have you stayed with them?'

Billy looked down at the ground, her voice wavering. 'For the last few years he's taken control of my money. Before I worked for his family I was independent and earned enough money to live. Over time he pressured me and said he'd invest all of my savings. I've never seen my money again. He made my life difficult and then made me pay for many things. Because he didn't pay me wages over the last few months, I haven't very much money. I found a small cleaning job but that does not pay very much. I need to find other work and that is also why I have left them.'

'Where are you living? Do you have somewhere to stay?'

'Yes, I have a small flat at Tullee. It's a long way from here but the buses run regularly. I've always swum here at the lake or brought the children here to the beach, because I thought he wouldn't see me here and that I would be safe. When I swim, or walk along the beach and watch the ocean, I forget my problems. Here he can't make me cover my head or body the same as his wife does.'

'Now it all makes a little more sense,' Liam said as he turned to her, her eyes looking straight back at him. 'I'd noticed that you sometimes had a scarf on and other times you didn't.'

'That was his and his wife's wish, and it isn't my practice.' Billy stood up. 'Thank you, again. I'm sorry that I've disturbed your swim today.'

'I'm just glad that I intervened. I thought he was your husband and it was a marital argument. Even then it would not have been okay for him to grab you like that.'

'He hasn't ever done that before. His wife will be angry that I have left because I did everything for them. Now she will have to do the work and look after the children.'

'Perhaps you should report the incident to the police.'

'I will do that, because I am worried that he will come back and try and force me into return- ing.' She stood up, rubbing her arm where he had grabbed her. 'Thank you so much for helping. It was very nice of you to intervene.' She looked up and down the road again. 'I think I'll get going. There will be a bus that comes soon, and I can go home on it.'

Liam stood up also. 'I think we should both go and still do our swimming. It's the best thing for taking your mind off anything that's worrying you.'

'I'm not so sure today.' She looked around warily.

'I think you should definitely go for a swim. It'll make you forget your troubles for a while. Look at the weather, it's the perfect day.' Liam stood up and waited for her. 'It'll be fine, I'll be there plus there's this ferocious dog to take into consideration.'

She smiled. 'It does seem a shame to waste the time that I spent getting here. It sounds strange, but I feel like I do know you.'

'We have been swimming here at the same time for a couple of years. I live just through the bush there. I'm a local.'

'That explains why everyone always waves or chats to you. I've often thought that you must live close by.'

'C'mon,' Liam said as he led the way, looking back to make sure she was following. He waited for her to catch up and the two of them walked silently down to the shores of the lake, Casso yapping noisily at their heels as he ran behind them.

'You're a good swimmer,' she said.

'Thank you,' he said, biting back the words he had nearly spoken. It had been on the tip of his tongue to ask her where on earth she had learned to swim, or maybe she had not ever learned. However, he kept the remarks silent, unsure of how she might take a humorous remark, not intended to be hurtful. Plus, she had just had a rough morning, perhaps now wasn't the time to tell her that whatever she did in the water couldn't exactly be classified as swimming.

When they reached the spot where she usually sat, she glanced back, towards the car park. 'I'm worried he'll return,' she said to Liam, 'I might give it a miss today. I don't think he'll just give in that easily.'

Liam put his towel and water bottle down on the sand. 'How about I sit here while you do your laps. I'll make sure he's not around. It will give me some time to give this dog some attention.'

Casso ran around, circling Liam in the hope of some playtime.

'Go on, you'll be fine. I can do some stretches and throw a stick to the dog. There's no hurry. Make the most of it, have your swim, you'll be amazed at how much better you will feel afterwards.'

'As long as you don't mind. Thank you. I do think a swim will be calming and then I'll be able to get on with what I have to do next.' She pulled her dress over her head and for a moment Liam saw the structured lines of her shoulders, her back covered by her bathers. He averted his eyes, instead finding a stick to throw.

'Take as long as you want. This dog will keep me busy.'

As she walked towards the water, her long legs

stepped out elegantly, her arms high above her head as she pulled her long hair up, twirling it expertly before tying it up on top of her head. Her body was toned, the colour of her skin a light brown, flawless and smooth, covered only by the black one-piece swimming suit. Entering the water quickly, she dived below the surface, before bobbing up further out in the middle. Soon she was moving across the lake, her arms and legs slapping the water, the familiar ungainly strokes clearly visible to Liam, who sat transfixed, watching her thrash across the water.

When she returned from her first lap, he couldn't help himself and he strolled down to the water's edge, wading in waist deep to meet her on her first return. 'You need to get your arms higher out of the water,' he demonstrated the correct freestyle action, 'and when you re-enter, use your hand, slice it into the water sideways, don't slap it down on the surface.'

She stood near to him, listening as he gave her some further instructions on how to move her legs. 'Try it.' He encouraged her. 'Just try it on this next lap. Think about what you're doing. Think about your arms and then your legs.' He did the actions again and she watched as he kicked the water with his legs and then moved his arms slowly so that she could see the action required. 'Go again, it's okay, I'm here watching, no-one is going to bother you.'

She giggled, a delightful sound, full of fun. 'I think you scared him. You're a lot bigger than him. I feel like I have a bodyguard.' She turned and dived deep again, coming up and then slowly swimming towards the other side. At first her arms flailed the water roughly and Liam shook his head. Before long though he could see that her arms moved more smoothly, and she seemed to swim quicker and with less water splashing around her body as she swam across the lake. Her legs however still smashed the water wildly and he chuckled as she turned on the far side, heading back to where he was sitting.

⋆ ⋆ ⋆

After the swim Billy seemed much more relaxed. 'Thank you. I felt like I was moving a lot quicker,' she said as she dried herself.

'You were. That was much better. Sit and play with Casso while I do my laps,' Liam said. 'He'll bark and nip at anyone that comes near you.'

'Thank you, I feel quite safe now. I don't think he'll come back when you're here. I'm glad we've finally met.'

Liam took off his shirt, redoing the tie on his boardshorts, aware that her eyes were following his actions as he walked down to the water's edge. Soon his arms and legs were moving powerfully through the water and his body clicked into the clocklike action of his regular swim strokes. Each time he swam towards the shore where she was, he checked that nobody was bothering her.

Billy, the butterfly girl, kept popping up in his life and this morning he had once again been surprised, having always thought of her as a young married mother. His mind ticked over as he swam, going over the events of the morning and then turning back to his thoughts of the previous night. Should he let her know that he had stared at her body for a very long time as she posed at the studio, or that he had an unfinished painting of her propped up on his easel at home? There was also the problem of his underlying desire to paint her without her clothes on. A real-life painting of the butterfly girl would finish off his collection.

14

After the morning swim, Liam escorted Billy to the bus stop. She assured him that she now felt safe and he had been right that the swim had taken her mind away from her problems. Travelling by bus was the usual way she came to and from her home to the lake.

'I have my own car,' she told Liam. 'But now it is in his garage and registered in his name. He changed the papers for it and then only let me drive it sometimes. I would not like to try and get it back. He's a dangerous man and my only good fortune is that very soon they will be leaving the city.'

'I could drive you home,' Liam said. 'I live just through the scrub there. Let me at least give you a lift.'

'You have already done much for me today. Thank you.' She held out her hand. 'My name is Billy.'

'No worries, Liam Andrews.' He shook her hand, disappointed at her refusal for him to give her a lift home and annoyed at the short conversation, due to the timing of the bus that now pulled up in front of them.

'Thank you, Liam.' She smiled and waved, hopping on the bus before giving him another wave through the window.

Stepping back from the pavement, he waved back. Casso was sitting for once, obediently at his feet. The bus pulled away, a belch of fumy smoke coming from its exhaust.

Liam mulled over the events of the morning. *What was her story*, he wondered. Her appearance was definitely Middle Eastern and she had said her boss was from Iran. She had a slight trace of an accent or sometimes a different pronunciation of some words, and she had argued with the man in both Arabic and English. He let out a sigh as Casso yapped at his heels, eager to start the walk home; no doubt thinking of the daily treat that was usually given after the morning swim and walk. Liam walked slowly, thinking ahead to the next morning when he would see her again, wondering how he was going to broach the subject of her posing for his painting.

★ ★ ★

The next day Liam made sure that he was at the lake earlier than usual. He sat down in his regular spot and after a while began his laps, making sure that at each turn he looked towards where Billy would generally be. He slowed down, drawing out the time, doing extra laps thinking that perhaps she wasn't coming this morning. Although swimming normally cleared his mind, today he couldn't get the image of Billy smiling and waving goodbye from the bus window out of his head. As he finished his last lap and begun to wade out of the water she was swimming in her regular position.

He was surprised by how excited and relieved he was to see her, and he watched as she swam back and forth. Liam spent a long time drying

96

himself and then positioned himself on his towel, using the time to throw the stick to Casso. He threw it for such a long time that Casso ended up exhausted and came to lie down at Liam's feet. The little dog was puffing and panting, probably wondering what was going on to have such a long playtime. Eventually to both Liam and Casso's relief, Billy finished her laps.

Trying to avert his eyes as she walked out of the water towards her towel, Liam busied himself patting Casso, only taking a sideways glance once he knew she had moved back to her usual spot. He tried not to stare as she deftly wrapped a towel around her waist, picked up something and made her way over to him.

He stood as she approached, Casso suddenly finding his lost energy to jump up and down as Billy stood next to them. 'I bought you something at the bakery. It's not much but it's to thank you for your help yesterday.'

Her skin was still wet, her long black hair tied up in a bun that dripped water down onto her shoulders. He hoped that she hadn't noticed him gazing at her bare shoulders and instead looked up into her eyes that stared straight into his. He opened the small brown paper bag, a smile lighting up his face.

'My favourite,' Liam said, peering into the bag, 'Macarons. There aren't too many places around here that make these.'

'My flat is above a French-style bakery. A Vietnamese family own it. These are the best macarons you'll ever taste.'

'Thank you,' he said, closing the bag, 'I'll save

it for my morning tea.'

She turned to walk away. Liam spoke quickly before she could leave. 'Would you like to join me for a coffee? There's a small café just up the road here.'

Turning back, she hesitated for a moment before replying. 'Thank you, it was very kind of you to help me yesterday, but I will say no to the offer for today. I'm off to do some job hunting.'

He watched as she walked back to her spot, picking up her bag and clothes before making her way up to the change sheds at the top of the beach.

'Damn.' He scuffed the sand with his toe, his gaze turning to the lake, the sunshine bouncing off the water's surface, the sky blue and cloudless. A beautiful day, but he knew he should get moving too. There were quite a few jobs lined up in his diary, and it was always good to get into the work while the weather was fine. He had wanted to ask her if the man bothering her yesterday had been any more trouble, but she had not encouraged conversation. Trying to push any further thoughts of Billy from his mind, Liam made his way back home, annoyed that he hadn't been able to entice her for a coffee and frustrated that he still hadn't asked her if she would be interested in posing for him.

★ ★ ★

Work kept Liam busy over the next week and he had rushed through his jobs, due to the poor weather that was forecast. Each morning he swam earlier than usual and then hung around, long after he finished his laps. This week there had been no-one else swimming in the lake. Now as the weather turned windy and rainy he wondered when he would see Billy again. There had been no sign of her at his art class and when he had checked the timetables of the classes where she normally posed, the director-in-charge had said that she hadn't turned up for a couple of her scheduled classes. He told Liam that they had tried the contact number they had for her but there had been no answer, and they had no other details for her.

Lottie and Annika had been curious about his attempts at getting her to pose for him and teased him about his interest in the model that they had only seen once.

'If only she knew what you could do with that paintbrush,' Annika said, fluttering a new brush in the air.

Lottie added into the discussion. 'Perhaps if she knew how much money you'd offer, maybe then the girl with the beautiful back would pose for you.'

'I just didn't get a chance to talk to her about it,' Liam said, his brush moving rapidly as he painted the buxom lady who faced them from out the front. 'I'm also a bit worried about what's happened to her. She hasn't been swimming in the mornings and although the weather has been fairly ordinary, she normally swims no matter what.'

Yared and Nadir had come to stand beside Liam, admiring the way his paint covered the canvas, the lines and curves that he had so quickly created, beautifully portraying the body that was lying on the lounge at the front of the room.

Nadir stayed near Liam but Yared moved to the side, his eyes focused on the abstract style painting that Annika was in the process of completing. He nodded politely, but Annika only looked sternly at him over the rim of her glasses perched on the end of her nose. His eyes widened, and his head moved to the side, oblivious to the glare that she was sending his way, instead transfixed with the style by which she had portrayed the model. He held his hand up and she looked shocked, thinking that he was going to touch her painting. Instead his hand moved over the air in front of it, his head moving from side to side. Annika spoke harshly, angry at the intrusion as she worked. 'What is it? What is your problem?'

Yared's stare was broken and he remembered where he was. He apologised profusely, his head bowed and nodding as he backed away. Liam put his brush down abruptly. He was annoyed at the way Annika was speaking to Yared.

'Yared, mate, what are you thinking?'

Yared gestured to Liam. 'Come.' He waved his hand beckoning for Liam to follow him as he walked back to his own piece of work. Both Yared and Liam stood and stared at Yared's work before both of them once again going back to Annika's.

Liam raised his eyebrows and spoke to Annika. 'You'd better come and have a look at this and don't forget before you open your mouth that Yared sits right off to the side and well in front of you. There's no way he could have seen your painting before he did his or you his.'

'What rot are you all going on about?' Annika

100

was annoyed but went with Liam as he stood in front of Yared's work.' Her eyes widened.

Both of their pieces were very similar, the abstract lines running in the same perpendicular angles, the thickness of lines that made up nearly identical shapes, the colours, everything was much the same. Annika quickly went back and took her canvas off the sheet it was attached to, returning and holding it next to Yared's work. Lottie and Matilda came and stood beside and they all looked at the two paintings, no-one speaking, just gazing at the similar pieces of art.

'They are very similar. Where did you learn to paint, young man?' Annika said in her most abrupt Dutch accent.

'I follow my heart and I teach myself how to paint in camp, slowly from the beginning. By crawling, a child learns to stand.'

'I can hardly believe it. All my years at art school, working with some of the finest and here today,'— she stopped and thought before she said what she was thinking— 'a man who has never had lessons, has mastered the finest strokes of painting nude abstracts.'

'I actually think his has finer tones and more defined lines than yours.' Matilda joined in the discussion. 'He has pieced together the fragments beautifully.'

'It is more detailed, perhaps a fuller explanation of the body,' Liam said.

Annika looked back at her work and then again at Yared's. 'I hate to admit it, but you're all correct. Just look at the way he's captured the light flitting over her upper leg. The chunkiness of the breasts, the shapes, my God, I've never seen anyone that has such a similar style to my own. What's your name young man?'

'Yared Tadese, but you can just call me Yared.'

'Well, Yared, my work is sought after and often my paintings sell for thousands of dollars. You and I may have to have some discussions once you get a bit more settled and get a collection going. Where do you paint at home? Do you have a studio or a room set aside?'

Nadir, who had been listening with interest, laughed loudly. 'We are only just newly arrived from refugee camps. Both Yared and I have very small houses, with lots of children and sometimes other people staying.'

Yared nodded and spoke directly to Annika. 'This is the only time I can paint. The people who help us, pay for our paint and canvas here one night a week. This is the only painting I can do, here with class.'

'Well, Yared and Nadir, we will have to see what we can work out for you both in the future. Perhaps there might be some room here for you to paint.' Annika's voice was animated, her face still revealing her surprise at the quality of Yared's painting.

Liam rolled his eyes, surprised at how polite Annika could be when she wanted to be. 'Shouldn't judge a book by its cover, should you now, Annika,' he whispered to her as they all went back to their places.

'Who would have thought that he could be such a talented artist?'

'Why not?' Liam shook his head.

102

'I've just never thought of them as people with talents.'

'They're just like you and me Annika; just their skin is a different colour. I've never understood why you would judge people by the colour of their skin.'

'Well, they're so black,' Lottie joined in, 'and they speak different languages, have different religions and eat different foods than we do.'

'Heaven forbid,' Matilda said. 'Fancy not looking the same as you two. There must definitely be something wrong with them.'

'You can be cutting at times.' Annika frowned at Matilda. 'Of course I don't judge people by their skin or religion.'

'Well, what exactly were you judging them by?' Matilda had fired up a little, obviously sick of the pompous attitude that Annika and Lottie often had towards the two new men in the art class.

'I just didn't know them very well. I mean I've never spoken to an African before. They actually speak quite good English.' Annika was trying to defend herself.

'And they seem so polite,' Lottie said, as she packed up her work.

'I think you both owe them some politeness and perhaps to be a lot more friendly next time they come to class. I'm surprised they've even come anywhere near us with the attitude you've shown them,' Liam said, his gruff voice signalling the end of his patience with the two older ladies.

The impact of Liam's words caused Annika to screw up her face, leaving her with nothing to say. Liam watched with interest as the three women left together, all of them nodding politely and saying goodbye to Yared and Nadir as they walked past where the men were ever so carefully packing up their things. Both men nodded as usual, their words gracious and polite, as they bid the three ladies goodnight.

15

A week had passed since Liam had seen Billy at the lake and although the thought of approaching her to pose for him was still there, he was more concerned about whether she had given in and gone back to work for her old boss.

Work had kept him busy and today Nadir had been his offsider, helping with some maintenance and carpentry work. Together they were going to look at a ute that was for sale. It was an older vehicle but still in great condition and ideal for what Nadir needed for his carpentry work. Liam had spent a large amount of time today trying to convince Nadir that there was no catch and he was prepared to loan him the money to buy a vehicle that would help him in his job. He was also adamant that he would loan extra so that Nadir could purchase the basic tools that he needed to work.

'There is so much work out there for a man like you Nadir. You just need a kickstart and once you start earning some money, you can pay me back in small amounts or whatever you can afford.'

'I am not sure why you would loan me money.' Nadir was apprehensive, obviously looking for the catch to go with it.

'There is no catch. You pay nothing extra. We'll write it all down on paper and both of us will keep a tally of what you owe. It'll be okay. It is not such a big outlay and I'll help you with quoting and finding work on the maintenance side. Not a day passes when I don't get asked if I can build or fix something and I only do basic jobs. I'm not a carpenter. I just stick to the lawn and pool maintenance. We'll work together and hopefully I can put on someone else to help me with the gardening work. It'll be a good team. Just take it, Nadir. I want to help you.'

Nadir had eventually given in, shaking his head at Liam's generosity. The ute was perfect for what he needed, and they filled in the necessary paperwork that would make it his, paid a deposit and arranged to pick it up later in the week. Liam smiled at Nadir's humility. The man deserved a break and now he could work for himself and run his own small business.

'I will be forever thankful to you, Liam. You are a good man and you will not be sorry for what you are doing.'

'It's nothing, we have it good here in Australia and I'm happy to help someone who wants to work.'

They had talked at length as they drove through the streets, the traffic thinning out as Liam neared the suburb where many of the refugees lived.

'They say sixty-two nationalities are here where I live.' Nadir spoke slowly and clearly. 'It is a big mixture and our children are growing up with children from all parts of the world.'

'It certainly is a huge melting pot in this area.' Liam had always been intrigued at the blend of cultures in the area and slowed down as he neared Nadir's house, a dozen or so kids running along the footpath, racing the car up the street.

'They are waiting for me,' he chuckled, his voice

deep. 'Next time you will come for dinner and meet my family. My wife speaks better English than me, and more languages also. I only speak four languages, she speaks five.'

'That's incredible.'

Nadir jumped out of the car, 'Perhaps we will teach you some Arabic. Goodnight Liam and may God bless you and all your children. The ones that one day you may have.'

Liam chuckled as he waved goodbye, careful to drive slowly as more children ran up the footpath, shrieking and laughing as they raced each other. They waved to Liam as he passed them, their smiling faces reminding him of other children who he had seen; children who had suffered so much and had so little. His thoughts turned to the blend of different nationalities that lived in the area and he wondered about Billy and where she lived.

There was a row of small shops further up the street and he slowed down, looking at the names of the variety of different ethnic stores that lined the street. He passed three or four shops and then spotted what he had been looking for, 'Le Saigon Bakery.' His gaze moved to the building above; an older block of flats, tan bricks leading up to small windows covered by black, wrought iron, safety bars. If he had remembered correctly she had said hers was the flat directly above the bakery. Slowing the car down he pulled into a park in front of the shops, noticing a wooden door next to the bakery that he imagined would lead to the rooms above.

For a while he sat in the car. He hardly knew Billy, and she would probably find it odd that he would come knocking on her door. They had however greeted each other for over two years and swum together every morning. It could possibly be regarded as being acquaintances. The overriding fact was that he had seen her being harassed by her boss. He was concerned about her well-being. The worst that could happen would be that she would be angry with him for tracking her down and tell him to leave.

A wooden door to the right of the bakery led Liam through to a small entry area. Narrow wooden steps beyond that took him up towards the first floor, which resembled a narrow corridor with two doors on either side. If she lived directly above the bakery it would probably mean that the door on the left would be hers. Without hesitation he knocked, having no idea what he was going to say when she answered the door. He knocked louder, noting the peeling paint and broken edges of the door. Billy's voice sounded from the other side of the door. 'Who is it?'

'It's Liam Andrews, the swimmer from the lake. I wanted to check that you're okay.'

Silence echoed in the corridor. Liam stood waiting. Was she looking at him through the spy hole window in the middle of the door?

'I was worried about you. You haven't been swimming. I just want to check that you're alright.'

The door next to the one Liam was knocking on opened a fraction, a middle-aged man peering through the gap at him. The man's voice was raspy, his breaths short as he spoke. 'Who are you looking for?'

Liam peered through the dimness of the slightly

opened door. 'Hello, I'm just checking on Billy.'

The man pushed the door open a little further, peering up at Liam who towered above him. 'I might be small, mate, but don't mess with anyone here. You'll be sorry,' the man said.

'I don't mean to make any trouble, I wanted to check on her to make sure she's okay.'

The man took a step towards Liam, his voice menacing, an oxygen bottle attached to him banging against the doorframe.

The other door opened and Billy came out. 'It's okay, Gus, this is Liam, the man who helped me the other day at the lake.'

Liam smiled, pleased that he had found the correct unit, and also that Billy had intervened before Gus became more agitated. 'I'm sorry to disturb everyone but I wanted to check that you were alright, you haven't been swimming and I was worried about you.'

She smiled, touching Gus on the arm. 'Thanks Gus, you're a great neighbour. I don't know what I'd do without you. It's okay though, you need to go and sit back down. I'm fine.' Gus turned slowly around, making his way back into his dimly-lit unit. 'Just you yell out if you need me. You know these walls are paper-thin.'

Liam held open the door and took the oxygen bottle from Gus, helping him back into the worn recliner where he had obviously been sitting before Liam arrived. 'Sorry, mate, I didn't mean to make you get up. It's good she's got you to look out for her.'

Gus settled back into his chair, his raspy breathing making his chest rise and fall heavily. 'Young girl like her, she shouldn't be living in this sort of place. There're all types living in this block. Don't know what's going to happen, because I'm going into care later this week. Who's going to look out for her then?'

Billy stood at the doorway. 'I'll be okay, Gus. Don't worry about me. I keep the place locked up.' She turned towards Liam. 'Would you like a coffee now that you're here?'

Liam and Billy closed Gus's door behind them, Liam pleased to breathe the less musty air as he followed Billy into her flat.

'Come in. My home is only tiny, but you are welcome.' Liam followed her through a narrow living room into a brighter room that was both kitchen and dining area. 'Please, sit, I'll make a hot drink for you.'

'Thank you,' Liam said. The flat was tiny, and he sat down at a small kitchen table that reminded him of the table his family had eaten from when he was a kid. There were two wooden chairs that didn't match, and a small room that doubled as a bedroom and lounge. Peering further past the kitchen he could see another room.

'That's the bathroom through there,' Billy said, watching him as he looked around the small area she called home. 'It's only small, but it's cheap and at the moment it's all I've got.'

She pointed to a chair. 'Have a seat. I'll put the jug on. How did you know where I live?'

'You told me you lived above the bakery. I was dropping some friends off just down the road, so I thought I'd check on you. I was worried you haven't been swimming.'

110

'Thank you,' Liam said as she put a large cup of coffee in front of him.

She poured herself one and then came to sit down opposite him. 'I don't usually let strangers in, but I guess I do sort of know you.'

'I feel a bit the same. It's not my normal thing to track down someone and knock on their door, but I figure we've really been acquaintances for the last two years. Also, I was concerned about you.'

Her eyes looked darker and larger up close and he stared at her long eyelashes that matched the colour of her hair, tied up in a ponytail.

'I just wanted to check that your former employer was no longer harassing you.'

She sipped her cup of tea, taking a while to answer. 'He has come around a couple of times and banged on my door, threatening me if I didn't return to work and yelling that he was going to make my life hell. Gus always makes an appearance when he comes but he knows that Gus doesn't move very quickly, so I don't think he's that scared of him.'

'Poor bugger, his breathing's terrible.'

'I know, he's got lung cancer and emphysema. He's got no family, and only occasionally will he let me clean or do anything in there, so I'm afraid it gets pretty smelly. He's a good neighbour but if he won't let me in I can't fix the place up for him.'

'At least he might get looked after if he goes into care.'

Billy sighed. 'I guess so, it's just so sad that there's no-one who really cares for him.'

Liam looked out the window, the narrow pane

of glass allowing only a small glimpse across to the similar style of old brick units across the street. His eyes returned to the door, the four security latches an indication of the protection needed for someone living here. 'How safe do you feel here? What safeguards, apart from those locks, do you have if your old boss comes calling again?'

'I went to the police and reported the harassment. They wrote all the details down.'

'I'm glad you went to the police.'

'I'm not sure it was the right thing to do, but it was my only option. I know it isn't the end of it. He won't give up that easily.'

'Do you think he'll be worried about the police?'

'Possibly, I don't think he'll want any trouble from them, but he knows where I live. I'm not sure he's going to give up. I think I'll need to move on.' She looked around the tiny apartment. 'I know it's only small, but it's my home.'

'At least you're not still working for him,' Liam was trying to point out some of the positives to her. 'There can't have been too many good things about that job.'

'I miss the kids. I've been with them for years and they thought of me as their mother. I know they'll be upset and that's why I stayed with them for so long.'

'Did you get any of your money back?'

She shook her head, her lip quivering as she tried to stop the tears from coming. Her voice was shaky as she spoke. 'I'm trying to get another job. It was so stupid of me to give him my money. There is nothing left in my name.'

'I want to tell you something.' Liam needed to

get some information out in the open. 'I know you work at the art studio, modelling. I've painted you.'

Billy's eyes widened, and she sat up straighter, looking directly into his eyes. 'You cannot have painted me. I have never seen you in the classes. I sit for a long time and I observe the artists. I have never seen you there before.'

'I don't paint in the portrait classes. I attend the life classes. You filled in one night when the booked model couldn't attend.'

'You are an artist?'

'Yes, my genre is life art. I exhibit at the city gallery and at the moment I make more money out of my art than my handyman business.'

'You painted me that one night?' she said in disbelief.

'Yes, I have the painting at home if you don't believe me.'

'Normally the artists paint my face, or from the waist up. That night was a one off. I wouldn't go again, they asked me several times.'

'Why not, you are very good at getting the pose correct and you sat perfectly, without moving.'

'Taking my clothes off is not my thing and even when they finally agreed to my conditions, that night was a bit much for me.'

'Well I'll be honest with you. I have come to check that you are alright, but I also have a proposition for you that may help you out of your unemployment situation.'

One of her eyebrows rose higher than the other and she sipped her coffee slowly, watching Liam carefully over the top of her cup.

'What is your proposition?' Her voice was inquisitive.

'I need to finish a segment of work for an upcoming exhibition. When I painted you that night, I knew that you were exactly what I've been looking for. Models who pose privately for artists can earn a good wage. The array of work I'm thinking about would probably take several weeks to work on and I would pay you a good amount to pose for me.'

Billy sat very still, the silence in the room only broken by a tap dripping in the kitchen sink. Finally, she spoke. 'Where would the work take place?'

'I have my own studio set up at home. It's very private, has excellent light and I can assure you that I take a very professional view to working with models. If you like I can show you some of the previous work I've done.'

'I do need to find some work,' Billy replied. 'But it's not exactly what I had in mind.'

A loud banging on the door of the flat interrupted Liam's next words. They both stood up as a loud voice yelled from the other side of the locked door. 'This is your last chance. You will otherwise shame your family name. I tell you to come with us now when we leave. I will make sure you get your money back.'

'It's him. Ervin, my old boss. He mustn't realise that you're here.'

Holding his pointer finger up to his lips to signal her to remain silent Liam began walking silently over to the door. Ervin banged loudly on the door again, his voice becoming angrier. 'You

114

are shamed, if you don't come with me you will be renounced, and I will make sure that everyone knows. I will tell everyone that you have dishonoured your family.'

Beckoning to Billy to move into the bathroom area where she would not be visible, Liam began to unlatch some of the safety chains. Ervin began pushing on the door from the other side, his last threat spoken as Liam opened the door. 'You will not be safe if you do not abide by my law and—'

His words were cut off as the door opened and Liam's tall frame filled the doorway. He towered over the stout angry man who stopped in his tracks, shocked at the sight of Liam filling the space in front of him. At the same time Gus opened his door, once again the oxygen bottle in tow. He stood silently, his eyes wide open, watching the interaction between Liam and Ervin. He mumbled loudly, 'Jesus Christ, not a bloody dull moment here today.'

Liam's voice was deep and intimidating. 'You are breaching a police order and I have now recorded everything you have just said. If you don't exit the building and leave your former employee alone, you are the one who will be unsafe, and I will track not only you down, but also look very closely at the business dealings that you're involved with. You won't be able to bother anyone from inside a jail cell.' Liam's words were calm, but his voice was threatening and left no doubt that he would do as he promised.

'The girl is like family. I just want her to come with us,' Ervin tried to stand his ground, looking upwards at Liam.

'She's not coming back to you and she's already employed elsewhere. The money you have taken from her will also be examined and our lawyers and investigators are already hot on your trail. They will leave nothing uncovered if this needs to go further.'

'It does not need to go any further, now she stays where she is. She is a dirty whore.' Ervin spat on the floor before turning around and walking down the stairs. 'She had no money before she came to me. I gave her everything. She is also a liar. Now she also has no family. She has nothing.'

Standing in the small hallway Liam waited as Ervin stomped down the stairs, slamming the door that led onto the street. He looked over to Gus, who nodded politely and smiled before shuffling back inside. The sound of the television faded out as the door closed behind him. A few minutes later, tyres screeching from outside the flats told Liam that Ervin had also left the area. The inside of the flat was now silent, and Liam came back in, locking the door behind him. He looked towards the bathroom doorway where Billy stood, her eyes wild with fear. 'He's a dangerous man. I'm glad you were here, it is like fate that you decided to come and visit.'

'That's twice I've seen him in action. He seems to think that he owns you. How the hell did you ever get mixed up with him?' Liam tried to hold back his anger but his voice was still loud as he walked back to her.

Billy hadn't moved and Liam lowered his voice. Her hand was shaking as she reached up and pushed her hair back, her face pale. He spoke

116

calmly to her. 'Come and sit back down.' He pulled a chair out for her. 'I'll make another coffee. Sit down.'

She sat down, her eyes glancing around, back and forth from the window to the door.

'It's okay, Billy, he won't come back. Did you notice his face when I mentioned dodgy business dealings? You can bet your life on it that you aren't the only person that he's ripped of. Usually his type have got their hands into all sorts of grubby dealings. I could see the doubt in his eyes when I spoke. He'll be involved in illegal activities, for sure.'

'How can you tell?'

'What? That he's dodgy, apart from ripping you off?'

'Yes. I mean you're right. I know from working there, he's involved in many dealings that aren't legal.'

'And he'll know that. He'll know that you might be suspicious and have seen activity that he didn't want you to know about. I took a guess. There's something about him and from experience, I can tell, he'll be involved with shady deals for sure.'

She looked worried again. 'They're moving on. He's got on the wrong side of some people here in town and they'd started to threaten him. I overheard him telling his wife why they needed to move.'

'There you go. I don't think that he'll risk contact with the police.' Liam placed a mug of coffee in front of Billy. 'How the hell did you end up working for him?'

'I worked at the fruit shop in the suburb where

they live. Many days his wife would come in, she would tell me how worn out she was, from his and the children's demands. She looked sick and tired and I kept telling her that she needed a nanny, a housekeeper, someone to help her out. I wasn't looking for a job at the time and didn't realise that she would think of asking me. I only thought that it would make life easier for her. Then her husband started to come and get the fruit. He'd talk to me about how tired she was, and I chatted to him and told him the same, trying to convince him that perhaps she needed some help.'

'No doubt he offered you good money.'

'He did, and he was always so polite and kind. He said I would become like family and then when he visited me the next time he had worked out that there was a connection between our families.'

'Or so he said.' Liam shook his head. 'He had you worked out.'

'He was very persistent and then he would bring the children in who also begged me to come and work at their house. The children were lovely and before I knew it I had agreed to work for him and become like part of their family.' Her voice steadied a little and she looked at Liam, her shaking hands wrapped around the warmth of the cup. 'I picked up the scorpion with my own hands.'

'Do you think you are related to him?'

'When Ervin came to the shop he asked me many questions about where I came from in Afghanistan. He is from Iran but had once lived in Afghanistan. He said he was related to my father's family there and that because my family was not here, that he would help me with money and my direction in life.'

She sat up straighter, her words now calm and slower. 'He offered me decent pay, more than I was getting at the fruit shop. His words were kind and he convinced me that I would be part of their family. At first, he was nice to me and so was his wife. The children, well, I loved them from the first day.' Her voice was soft, her words drawing Liam in, as she told him how she had become the carer for the children, their own mother drawing further and further away from them as she allocated more of the time with the children to Billy. 'I think they did it on purpose, the two of them. They knew that I was very close to the children and every time I even looked like I wanted to move on, they dangled that in front of me. Also, by then I had stupidly given over my savings, which weren't that much, for him to look after.'

'Why would you do that?' Liam asked.

Billy's eyebrows lifted, a hint of annoyance in her tone. 'I'm not stupid, and I'd managed to save a good amount of money.'

'I can tell you're not stupid, that's why I'm intrigued why you gave him control over your money.'

'He wrote it all out for me on paper. The way he made it look showed that I could make a lot of money if I let him invest it for me. He told me I would be able to have enough to put a deposit on a flat, that he would make sure he worked out the deposit and a loan that would set me up for life.'

'Don't feel bad, a lot of people get done out of their money in the same way. He would have been convincing, particularly if he was helpful to start with. It's easy to see how you might have trusted him.'

'I was a single woman and he believed that he could rule over me.'

'So, what made you decide to leave? Was that the other week when he tried to hassle you in the car park at the lake.'

'About a month ago he started to get really weird. He bought me presents and then he'd arrange for me to be at home when his wife wasn't there. He started to say sleazy things to me and then he came straight out and told me that I was to be his mistress and that if I told his wife he would make my life difficult and that he would hurt me if he had to.'

'What a mongrel! Have you told the police all of this information?'

'I have told them most of it, but all they've done is take statements from me at this stage.'

Liam took long sips from his coffee, his mind turning over what she'd said. She was from Afghanistan. Of course, he thought, it made sense, the shape of her face and eyes, the tone of her skin.

It had been unusual to see a woman when he was in Afghanistan. They were rarely seen out of their houses and if they were outside, they were completely covered up. Billy hardly had an accent so he had not picked up on her Afghan background.

Ervin was another story. Liam leant over the table, concern written on his face as he spoke. 'I know you hardly know me but I'm not leaving you here. I'm not sure I've scared him off completely and he might try to break in.'

'I have nowhere else to go.'

'Do you have any family or other friends where

120

you could stay?'

He could hardly hear her reply. 'No-one. I have no-one in this town.'

'Then you're coming with me. I have a couple of small cottages on my property. They're pretty basic, but comfortable, and no-one is living in them at the moment.'

'I can't come with you. I don't even know you.'

'Listen, we've swum at the same place for the last couple of years.'

'But I still don't know you. I can't even believe that I've let you in here today.'

'You have to trust me. What we can do is go via the police station and let them know exactly what's going on. We can leave the details with Gus too. You won't be living in the same house as me and your cabin is completely self-contained and has locks. You can check with the director at the art studio, they've all known me for years. I can ring them right now if you like.' He took out his phone and held it out, offering for her to ring. 'It'll be just the same as renting here, except you'll be living somewhere a bit harder for him to find, plus my house is close by if you need any help. Just think of it as a rental agreement.'

'I don't have much money to pay rent, but I will get a job straight away. I have one small cleaning job already.'

'You can live in the cabin for free until you get a job, it doesn't make any difference to me, it's empty anyway and you'll be completely independent.'

'I don't have much of a choice,' she said, looking around the tiny flat. 'I can't stay here any longer.

121

Perhaps I could rent your cabin for a while, maybe just until Ervin and his family move away.'

'Exactly, even just for a short while. Once we can confirm that they've left town you'll be a lot safer. Plus I want to go and have another talk to the police. They need to step up their handling of this harassment. That way we can let them know at the same time where you're going to be staying.'

Liam breathed a sigh of relief when she nodded. 'It's fairly basic accommodation but it's got everything in it that you'll need. I often rent it out to people on holidays, and I've been thinking about renting it out on a long-term basis anyway.'

'I don't have a choice.' Her eyes moved across the small room as she sighed. 'It's a very generous offer.'

Liam smiled. 'You'll have to dust and wipe away the cobwebs, but you can stay there for as long as you want.'

'I'm going to go next door and talk to Gus. Can you write down the address for me and I'll see what he thinks.'

* * *

It didn't take long for Billy to return and she appeared to be more at ease with the idea of moving to a new place.

'Gus thinks it's a good idea. He's been worried about how I'll go once he moves. I've left the address with him and I'll get back to see him later this week before he leaves. I will need to gather my belongings.'

'Just bring what'll you need for tonight and

122

tomorrow. Tomorrow afternoon we can come back and pick up the rest of your things. That way you can also have a good look at the cabin and the living situation.' A frown crossed her face and Liam wondered if he was pushing her into a situation that she didn't really have time to think properly about. 'If it isn't going to suit you then you can just stay there for a couple of nights and then I'll help you find something that's safer than here and that suits you better.'

'So, it's a completely separate house?'

'Yes. I have a large property, so the cabins are spread out. You can see the main house from the one you'll be staying in, but it's all separate living. I'm at work during the day and often out at night.'

She sounded hesitant and he could tell she was going over the doubts that she had about going with someone that she really didn't know. 'Can we stop at the police station and let them know where I'm going to be and also if you could ring Jason down at the art gallery, I'd like to speak to him before we go,' she asked.

'Yes, of course. I promise you the cabin is safe and lots of other people have rented it similarly over the years. You can have the place to yourself, it's close to the lake and ocean and the bus stop is right there if you want to go out anywhere.'

'And you were going to rent it out, did you say?'

'Yep, I just haven't got around to it. I leave the other cabin free for when family come but the one you can rent was actually going to be advertised next week. If you decide to stay we can talk about the rent later, and it won't be much. Right now, I'd really like to get moving and call in at the police station.'

Billy stood up. 'I can't stay here, soon they will be chasing me for another month of rent and then I will have nowhere to go. Thank you. I will come with you.'

16

'I just spoke to Jason at the art gallery,' Billy said.

'And?' Liam raised his eyebrows.

'He said he's known you for years and that I can trust you.'

'You will be safe on my property.'

Billy moved more quickly now, placing clothes and some linen in a bag. Liam found a cardboard box and packed the contents from the fridge into it, noting the small amounts of food that she obviously existed on. She took one last look around the apartment before following Liam out into the hallway, hesitating for a moment after she locked the door.

Liam stood next to her. 'I promise you it will be fine, Billy.'

'I'm used to looking after myself and I hardly know you.'

'I understand, and I can tell you it's not normal for me to invite someone I hardly know to live on my property. But given the circumstances it just seems to be the right thing at the moment.'

'I know.' She spoke softly, her eyes meeting his, her face now calm as she resigned herself to the situation. 'It will be alright. I have a feeling he is going to come back.'

The old wooden steps creaked as they walked down them, Liam stopping and turning again to take the small suitcase from her, 'C'mon, let's get you settled in.'

The cabin consisted of a large room with kitchen, dining and living room all in one. A door off the room led to a bedroom and bathroom, which was small but comfortable. Liam placed the box of food on the wooden table, before opening the door, showing Billy where she could put her clothes. 'It's dusty and you'll need to give it a good sweep out tomorrow, but it's comfortable and I'm close by if you need.'

'It's lovely, thank you. I'm grateful for your help.'

'I've turned the fridge on, and tomorrow we can sort out food and whatever else you need. It's only me up at the main house and there's plenty of food and linen or anything else that will help.' He passed her a card. 'This is my phone number. If you need anything, just ring. I'll be up early in the morning, so we can talk about what you'd like to do. I hope you sleep well.'

'Thank you,' Billy said. 'I will be asleep before my head hits the pillow.'

'Goodnight, Billy.'

'Goodnight.'

★ ★ ★

The next morning Liam woke early and began his normal routine. As he finished his exercises and prepared himself for his swim there was a knock on the front door.

He opened it to find Billy standing there. She wore a casual short dress and had a towel hanging

126

over her shoulder. 'I wondered if you were going swimming. If you're not, I'll find my own way there.'

'No, no, I'm just about to go. Come in. Have a seat and I'll get my things ready,' he said before he went down the hallway.

When he returned he stopped short, his breath taken away. She stood with her back to him, her hair pulled up in a messy bun, tresses of black hair twining around her slender neck. Her head was at an angle as she looked at the print that hung on the wall. He could see the top of her back, the skin a beautiful dark brown, the shape of her shoulders symmetrical and defined. He stood beside her, both peering up at the large framed print that took pride and place on his lounge room wall.

'It's not a painting is it?' she asked, her eyes never leaving the print.

'No, it's a print of my favourite painting.'

'What is it about it? There's sadness, but also a happiness. Everyone is having fun. Why is it so sad?' Her eyes filled with tears and she wiped them away with the back of her hand. 'I'm sorry, I'm not normally so emotional, but I feel drawn to the people in this picture. There's so much love in this.'

Liam reached forward and straightened the large frame, moving it ever so slightly until it hung even. They stood for a long while looking at the picture.

His voice was deep and husky. 'It's my family and that's me holding the bat. I was about five.'

'Who painted it?'

Liam reached up and ran his fingers slowly

127

across the figure of his mother. 'My mother, Jean did, that's her there. Her favourite pastime was to have us all together in the backyard. When she was told she only had a short time left to live, all that she wanted was to be at home doing the everyday things that mothers do. They could have travelled anywhere in the world or done anything that she wanted. But my father told me that every minute she had, she spent at home with all of us. That was what she wanted to do.'

He stopped, surprised at himself. It was unusual for him to voice his emotions and talking about his mother to someone he hardly knew was rare. A lump formed in his throat and he looked again at the print, struggling to keep his voice steady.

'She died shortly after she finished this painting. My dad was left to bring up the four of us boys. Chris, Jack, Nate and myself,' he said pointing to each of them.

'Your mother is beautiful and so is the print. Does your father have the original painting?'

'He does.'

'How sad. Four little boys.' She drew herself up and took a deep breath. 'I need to swim.'

'So do I,' Liam said, also dragging his eyes away from the print. 'Let's go. Maybe we can do some work on your stroke this morning. If you're going to stay here for a while perhaps you could improve your swimming.'

* * *

Before they started, Liam gave Billy some tips on swim strokes. He watched as she did a couple of laps, waiting for her to return, before giving more directions. 'Your legs are bending too much and there's no rhythm.' He demonstrated how her legs should be working. 'Concentrate really hard and think about every movement you make.'

After a while he also began doing his laps, his mind turning away from the events of the last few days, instead focusing on his own strokes and movement through the water. They passed each other a few times and he noticed that she had finished her swim and moved up onto the beach. She had placed her towel and bag down in the spot where he normally sat. A few times he noticed her looking around, obviously wary of any cars or people walking further up the shore near the car park. By the time he finished swimming she seemed relaxed and lay sunbaking, watching Liam as he walked out of the water towards her.

'You swim like a fish,' she said, sitting up and shielding her eyes against the glare of the sun. 'It's like you glide across the surface of the water.' Liam laughed as he dried himself, as usual the freshness and exercise of the morning swim invigorating and allowing him to get his world into focus.

Billy stood up. She was quite tall, her legs long, her muscles defined from the hours of swimming giving her an athletic physique. Liam could feel her eyes on him and he knew that his physique often attracted attention because of his bulk and strength. Although he loved the fitness aspect of his exercise, his appearance was not of interest to him. From experience, he knew it was the health of the mind that mattered the most.

He chuckled.

'What's funny,' she asked as she wrapped a towel around her tiny waist.

'Well, don't take it the wrong way. But before I knew your name I always thought of you as the butterfly girl.'

'Why?'

He pulled a comical face. 'Well, if you could see yourself do the butterfly stroke.'

'What are you saying?' She looked up at him as he dried his hair.

Liam towelled his hair carefully, trying to flatten the thick curls that he knew would be springing up in an unruly fashion on his head.

'Um, let's just say it needs a lot of work.'

'I thought that was my best stroke. I am good at the butterfly.'

'Well it's what you think that counts, but I'm telling you that stroke needs some work. Come on, it's time for a coffee and then I have to start work.'

She followed him through the bush, picking up her pace to keep up with his huge strides. When they reached his property, he led her to a covered area, the rough wooden structure covered in a vibrant hanging wisteria plant, its stems twining in and out of the beams. Purple flowers hung thickly from the vine, the foliage forming a thick covering that provided a shady recess in the corner of the garden. The petals dropped onto the cobbled paved area below, a purple blanket that added a whimsical colour against the green of the grass. An old wrought iron table and chair setting in the middle of the pavers provided a comfortable place to have morning tea and Liam gestured for Billy to take a seat. 'Sit here and enjoy the garden. It's at its best in the morning. I'll bring out a coffee for us.'

★ ★ ★

They sat together, Billy curious about the garden and the various buildings on the property.

'Who looks after it all?' she asked, her eyes wide.

'Well, that's what I do for a job now, but as you can see this place is getting a bit rundown. My dad's coming to stay in the cabin next to yours in a few months, so I'm hoping he might want to do some yard work.'

'I'd really like to potter around here in the garden while I'm looking for a job.'

'Really, you want to do yard work? Have you ever gardened before?'

'Of course I have. I've worked on farms in various parts of Victoria over the years, plus I used to do the gardening and mowing at Ervin's house.'

'I didn't even think . . .'

'What? Because I'm a female?' She plonked her cup down on the table. I may have a foreign background, but I am a very independent modern Australian woman. I can turn my hand to most things. I've had to do various jobs to survive over the years. I'm a competent gardener and I can mow and use a whipper snipper.'

'Hang on a minute. Maybe there's more here than what I've been thinking. If you can garden and you're interested, I was actually about to advertise for a gardener and an offsider for light landscaping work. The business is really starting to pick up and I can't do it all myself.'

'I have references. I would do a week trial for free if you wanted?'

He laughed loudly. 'Don't undercut yourself. How about we start the day after tomorrow and see how you go. You can work the first week here in my yard and then after that you can come out on the jobs with me. We can talk about your wages.'

Billy twirled a wisteria flower in her hand, watching it as it spun in the air. She tucked it behind her ear, the purple standing out against the darkness of her hair. With her hair drawn up she really was the picture of beauty, her high cheekbones leading up to her exquisite eyes, framed by thick eyelashes, dark green eyes peering out from beneath.

'There is something else I'd still like to discuss.' Liam had her full attention now, her gaze drawn away from the movement of the flower in her hand. 'Do you remember I asked you about posing for me. I would like to know if you are interested. The money will be far more than what you earn with the gardening.'

Liam thought for a while and then watched her eyes widen as he told her how much each sitting was worth. 'I'm very professional and I have been completing and exhibiting nude portraits for a number of years. I can show you some of my work if you'd like.'

She stood up abruptly. 'There is no need to discuss this any further. When you asked me last night I did not think you were talking about posing nude. I thought you meant perhaps a pose like the one I did at your class weeks ago.'

'Well, it is something you could consider. The money is well worth it and you have the perfect body for what I'm looking for.'

Dark eyes flashed angrily at Liam, and he was taken aback at the fury written on her face. 'I don't sell my body. I think you have taken the wrong impression from me. Do you think just because I need a job I would sell myself? Is it because my skin is dark? Is that why you presume such things?'

Liam stood also, alarmed at the response and the way she had reacted to the proposal. Painting unclothed models had become commonplace in his life. The women who posed were professional workers who took the sittings seriously, vying for the opportunity to work with an artist whose work was hung in some of the best galleries in Australia. 'You aren't selling your body. You simply pose and as a professional and a highly regarded artist I paint your body. It's a matter of lines, colours and shapes. It isn't a sleazy sexual approach but rather a form of beauty, and for models, a very good way to make a lot of money in a short amount of time.'

'I will not pose nude. I think you have misread me and now I'm going to pack up my belongings and move back to my flat. I thought I could trust you, but now you ask me this. Don't get up, I can easily catch the bus back. Was this your motive the entire time, to entice me here and then ask me to take off my clothes? What do you take me for?'

Her words came out fast and the angrier she got the faster she spoke. Her hands started waving around in the air and Liam took a couple of steps backward, surprised at the force of her arguments as she directed more words of anger towards him.

'I apologise. I don't see a problem and many life models start their careers posing as you did the other night. However,' he held his hand up to stop her going off again. 'If it is definitely not your thing than I won't ask again. I guess I have painted so many unclothed models that it doesn't seem such a big thing to me anymore. I apologise again, it makes no difference to my original offers of rent and a job. Forget I asked about the paintings. The offer for the gardening still stands. I do actually need someone to work for me and I can assure you that when I offered for you to stay here it was purely out of concern for your safety.'

'Do not take me for a fool.'

'I apologise again.'

She had turned her back to him and looked out across the garden, her shoulders moving up and down as she drew herself up straighter.

Liam knew she would be weighing up her options. If she returned to the flat she wasn't safe and not able to pay the rent. It could take ages for her to get another job and by then the landlord would have kicked her out and she would go backwards even further with the little money she had left. Living in the cabin was the ideal situation, and he could tell she was drawn to the garden. Liam watched her as she looked around the garden. It was beautiful, and he knew she would enjoy living and working in it.

At first, he had thought it wouldn't make any difference to him if she stayed or not. Last night it had felt good to be able to help her and to scare her former employer away, however he was not convinced she would stay and had decided it was good for her to work that out for herself. This morning however, he had enjoyed her swimming with him. It had been nice to have someone there when he started the day and she was good company, the two of them talking easily to each other and relaxed in each other's company. Now he waited for her to calm down and perhaps think about the benefits of somewhere safe and pleasant to live, along with the prospect of employment in the gardening business. He was also experiencing a niggling feeling deep down. He didn't want her to go. He wanted to see her again and share coffee, a swim and to sit and chat.

He held his breath as she turned around.

'I am not scared of you. Just because you are a man and much bigger than me, you don't intimidate me at all.'

Liam's eyebrows rose. 'I would hate it if I did. Why would you even say that?'

'Because that is often what men think life is like. That they can tower over the woman and scare them. Get them to do what they want and not be who they really are.'

'For God's sake. I'm not like that.' Liam wanted to say more but she flashed her eyes at him and held up her hand to silence his words.

'I need to be honest with you. I do feel like I know you a little, however I misjudged your original request to model and I hadn't given it another thought until you brought it up now.'

'Forget about the modelling. It has nothing to do with the other arrangements that I have offered.' Liam watched her and knew that she was summing up the offer, extra cautious because of her past employment experiences.

'I have learnt that what comes easy is not what it always appears to be.'

'That is sometimes true but there are also times when you need to take opportunities and grab them with both hands. The cabin is comfortable and cheap, this may be a job for you and besides you need swimming lessons, badly!'

He watched her stifle a smile. 'Sometimes your own swimming is not calm or structured. I have seen you making many splashes and making the water around you angry.'

Sometimes Liam swam peacefully, his body gliding effortlessly, his strong arms and legs at one with the water. On other occasions though there was an aggression, a pent-up frustration as his body pounded the surface, moving at speeds faster than usual.

His face was stern when he replied. 'Sometimes swimming helps me calm my mind. It takes my thoughts away from where I don't want them to be.'

They stood staring at one another, Liam waiting for what would be her decision.

Angry flashing eyes looked hard at him and Billy crossed her arms. Liam sat down again, waiting for her to compose herself before she spoke.

'I will work as a gardener and rent the cabin. You'll need to draw up a contract for both, including wages and rent costs and conditions. I will not however *ever* pose nude for you.'

Liam stifled a chuckle, watching as she stomped off over the lawn back to her cabin. Well, he thought, he might just have a new worker and tenant. He would have to see how she worked before getting too excited, but hopefully she was as competent as what she said. As for the artwork, he could see it just wasn't going to happen. He would have to look elsewhere for a model or perhaps at class someone else might appear, a model who would suit his needs. Resigned to her refusal of his offer, he sighed loudly and stood up, stretching his arms high above his head before making his way back to the house.

The artwork would need to be pushed aside for the moment; he had a lot of jobs to attend to, as well as now organising tools and gear for an extra worker.

17

By the following morning Liam had drawn up not only the contract papers for work and rent of the small cabin, but also a list of the work he wanted done around the yard. Most of it was light gardening, weeding, mowing, mulching and some trimming around the edges of the gardens. It would be a good way to start Billy off and then he could gauge how well she worked.

She had joined him in the morning for their swim, neither of them talking as they made their way to the lake. Casso as usual ran ahead, scurrying after every lizard or grasshopper he could find.

There had been no swim lessons today, instead both of them wading out and swimming methodically across the lake, Liam quickly passed Billy as he pushed strongly through the water. By the time he finished his laps she had disappeared. Casso had gone also and Liam shook his head at the dog's lack of loyalty. He dried off, enjoying the warmth of the sun on his body. The discussion from the night before bounced around in his mind and he smiled, remembering how her eyes had flashed when she had become angry with him. He admired that she had stood her ground, even though it annoyed him that she couldn't see the reasoning behind posing for his paintings. By the time he returned to the house she was sitting waiting for him under the pergola area, Casso lying angelically at her feet.

'You look like you're ready to start,' he said, looking her up and down. He liked the way she dressed; long khaki shorts with a collared T-shirt, her hair tied up in a ponytail and work boots and socks on. A straw hat sat on the table next to her.

'I'm keen to begin.'

'I'll be back out in a minute. Just let me get changed and I'll bring the contract papers out for you to look at before you start.'

* * *

While she sat waiting, Billy went over the events of the last couple of weeks. She was excited and amazed at how the change of circumstances had fallen into place. Because of Ervin's threats, she now had a cute cosy cabin to live in. It was perfect for her, set in a beautiful garden and close to the lake where she could swim each day. Not only that, but if she worked hard and proved she was capable, she may just have landed herself a job doing something that she actually enjoyed. Keeping active would be good for both her body and spirit and she was most happy when she was doing physical work. This job could be the mixture of both and if she was determined, she could make it work.

Although Liam had handed her the job without hesitation, he would expect her to pull her weight; he had made that clear. She would need to work solidly and be reliable. More importantly she was confident about her refusal to pose for his paintings and hopefully he wouldn't broach the subject again. Even though he was twice the size of her, he had backed off immediately when Billy had let him know how she felt. She was well accustomed to sticking up for herself, after all there had never been anyone else who would do it for her.

At first when she worked for Ervin she had been compliant, and his demands had not been too unreasonable. However, as the months passed, and he gave her more tasks as well as making strange and difficult requests, she had tried to stand up for herself. It was not her nature to go along with things she did not agree with. Ervin however, had been cunning and in the end had used the children and the money he had swindled from her to coerce and intimidate her into doing what he wanted her to do.

When she first started with the family he had insisted that she wear the traditional Islamic dress, telling her that she was a bad example for his children and that men such as himself could be tempted by her uncovered skin. She had argued with him and told him that even though her heritage was Islamic, she was no longer of the faith. She had grown up in modern Australian society and was an independent woman. He was however persistent, and after continuous arguments and the fear of losing her job, she had given in and worn the traditional garb when she was in the children's company. As the months went by he had tried to manipulate other facets of her life and continually tried to get her to think as he did. When he had started sending his wife away on extended holidays and leaving Billy alone and in charge of the children, she had become frightened and worried

140

what he was capable of.

Ervin began to spend more and more time at home with her during the day, instead of working from his office. A huge argument had erupted between them when he ordered that she move from her tiny flat into a spare room that he had in his house. She had refused, knowing that he would have total control over her if she was under his roof. By then she had begun looking for another job, however her car had disappeared and when she tried to get access to her money he had invested, she found that there didn't appear to be any trace of it.

She had questioned him, but he had only smiled scornfully and asked her what money and car she was talking about. The next day he had grabbed her arm roughly and tried to talk to her about the financial favours he was doing for her and how she needed to do some favours for him. He hadn't come straight out and said what he wanted, but from the way he looked at her and then stroked her arm, she knew what he had in mind.

She had quit that afternoon and Liam had interrupted the argument at the lake the next morning. Ervin had followed her in his car and when she got off the bus had grabbed her around the waist, pushing her back towards his car. Thank goodness Liam, who had towered over Ervin, had been there, because who would know what would have happened if he hadn't intercepted.

Billy's only saving grace was that the family was about to move away and, hopefully Ervin would leave her alone. Perhaps the fact that Liam had also now warned him, as well as the police being involved, would be enough to keep him away. During the time Billy had worked for the family she had seen and overheard conversations that implicated Ervin in some serious illegal matters. Liam had hit the nail on the head when he suggested to Ervin that he would report him to the police in reference to his illegal dealings.

★ ★ ★

Life had been a rollercoaster of emotions and worries over the last months. Closing her eyes, Billy breathed in the musky fragrance of the wisteria above. She made a wish that today might be the start of a new chapter in her life. She opened her eyes, the sun bright and warming her skin. Also enjoying the sunshine were tiny honey-eating birds, their backs bright yellow, slender beaks fine and long as they darted in and out of the wisteria. She watched them closely, admiring their speed and deftness, their bright bodies flying neatly through the twisted vine, their beaks tapping the pollen hidden between the purple petals of the flowers. Overhead the vivid blue sky created a contrasting backdrop, a few fluffy white clouds scuttling across the vastness before heading east, out across the nearby ocean.

Last night she had lain awake for hours, listening to the soft noises in the bush around her. Stillness and solitude surrounded the cabin and even though it was small it was spacious and quiet compared to the noisy cramped flat she had lived in for the past couple of years. It had never been completely dark in the unit, no matter what she put up to cover the windows. Glaring lights from the shops below and the traffic lights that flashed brightly in the street, always allowed some light in. The pitch darkness that had pervaded the room she had slept in last night was like a cloak of safe comfort and a calm backdrop to what had been a tumultuous year.

As she lay on the bed she had tried to work out some of the different sounds that could be heard. Crickets chirped lightly in the trees outside her window, and a cooing noise, probably an owl, could be heard from the taller bushes behind the cabin. Every now and then the muffled croaking of a frog echoed up and down the downpipe that was outside her room. Background to it all was the distant sound of the waves crashing onto the beach, situated beyond the lake where she swam each day. The sound of the ocean and the noises of nature had lulled her to sleep; a deep slumber and the best rest she had experienced in a very long time.

18

The first week flew past and Liam was impressed with Billy's ability to think ahead and see what needed doing, without being asked. When it came to the heavier and dirtier jobs in the yard she completed them easily and had actually seemed to enjoy the work the harder it became. Each afternoon he had checked in with her, laughing at the state of her clothes now covered in stains and dirt. An outside laundry under an old lean-to provided them both with a place to wash their work clothes, a job that she automatically took on as her own. 'I didn't really employ you to do domestic work,' Liam said one afternoon as he threw his dirty clothes into the basket she had placed in the laundry.

'Hanging out the washing is one of my favourite jobs to do. It's outside and it's relaxing, sort of like hosing a garden.'

'Well, as long as you don't mind.' He shrugged, secretly quite happy that there was one less housework chore for him to do.

At the end of the week she had accepted his offer to take her back to the flat and pack up the remainder of her belongings. Together they had filled boxes with her possessions. Liam had organised Yared and Nadir to help load the few pieces of furniture that she owned into his trailer. It had been amusing to watch the two men who appeared quite shy and kept nodding their heads when they were introduced to Billy. Once they were loaded up, Liam led them all towards the small coffee shop next to the bakery. Billy had been quieter than usual, and Liam had made a concerted effort to get her to join in the conversation. Yared who was much the same build as Liam, sat next to her and had been very polite, ensuring that he passed her the sugar and the milk, asking if she wanted anything else.

Liam had instigated the talk with some questions, picking up on the fact that all three were wary of the others' culture, and although friendly, were cautious about what they were saying. The longer they sat, the more they all relaxed and soon Liam's questions and laughter had drawn them together. Even Billy appeared more at ease, her beautiful smile and relaxed chatter making the initial wariness of the two men disappear.

Yared and Nadir talked enthusiastically to Liam about the work they were now doing and how Lottie and Annika kept passing their names on to other friends, ensuring the flow of work. 'They have been very, very good to us,' Yared said. 'Last time they even sent us home with books for our children. I think they may have realised that we aren't savages or head-hunters.' He laughed loudly, a deep chuckle that made the others laugh as well.

'Just because we have dark skin, does not mean we were not educated before we came here,' Nadir said. 'Some people say the funniest things to us. You think they had never seen an African person before.'

'They all think I'm a terrorist because I'm

Afghan,' Billy said. 'They don't realise we flee from the same people they are terrified of.'

'How long has your family been here in Australia?' Yared asked.

'There is only me and I came from a camp in Pakistan when I was only a child. I have no family because they were killed in Afghanistan as we tried to leave.' She looked down and Liam could see Nadir and Yared straighten up as they looked at each other.

'You too have suffered,' Yared said. 'We who have come from different camps understand the hardship. We have our families though, well some of them. But you say you have no-one.'

'No-one. Another family in the camp took me in as their own, but once we arrived here that did not last. The rest is a very long story.'

'But you have survived.' Yared nodded at her in respect. 'As we have also.'

'I have lost my culture though. I am more Australian now than Afghan.'

'It is difficult.' Nadir was serious for once. 'We too try and keep some old ways and to make sure our children retain our language. They will be Australians but they will also always be Sudanese or Eritrean, just like you will always be Afghan. The war, the camps and the separation from country, cannot take away that part of your identity.'

Liam loved listening to them talk. The two men, like Billy, always had such a philosophical take on life and were eager to accept and learn as much as they could. 'Can you still speak any Afghan, Billy?' he asked.

'I can, because growing up I had many friends

146

who spoke Farsi and Persian. I can speak and write three languages fluently other than English.'

Liam ordered another round of coffees and they sat chatting for ages. Billy asked Nadir and Yared about their wives and families, the two men eager to share their stories and to talk to someone about the difficulties of settling into a new country. Yared's wife was having problems with improving her English and Nadir's wife had trouble choosing the food that she saw in the supermarkets. 'Everything is different; everything we go to do is new. We're loving life here, with so many opportunities for our families and education for our children, but it is sometimes not easy to settle in.'

Billy suggested that when the men were at art classes she could meet with their wives and help to improve their English. They nodded enthusiastically when Liam added that when he dropped the two men home from art class he could pick Billy up and bring her home. Nadir and Yared kept thanking Billy, telling her that it would be a great help as their wives were finding it difficult and needed help filling in forms for the children, as well as working out where to pay the bills.

'Nadir and I have our art classes. It gives us time to do something ourselves, but our wives would find it very, very difficult to mix with those they do not know. It is greatly appreciated.'

'No worries,' Billy said. 'I know how hard it can be. I would love to help them out. It will also be good for me to have some company. It is important for them to learn English, it will make life much easier for them.'

With that the talk turned to the art classes and

Billy stayed silent, listening to the men talk about the different pieces they were working on and some different exhibitions that Liam wanted to take them to.

'Do you paint?' Yared asked Billy.

'No, no, I am not an artist.'

'Have you seen Liam's work?'

Liam started stacking the plates and cups up, signalling it was time to go. 'No, she hasn't seen any of my work. I've been keeping her busy with work in the yard. Now she needs to set up the cabin with her belongings from here. It's going to be busy working with me out on the jobs.'

The four of them stood; Yared and Nadir bowing their heads to Billy and shaking her hand. Nadir spoke earnestly, 'A small house will hold a hundred friends and today we have made new friends.'

19

The cabin provided a perfect new home for Billy and Liam's once overgrown garden was now well-maintained, the summer months providing plentiful rainfall to keep it looking lush and green. The arrangements were working out fine, and not only was Billy an excellent tenant but also a reliable offsider for Liam's gardening and maintenance business. Although she had told him that she had previously done farm work and gardening, he had been surprised by her knowledge and ability to do all the work he had given her. Today Liam's dad was arriving, and Billy had volunteered to clean out his cabin and make sure that everything was right for his stay. Liam was excited about seeing his father and Billy suggested she would like to do some cooking for them, so that they could have some special meals.

'That's fine, Billy, but only if you agree to join us on some nights.'

'I don't want to impose. We usually eat at our own places.'

'I know that, but I think you'd really like my dad and he'll be keen to talk to you.'

Over the previous months Billy and Liam had worked together each day, swum at the lake each morning and occasionally had a cold drink under the pergola in the afternoons. The nights and weekends however, they had kept separate; Liam often at art classes or working in his studio,

Billy helping out the women with their English or spending her time in the garden. They had purposely given each other their own space. If the arrangements were to work, they would need to have their own time away from each other.

The ladies at art class had been curious about Liam's new tenant and worker, and even more so when they learned that she had been the clothed model who had posed for them many months ago.

'So,' Matilda said. 'Just work, hey? We weren't born yesterday, young man. A woman of beauty like that. I don't think you'd be just mowing lawns with her.'

Annika chipped in. 'Have you got some nude paintings of her? You should show us.'

Lottie joined in. 'We thought you looked happier than usual. C'mon Liam you can tell us. We can keep secrets, ask anyone.'

They had all laughed and made further jokes. Liam had smiled but had insisted that it was purely a work relationship and it was nothing more than that.

'And, although I did ask, she told me in no uncertain terms that she will not pose nude for me. End of story.'

'Argh, how much did you offer? Maybe you can offer her more money,' Rolande raised his eyebrows.

'No, there is no way, it wouldn't matter how much was offered, she won't do it. She looks like a gentle person, but I can tell you, I wouldn't like to push her too far. She's very independent and after the problems at her last job, she's certainly not going to let anyone push her around again.'

Pierre shook his head. 'Such a waste, those lines and curves. The perfect model's body and right under your nose, Liam. What a shame.' He chuckled as he walked away, all of them going back to their own work as a naked woman took her place on the chair in front of them.

Matilda turned around and whispered to him. 'Cellulite is difficult to draw, is it not? Ugh, and so much of it!' She rolled her eyes dramatically before turning back to her work.

Liam had not forgotten about his wish to paint Billy, but the more he came to know her, the further he pushed it from his mind. She was a modern woman with progressive and independent thoughts and she also had a certain degree of modesty about her. Besides, he liked the way the arrangement was working. She was great company at work and often when something fired him up, or customers were troublesome, she would take over and handle the situation much better than he would have.

There was a calmness to her and it was a good balance for him, keeping his thoughts positive and motivated. She was, he thought, a glass half-full person and she never complained about anything. Instead she just found a way to work around whatever the problem may be.

He looked over to where Yared and Annika were in deep conversation. Annika looked closely as Yared worked, the two of them talking about the method that he was using. Annika and Lottie had changed their opinions about the two men and not only had they helped them both start their businesses, but also now on weekends they often had them and their families over for a backyard barbeque. Lottie was teaching Yared's two girls to play the piano and Annika had started taking Nadir's boys to tennis lessons on a Saturday morning.

'Well, I always took my own boys,' she said. 'For years they played tennis. I miss that and besides the two boys are just lovely. I've grown very attached to them. They've asked me to come to their sports day at school next week. They tell me they are very, very good runners.' She did a good imitation of Nadir's accent.

The jokes were now in good fun and Liam was pleased that once the women had got to know the two men and their families, they had not only been friendly but had found numerous ways to help them out as they settled into their new lives. It had been beneficial for all of them.

20

This morning Liam and Billy finished swimming at the same time. They stood at the water's edge and chatted, both refreshed and enjoying the warmth of the sun. Liam demonstrated some arm movements to Billy, who was still trying to improve her strokes. Although her style had come a long way, she still needed to work on it. She copied Liam's actions, and he showed her again, trying to perfect the ways her arms were supposed to move.

They both laughed before turning around to see Liam's father, John, walking towards them. His hand stretched out to Liam's, both of them grinning broadly as they wrapped their arms around each other.

Billy watched with interest. It was obvious they were father and son. They were both tall and solidly built, their faces similar, the same friendly blue eyes set in a handsome rugged face.

'You look good son,' John squeezed Liam's shoulders.

'You too, Dad,' Liam replied.

'And this must be Billy. I've heard so much about you.' John held out his hand, his smile widening even more as Billy's vivid green eyes met his, her slender hand squeezing his in return. He turned back to Liam. 'You two look so good. The swimming and work must be keeping you fit and healthy.'

'Pleased to meet you John. Liam has told me many stories about you,' Billy said.

'All good, I hope.' John chuckled.

'Of course,' Billy called out as she made her way up the beach to where her towel was.

John turned to Liam, 'You look so happy son, it's the best I've seen you look in a long time. The stress seems to have gone from your face.'

'It has been a good few months, Dad. I feel well,' Liam said, 'and it's been great to have Billy working with me.'

'You said that was working out for both of you. You failed to mention though, how beautiful she is. She almost took my breath away. Are you sure there's nothing more than friendship between you? I watched you both from up on the dunes, you seem so at ease with one another.'

Liam laughed. 'Don't start matchmaking the minute you get here. We're just good friends.'

John chuckled and shook his head, before hugging Liam again. Their conversation continued, only stopping when Casso came bounding out of the bush, yapping excitedly around their legs. Liam picked him up, patting his scruffy coat.

Billy had returned and stood beside them, the water glistening on her skin, her dark wet hair trailing down to her waist. Both men watched as she expertly wound her hair around her fingers and tied it up loosely on top of her head. John closed his eyes, his hand reaching for Liam's shoulder.

'Are you okay, Dad?' Liam asked.

John cleared his throat, shook his head and slowly opened his eyes.

'I'm sorry,' John said, 'Jean always tied her

154

hair up in exactly the same manner. She used to twist and twirl it around and then, hey presto, an elegant bun would sit on top of her head.' He chuckled. 'She used to get annoyed at the ringlets that escaped and hung down her neck and around her face.' He smiled and looked at Billy. 'I loved those stray bits of hair; they were like her, wild and free. That just brought back a lot of beautiful memories.'

He threw his arm around Liam's shoulders. 'God son, do you ever stop growing.' He pummelled Liam's biceps. '*Muscles*, that's what we used to call him, Billy. *Muscles*, even when he was small.'

'Dad, don't start with all the embarrassing stories.'

Billy walked ahead of them, letting the two of them catch up, trying to walk away unnoticed when she got nearer the house. The sight of them together had stirred deep emotions for her and there was a lump in her throat as she thought about the special connection between a father and son. Billy was used to the loneliness, the throbbing aches, a reminder that she had no family. There was nobody to call her own.

21

John swam with Billy and Liam each morning, offering Billy some further advice on her strokes.

'Um, I'm just not sure where to even start with your butterfly style though.' He pulled a face at her. 'It's probably the worst I've ever seen.'

'I thought it was my best stroke,' she joked back, before taking off across the lake, both arms raised together, thrashing the water, her body only moving forward a tiny bit at a time.

⋆　⋆　⋆

'I moved a lot quicker that time,' Billy said as she stood next to John, the water dripping from both of them as they allowed the heat of the sun to dry their bodies.

'It was a smidgen better, but we need to do a lot of work on your swimming style,' John said, shielding his eyes as he looked out across the water at Liam, who as usual, was gliding strongly across the lake.

'You know his mother was a good swimmer,' John said. 'She would swim every morning in the public pool near us. When the kids got old enough, she taught them how to swim. They're all good in the water.' His voice was melancholic, his eyes tinged with sadness. 'She would have loved to have watched him swim like that.' He gestured out across the lake. 'As a man. She never got to see any of them grow up.'

'It's a sad story, John. I often look at the print on Liam's wall. There is so much love in that picture.'

He coughed to clear his throat, the emotion obviously still so close to the surface. 'Never was a mother so sadly missed. But we have survived, and they have all done well for themselves. Liam's probably had the worst time, but he's doing fine now as well. Has he ever talked to you about when he was overseas?'

Billy shook her head. 'No, he has never said anything. I don't know that much about his life.' She took a deep breath. 'I guess I don't share many of my thoughts or memories with him. That is why we work well together. We are friends but more work colleagues than anything.'

John turned to look at her. 'That's his problem, he doesn't talk to anyone about what troubles him the most.'

'I suppose we all work through our problems the best way we can. The road travelled is often difficult.'

John went to speak again but stopped before any words came out. He watched her as if waiting for her to speak. But she was silent, her gaze fixed on the dunes behind the lake.

Finally, John spoke. 'You have had a difficult life. I can sometimes see the sadness in your eyes.'

Billy looked back into John's eyes. 'It has not always been easy, but it is a long and complicated story and now there is much happiness in my life. I am blessed.'

'Liam said you came here as a refugee from Afghanistan.'

'It is about seventeen years ago now, but yes that is correct. I came by boat with others who were not my family. Although I was only a child I can still remember the terror that was constant for everyone who was crammed on there. The seas were rough, and I remember vomiting over and over.' She stood up straighter. 'No-one helped me. A lot of time passed and the next thing I remember was people shouting as we were taken from that boat to a large ship. They burned the boat we had come on. I still remember the flames.'

'Who looked after you? Where was your family?'

'My mother died in the camp just before we came on the boat. I do not know what she died from. My father and four brothers were all killed when we tried to escape from Afghanistan to Pakistan.' Her voice choked up and she tried hard to compose herself. 'I do not remember what they looked like and I only remember my mother's face a little.'

John hugged her, his eyes brimming with tears. 'That is a tragic story. There has been so much sorrow in your life.'

'That is why I love the print on Liam's wall. Your whole family is there, forever, even if they are not in this world they can be remembered by the painting. And your wife captured the emotion and love, the sadness and happiness, it's all there in that one painting.'

They both looked up as Liam strode up the beach towards them. 'Right you two, what happened to the swimming lesson?'

'We have been having a heart-to-heart,' John

said. 'It's helpful to talk to someone about the obstacles in life.'

Billy gathered her thoughts. 'Thank you, John. It is good to talk.'

Liam grabbed his towel and stood waiting for the two of them. 'Let's go, we have a lot of people coming for lunch. I'm going to need all your help in getting it ready.'

John wrapped his arm around Billy's shoulders and gave her another hug. 'Righto Billy, we've got it all covered, haven't we.'

'Everything is organised,' she said, directing her words towards Liam. 'Your father and I have it all under control. There will be twelve adults and eight children all up, including us three. Oh, and an extra one, Matilda's daughter is coming also. That makes twenty-one.'

The gathering had been organised at art class the previous week as a welcoming get together, so John could meet Liam's friends. Yared and Nadir had talked of nothing else at class and it sounded like they were bringing enough food to feed the entire neighbourhood. Pierre and Rolande were responsible for bringing the drinks and Annika and Lottie were vying with Matilda to claim who could bring the best dessert. All Liam had to do, with Billy and John's help, was to set the big long tables under the pergola in the shade and make sure there were enough chairs, plates and cutlery.

★ ★ ★

It had taken the rest of the morning to ensure that everything was the way they wanted. Liam and

John set up the chairs and table and Billy spent a lot of time arranging the settings. She cut large bunches of native flowers from the garden to fill the vases positioned in the middle of the table. The grass had been cut, the hedges trimmed, and the garden looked, as Liam said, the best it had ever looked.

'Take it as a compliment Billy; it's your doing. You definitely have a flair for gardening and keeping everything in the yard looking as it should.'

'It's a beautiful garden and I love working in it.' She was modest about her achievements in the yard and made sure to add that John had also been busy helping her since his arrival.

Before long the guests began to arrive. Liam and John were ready to greet them and showed them around the yard, pointing out to the kids where the bats and balls were, as well as a badminton net in the side yard to keep them occupied. Nadir's wife's name was Atifa, and she wore long tailored pants and a long-sleeved shirt, matched with an exquisite blue satin headscarf that only showed a small amount of her fringe. Like Nadir she was tall and slender and the two of them made a striking couple. Nadir was dressed in a collared shirt and long trousers, a tie completing his outfit. He introduced his four small children, all of them with curious eyes that looked out from behind thick eyelashes. Atifa was quiet and smiled shyly as she handed Liam the pots of food they had brought to share. The children clustered around her, the two smallest ones hanging on tightly to her trousers, their big eyes looking up curiously at Liam.

Yared's family joined them and his wife, Meron,

was soon chatting and laughing with Atifa. She also was tall and elegant, her hair done up in numerous tiny plaits that hung down to below her waistline. Colourful printed fabric twirled around her body, forming a traditional style dress that was matched with vibrant bangles and a bright orange necklace that contrasted sharply against her dark Eritrean skin. A wide smile appeared to be permanent on her finely structured face and before long she had Atifa smiling and laughing too. Yared and Meron also had four children aged from ten down. Each one shook Liam's and then John's hand, repeating the same greeting as they met. 'Good afternoon. I am very pleased to meet you and I thank you for welcoming my family today.'

The two men smiled at the well-rehearsed words that the children would have been asked to practise before their arrival today.

Annika, Lottie, Pierre and Rolande arrived together and the backyard was soon filled with noisy chatter and laughter as everyone was introduced to each other. In the midst of the noise Billy quietly joined them. She had become friends with the two wives through helping them with their English and now they welcomed her like she was part of their families. It didn't take long for the children to spot her and Liam watched how they all vied for her attention, pushing each other to get the closest to her. The youngest boy held his arms up to her and she picked him up as he planted a sloppy kiss on her cheek. Liam caught his breath, drawn in by not only her beauty, but by the warmth and love she showed towards the others in the group. He stared hard, surprised at how different she looked in a flowing floral dress, her long hair loose, pinned back on one side. His eyes moved over her body, admiring her graceful stance and long legs, delicate tapered ankles and strappy sandals showing off her slender feet.

'You're staring, son.' John had come up beside Liam.

'Oh, sorry, Dad. Billy just looks a bit different dressed up.'

'Ha. She always looks beautiful. I'm not sure what you're waiting for.'

'I, um, well ...' Liam stuttered over his words, caught off guard by John who went to say something more, however was interrupted by the arrival of Matilda and her daughter, Ruby.

More introductions were made as Ruby was introduced to everyone and Billy and Liam were kept busy making sure everyone had a drink and something to eat. At first Billy stayed with the African women, comfortable in their presence and enjoying their funny stories about their new life in Australia. Eventually she relaxed and also started talking to Matilda and Ruby. Both women were friendly and Billy laughed at Matilda who loved to shock everyone with her flamboyant language and crude jokes. 'Just because my body is old, doesn't mean my mind is,' she teased. 'I'd give you younger ones all a run for your money.'

John came over to join the group and was soon in deep conversation with Ruby, the two of them hitting it off instantly. Billy had formed a strong attachment to John and she smiled as she watched him. Today he was dressed up and enjoying lively conversation with Matilda's very attractive daughter, who was a similar age to him.

Billy moved away from John and Ruby as Annika and Lottie both beckoned for her to join them. Soon she was deep in conversation with the two ladies, who were also keen gardeners.

Today the backyard offered the guests a kaleidoscope of colour, and the bright azaleas surrounded by the whites and purples of the alyssum flowers made a colourful border near where they all stood. Tall shady trees dropped their jacaranda blossoms and in some areas the ground was covered in purple hues. Freshly mowed areas offered a stretch for the kids to run around in and two of the younger girls climbed the trees. The sound of them singing a song in their own language offered a cultural melodious background to the excited chatter of the older guests.

★ ★ ★

Yared called all the children in from playing and now they all sat on either side of the long table that had been set up in the cool of the pergola. Large jugs of cold juice and bowls of different foods were scattered along its centre, the mixture of Eritrean and Sudanese food a delight to the others, who said they hadn't tasted anything quite like it before.

Annika and Lottie made an emotional speech, welcoming the two new families and letting them know that this was now their Australian family. Apart from the words of welcome the backyard was quiet, even the smallest of the children sitting silently as the two ladies talked about the opportunities and hope that living in Australia would bring Yared, Nadir and their families. Billy sat between John and Liam, listening quietly. This was a rarity for her, a large happy gathering, an atmosphere to soak up and a day that hopefully would never end.

Yared and Meron's smallest boy had taken a liking to Billy from the start and had continued to bring her small flowers that were growing in amongst the grass. When he finished his meal, he had not followed the others to play but had instead come straight to Billy and climbed up on her lap. He cuddled in closely and put his thumb in his mouth. There was tenderness in her touch as she stroked the small boy's tight curly hair and his big eyes peered out at Liam from under her arm. Liam winked at him and he smiled and closed his eyes, snuggling in closer to Billy.

'He's not silly,' John whispered to Matilda, 'He's got the best spot in the house.'

Liam's eyes never left the small boy who appeared to have fallen asleep in Billy's arms. A familiar tingle ran across his skin and he felt the beads of sweat form on his forehead. He clenched his hands together, aware of the warning signs as his legs began to shake under the table. Through the mist that started to envelop his mind the clear voice of Billy could be heard. He shook his head and tried to focus on her face instead of the small boy's.

The others were busy talking and had not noticed the change in Liam.

Billy reached over and gently tapped his arm. 'Are you alright?'

Her voice came through the fog and he gulped hard, taking deep breaths and looking straight into her worried eyes. 'Look at me, you are okay,' she said gently.

Liam nodded and inhaled deeply. 'Thank you.' He took the glass of water that she passed to him. He sipped it slowly, his eyes following her movements as she handed him a serviette to wipe his brow with. She nodded her head towards him as he finished the water. Their eyes held and Billy smiled warmly, her gestures reassuring him that he was okay.

Yared clinked his knife against a glass, gaining everyone's attention. 'Thank you, Liam and your family and friends for welcoming us here. We are all here today together, like a fruit salad, the more mixed the fruit the sweeter the taste. We do not stand alone now, as we have many new friends. We are lucky to be here with you, our new Australian family.'

Everyone clapped and raised their glasses, a toast, to the heartfelt gratitude of those who had come to live in a safe and free country.

* * *

As the afternoon wore on and the shadows grew long across the yard, children were rounded up, toys picked up and soon everyone was hugging and shaking each other's hands. The noisy clatter and talking escalated and then faded into the distance as the guests departed.

Liam, John and Billy sat together in the garden, watching the sun dip quickly behind the tall trees that bordered the garden.

'It's so quiet now,' Billy said, her eyes moving across the yard.

Casso slept at their feet, exhausted after running around all day with the kids.

'What a day,' Liam said. 'Billy, you and Dad did a great job organising that. They all loved it.'

John stood up, stretching and yawning. 'Those kids are amazing. They have the best manners I've ever seen, and they just play and do their own thing. Not one of them complained or asked for anything. So well behaved, I must say I was impressed.'

'They are beautiful children,' Billy added. 'And all very clever.'

'You look tired, Dad,' Liam looked up at John.

'I am. I'm not as young as you two. I'll leave you both to sit. I'm exhausted. Shower and bed for me. Goodnight.'

'Goodnight,' Billy and Liam answered in unison.

22

A full moon rose in the sky, its golden haze throwing a misty sheen over the backyard where Liam and Billy sat.

'You did a great job getting all that ready. Thanks, once again.' Liam found himself unusually lost for words as he turned towards Billy, the moonlight throwing its light across her face.

'You're lucky to have them all as friends,' she answered.

'They are your friends also. They think of you as that.'

'Do you think so?'

'Of course, they do. Ruby wants to return tomorrow, so you can show her around the garden.'

Billy laughed. 'I think she wants to come back to see your dad again. They really hit it off.'

'It was nice to see Dad enjoying himself and maybe it's about time he had some female company. He's never bothered meeting anyone else since Mum died.'

Billy sat silently, watching as the moon rose higher in the sky. Stars twinkled brightly above, and crickets began to chirp noisily in the bushes.

A long while passed before Billy finally shifted in her seat. 'There is something that bothers you. I could see it in your eyes this afternoon.'

Her face was beautiful in the soft light, her long hair tousled from playing with the children. She twirled it with both hands, her fingers working easily to form a messy bun on top of her head.

'What is it, Liam? What is it that makes your mind frantic or makes you swim like the devil is chasing you?'

Liam shook his head and looked down to the ground. 'Sometimes it does feel like the devil is chasing me.' He looked up at the sky before bringing his gaze back to Billy's face. 'Some memories are hard to let go of. They haunt me.'

'It was the boy wasn't it? It was Yared's son.'

Liam drew a quick breath. 'Yes, it was.'

'What is it that bothers you?'

'It's nothing. Today I slipped up. It won't happen again.'

Billy stood up, her floral dress accentuating her slim body. 'I'm here to talk to if you ever want. Sometimes a problem shared is helpful.'

Liam smiled at her as he too stood up. 'I am fine. Thank you, but everything is okay.'

They looked at each other, neither speaking for a long while.

Eventually Billy spoke. 'Thank you for a lovely day. I think I'll head off to bed. Goodnight.'

'Goodnight Billy.'

★ ★ ★

Liam had sat for hours after she had left. He watched the stars sparkle above him and the clouds move quickly across the brightness of the moon. The air was still and the sounds of the waves in the distance echoed and crashed down onto the beach as the incoming tide pushed its waters up over the sand. Closing his eyes, he let the sounds soak into his mind, his body totally relaxed, the freshness of the night air cool against his skin.

When he opened his eyes, the blackness of the night surrounded him, the moon now hidden by heavier clouds that moved across the sky. The cabin his dad was staying in was dark, the outline of the roof just visible in the darkness of the garden. Incessant yapping sounded near Billy's cabin and Liam whistled a few times, pleased when Casso stopped chasing whatever he had been pursuing and came running back to where Liam sat. A dim light still shone in Billy's cabin and he wondered what she did at night. Apart from helping the two families with their English a couple of nights a week, she didn't leave the cabin at any other time except to work with him, or help in the yard. Today she had taken his breath away and it had taken all of his effort to stop staring at her as she laughed and talked with the friends who had filled the backyard with their food, laughter and chatter.

Her smile had saved him from the darkness and confusion that had surfaced when he looked at the small boy, and he had come close to confiding in her what had fractured his soul over the years.

This afternoon he had looked at Billy in a different light. Usually she was his swim partner, his offsider at work and friendly company when they met up with the families of Yared and Nadir. Now though, he wanted to see more of her, to talk and hear the sound of her voice. He wished she hadn't gone to bed but had stayed and talked with him. But she hadn't, because he had not been able to think of anything to say to her. His words had got stuck in his head and he had almost stammered as he thanked her and said goodnight.

An owl called out from the bushes and the light from her cabin flicked off, leaving Liam sitting in pitch darkness. He closed his eyes again, letting the night air wash over him, hoping that it would make the unusual feelings he was experiencing go away. He knew what was happening, but he did not want to complicate or ruin a lovely friendship and mutual understandings. Arrangements needed to stay the way they were.

23

For a few weeks after the gathering, life ebbed and flowed just as it always had. The only thing that altered was that John and Ruby were seeing more and more of each other. Ruby was only a few years younger than John and they both enjoyed similar pastimes. Since the day of the lunch they had spent a lot of time together and John had told Liam that they were planning to go on a trip in Ruby's van together.

'I haven't felt like this since your mother.' John confided in Liam one afternoon, the two men sitting outside in the cool, both drinking a cold beer. 'She's just so lovely and we have many things in common. Who would have thought at this age that I'd be lucky enough to find a woman who I can enjoy life with?'

'You're still only young, Dad. It's great that you've met Ruby and I know Matilda is also ecstatic to see her happy, and with you.'

'I feel like I'm twenty again.'

It was the happiest Liam had seen his dad for as long as he could remember and that night he enjoyed repeating all the news to his sister-in-law, Kath, on the phone. She too, had been pleased to hear that John had found happiness and that he was already making arrangements to visit them when his and Ruby's travel plans took them to Western Australia. Kath also wanted to find out what Liam had been up to and she asked a lot of questions about the young woman, Billy, who John had told her was living in the spare cabin on Liam's property.

'She's a workmate, Kath. I've known her for a while now and there's nothing more there than friendship.'

'Your dad told me he thinks there's more to it than just friends. He said Billy is very beautiful and cares a lot for you.'

'You two are just old romantics. She works for me and she's grateful for the job and the cabin, but there's nothing else to it. You know I wanted her to pose for me, but she wouldn't be in it.'

'Smart girl, I like her already.'

'Why? So many of those life models make good money posing. She has the perfect body for what I wanted in my collection, but there was no way I could talk her into it.'

'Well, look at how the last model who posed for you worked out. Good old sour-faced Amanda. I hear you've got her dog there at the moment.'

Liam chuckled. 'I have and he's having the time of his life. Amanda would have a fit to see what her precious city dog has been up to, or rather rolling in.'

They chatted for ages; Liam always grateful for the closeness and care that Kath continued to give him. After he hung up, he thought as he always did about the advice she always loved to share with him. For so long she had held the family, and his life in particular, together. Now she was encouraging him to look a bit deeper into his feelings, to think about what his real connection to Billy was.

After returning from overseas he had found it difficult to look for and find love. Amanda had been the instigator of the last romance and when he thought about it, he had just gone along with what she had wanted. Once he had rid himself of so many of the demons that had plagued him, he had come to the realisation that he didn't love her, but instead was just going through the motions of living with someone else for companionship.

He had come a long way with his healing process since then and although he knew there were times when he went backwards emotionally, there weren't so many spiralling downward plunges like there had been in previous years. He had to admit to himself though, that since the afternoon party in the backyard, his thoughts kept returning to Billy. Not just about what work he'd lined up for her, or how he was going to improve on her swimming, but deeper thoughts. Emotions that were bubbling to the surface each time he talked to her or watched the way she moved. Trust Kath to get him thinking about his emotions instead of just working and moving along with his everyday life. He shook his head as if trying to clear it and called Casso, picking him up before heading down to his studio.

Painting, he thought, *that's what I need to do. Get these thoughts into line. Sort out my brain.*

★　★　★

Soon he had set up in the studio, his mind now focused on the latest piece he was working on. Casso jumped up on his favourite position on the old lounge as Liam sorted out the colours and brushes he would need for the afternoon. It was a quiet Sunday afternoon and when he pulled the curtains back, streams of sunlight filtered in through the windows, throwing the perfect lighting for working into the cluttered, colourful room. It didn't take him long to become engrossed in his work, Casso snoring softly, the only other sounds the clatter of a jar as he moved the colours around, or the soft brushing of his paintbrush over the canvas.

Standing back, surveying the section he was working on, he was disturbed by the creaking of the large timber door that was the entrance to the studio. He turned around to see Billy carrying a stack of chairs in front of her, pushing the door open with her foot as she struggled with the load.

'Whoa, careful, let me grab them,' he said, as he rushed towards her, taking the chairs from her arms.

He placed them down carefully in the corner of the room, noticing her eyes flitting curiously around the room. 'I'm sorry. I didn't know you were in here,' she said. 'Your dad asked me to bring these in here. I told him that's not where they belonged, but he was adamant I needed to bring them in here now.'

'They don't belong in here. I'm not sure why he thought they did.' Liam squinted suspiciously past Billy through the doorway, looking for his father who was nowhere to be seen.

'I can take them back out if you like,' she said.

'No, it's fine, just leave them here. I'll fix them up later.' He could see her eyes still moving around the room. 'Welcome to my studio.'

'I've never been in here before. I would never intrude on your privacy, it's just your dad said they needed to be brought in straight away.'

Liam shook his head, wiping his hands on a clean rag before shutting the door behind her. 'Well, this is where all the work gets done. Have a look around if you like, I'll keep going if you don't mind. I'm right in the middle of fixing a section of this painting.'

She followed him back to the canvas he was working on, the easel slanting so that the light fell upon it, showing up every tiny stroke and line.

'This was my mum's easel. I always use it when I work in here.'

Billy looked closely at the painting. 'It's so large and the colours have no edges, they just push across the surface, making up the portrait.'

Liam was pleased with the way the painting was coming together and he started to explain the different techniques he was using and how he was trying to fix a particular section, so that the woman's nose in the painting didn't appear so long. 'Something went wrong here. She was a model at the classes and sometimes there just isn't long enough during class to perfect what I want to do.'

'Why didn't you just offer her money to pose here?' Billy raised her eyebrows, her voice carrying a hint of sarcasm.

'It's highly unusual for me to make an offer of a private sitting.' Deciding to ignore her dig at the offers of money for sitting, Liam picked up a rag and wiped some paint from the woman's face.

'Have a look around. I'd like you to see what I actually paint.'

'How did you do the shading on her legs? There are no lines, just strokes and shadows, yet it looks so realistic.'

'There are so many different techniques to use. Sometimes I'm not sure myself how I get the picture to take shape. The brush is an extension of not only my arm, but also my mind.'

'It's beautiful. I mean it's a bit risqué, but it also captures that she's content with her body. That the bulges and saggy parts don't worry her.'

'Very good! That's exactly what she was like. Most models are. They're comfortable with their bodies and the beauty of the lines, regardless of what's seen or expected as the correct or perfect body shape. It's art and it's all about the uniqueness of the human body. Everyone is different.'

★ ★ ★

Billy crossed her arms as she stood next to Liam, drawn in by the beautiful colours that filled the canvas. Sometimes when she worked in the garden near the studio she had been tempted to look in through the windows, to see what it was that filled the space where he painted. But she had respected his privacy and not wanted to pry. He already shared so much of his home with her and it hadn't taken her long to work out that the studio was the area he retreated to when he was unsettled or not happy.

She looked more closely at the painting, trying to work out how he had mastered the expression on the woman's face. Suddenly she was aware that she was in his way and he was waiting for her to shift so that he could move freely in front of the painting.

'Oh, sorry, I'm just drawn in by how life-like it is. She finally drew her eyes away from the large painting. 'Can I have a look around?'

'You're welcome to look at anything that's in here. Open house.'

Moving off to the side, she smiled as she saw Casso asleep on the couch, his nose tucked in under an old quilt that covered the tattered upholstery.

Billy wasn't sure where to look first. The room was large and full of paintings, some stacked and leaning on the walls, while others stood on easels scattered throughout the room. A large bench off to the side was full of drawings and books, every sort of oddment that you could imagine, cluttered onto the top of the wide dented boards that made up the surface.

There were hundreds of drawings on cream paper scattered on the bench, some with sections ripped off and others with tiny samples of ideas scrawled across them. Notepads full of writing and sketches were strewn towards the back and a pile of recent nude sketches stacked in the middle of the bench. Her eyes flitted from one section to the other and then back to the painting Liam was working on. She took her time, looking carefully, delicately turning over paper drawings to look at the ones below.

Towards the back of the bench there was a cardboard box and she pulled it over closer to the front, peering inside at the stack of small notebooks. A fine dust obscured the intricate patterns carved into some that had leather covers. She wiped her hand across them so she could see them more clearly. The top one had a worn brown cover, the pages tied together with a string of leather. Pressing the notebook to her face she breathed in deeply. There was a smell of raw leather; a mixture of pelt accompanied by a smoky aroma. Untying the string she carefully opened the pages that were made from thick recycled paper. Her eyes opened wide, her hands turning the pages silently as Liam remained focused on his painting.

Each page contained a drawing; intricate pencil and crayon sketches, filling the book with a variety of different pictures. Her fingers turned the pages slowly, her eyes moving over the scenes on each page. There were images of children playing in the dirt, women walking in their long cloaks along a dusty street, men with long beards and winding turbans, sitting drinking out of tiny cups and scenes of bazaar dealers plying their wares. She peered curiously at the drawings depicting markets. Rickety trestle tables filled with colourful trinkets and rugs for sale, looked upon by children wearing long trousers and vests, their faces hopeful at the expected sale of the goods on display.

The noises and smells of the markets with its cooking pots full of food and colourful goods for sale emanated from the drawing and she passed her hand over the steam from the pot, wispy pencil lines rising up into the air.

Another page revealed a drawing of an old man, his face wrinkled with a thousand deep lines, eyes peering out from under his dusty turban; piercing eyes that told a million stories, eyes that had wept endless invisible tears. Billy's eyes welled as she continued to look through the pictures. So many drawings of children, playing, sitting together in the dust, their ragged clothes and tatty hair testament to their poverty. A small boy sitting on an old rusty chair trying to form letters with a stump of a pencil, the look on his face one of determination as he gripped the pencil, scratching it across a battered slate, his tiny legs swinging barefoot in mid air.

Her hands moved silently over the papers. Beneath the small book were others, all full of similar drawings, hundreds of them, some in cities and others in villages in the countryside; depictions of another time and a foreign place. She opened a battered green book containing pages filled with drawings of soldiers. Some sat on rocks on the sloping side of desolate mountains, their eyes peering out from under a helmet as they smoked a cigarette or talked to another soldier. Soldiers sitting crouched in the dirt, their heads down, their stance one of defeat or, she looked again, perhaps more of absolute exhaustion.

Every face was different, their emotions portrayed in just a few strokes of a pencil, or rough shading done with a crayon. She held the book up to look more closely at a sketch of an Australian soldier, his body covered in dust and grime, but his face lit up by a huge smile that stretched across his young face. The drawing underneath also drew her attention and she stared intently at the page. Lifelike, the images peered back at her; a drawing of a group of foreign soldiers, their turbans wound high on their heads, their craggy darkened hands holding tight to long guns from another era. At their feet a couple of small boys played with stones, drawing in the dirt, sketching around the shape of the boots that the soldiers wore.

She held a drawing up to the light, so she could see it better. Four small boys flew a kite, their clothes ragged, and hair matted. Billy's chest heaved, and her eyes welled with tears. The kite was high in the sky and the boys' feet were off the ground as they ran along with the wind, their spirits soaring like the colourful sail attached to their strings. The background was a backdrop of rugged mountains, their steep slopes jagged and sinister, menacing against the innocence of the children playing.

She had been so absorbed in the drawings that she hadn't noticed that Liam had come to stand beside her, his hands also now flicking through one of the notebooks filled with his drawings. His voice was husky, and he talked quietly. 'I haven't looked at any of these for many years.'

'These drawings are of my country,' Billy said. 'These are my people.'

'They are,' Liam said as she turned towards him, their eyes locking.

'I don't understand.'

'I was in the Australian army for many years. I did three tours in Afghanistan. Sometimes I feel like these are my people also.'

'You have never told me that you have been there.'

180

'I don't talk about it. There is too much sadness.' His voice was shaking and he thumbed further through the drawings, finally placing all the books except the one that Billy held, back into the cardboard box.

In her hand she held open a book, her hand running softly across the page without touching the paper. 'This one is special,' she said as she passed it to Liam. 'There is something in this drawing.'

'You are very good at reading my drawings. Yes, you're right, this one is special.'

He looked at it for a long time before closing the book and placing it back in the box. You haven't looked at the paintings yet.' He gestured over to the sidewall that was stacked with painting of many different sizes.

Billy moved slowly, a confused look on her face. Why had he never told her that he had been in Afghanistan? Those drawings, they should be displayed, not tucked away in a box that no one ever looked at. So many things that neither knew about the other. They talked a lot to each other, but not very often about anything too intimate or personal.

She had so many questions. Who was he? What had he seen? Where had he been? The drawings she had just seen depicted the everyday life for Afghans and it was obvious from the detail and the emotions depicted that he had a strong connection to the people, particularly the children he had crossed paths with.

Liam pulled a sheet away that covered a stack of canvas paintings, drawing Billy's attention away from her thoughts. She gasped as she tried to take in what was displayed in front of her. These works were vastly different from what she had just been looking through.

The first canvas was large, wider than Billy was tall and nearly as high. The young woman in the painting was sprawled out on a large bed, her hair long and dark spread out around her. Her body was fully rounded, voluptuous and her breasts huge with dark nipples pointing straight out from the canvas. She posed lying on her back, her back arched, her hand resting on the curly black hair between her legs. Her neck was arched backwards, and her eyes closed as if she was sleeping. Billy put her head on the side, her gaze intent. The woman in the painting had a beautiful face, full red lips and long dark eyelashes that were prominent against the waxen paleness of her skin. Shapely legs stretched out and her feet rested across each other, bright red toenail polish adding a splash of colour.

Billy jumped as Liam's voice sounded over her shoulder as he came up behind her. 'These are part of the collection I'm getting ready.'

'Oh.' Billy moved onto the next painting, colour flushing her face as her eyes were drawn to the same woman but in a different pose. 'She lay like that while you drew her?'

'Sure, it's just a different position. I know that you're thinking that those parts are normally covered, but to me it's just another part of the body to draw. Painting nudes can include incorporating many different poses and sections of the body.'

'Oh.'

The colour heightened in her face and neck

and Liam chuckled. 'You're a woman. You have seen all this before.'

'It's just different to see it painted and on such a large canvas.'

She flicked through some canvas drawings stacked against the wall, blushing further at the positions that some of the women were drawn in. 'Who would buy one of these paintings?'

'Oh, you'd be surprised. Particularly these larger ones, they're sought after by a lot of the top buyers.'

★ ★ ★

Liam continued explaining the different techniques and angles, hoping that Billy would become used to the fact the women were naked and instead look more deeply at the shape and curves that made up the different body types. Some were thin and tall, some short and rounded while others were muscled, buxom and large.

Billy held her hand to the streams of light coming in through the windows. Specks of dust floated through the air and she inhaled. 'I love the smell of the paint and there's a warmth in this room, almost like it soaks into your soul.' She looked at Casso, snuggled in between the cushions and rugs. 'That would be a good place to sleep.' She closed her eyes and took deep breaths. It was a comforting space, the colours, the smells and the light that filtered in from the outside world.

'I have something else to show you,' Liam said. She followed him to a space behind the lounge couch where a small easel was covered up with a shawl. She looked closely, her eyes widening as she reached out to touch the colourful piece of fabric. 'That is my shawl. I lost it at the beach.'

'I know. I picked it up and meant to give it back to you the next day. But I forgot, and it's been here since.'

Liam removed the shawl slowly, revealing the painting that was positioned on the easel under it.

Silence filled the room as they both stared at the canvas that had been covered by her bright shawl.

Billy ran her hand gently over the surface, touching the curves and lines that made up the woman on the canvas. 'It's me,' she whispered. 'How can you paint that? It's exactly me.'

Liam laughed loudly, his chuckles echoing around the large room causing Casso to give a short bark, look up at both of them and then go back to sleep.

'I'm an artist. That's what I do and that's why my paintings are displayed in galleries. It's my genre. It's what I do the best—the female body. The only difference is that this one of you has clothes on. Just your shoulders showing.' He shook his head and rolled his eyes in frustration. 'This is the night that you posed at art class, it is my favourite piece of work.'

'You make me look beautiful, my arms, even the bottom of my feet. It all looks natural and like, well like a painting you see hanging on a wall.'

'Billy, I didn't make you look beautiful.' He held the painting up, looking at it closely, wanting to say so many more words, but holding them back. 'I'd like to paint it over again. Extra time

184

that night would have helped. There needs to be more of your back though. Well I'd like to paint all of you, but I know that's out of the question.' He placed the canvas back on the easel, holding out his hand for her to give him the shawl back. She passed it back to him, taking one last look at the beautiful painting he had completed.

'Well, now you've seen it; you've seen what it is I do.'

'Your work is incredible. I'm not sure if I like the paintings the most or the drawings.'

'The drawings were just to fill in time and get some memories out of my head and down on paper.' Liam packed everything away and pulled the curtains closed. 'C'mon, let's go and find Dad. You can tell him that I didn't want the chairs after all. They've never been kept in here and he knows that.'

24

Dark clouds scuttled across the sky the next morning and Liam could sense that Billy had not particularly enjoyed her morning swim. The water appeared murky and the surface choppy, tiny waves making it harder for her to push her body through the water. His own routine as usual had been consistent, his arms propelling his body through the water. His were constant, methodical strokes that worked as a therapeutic exercise and mind healing process, regardless of the weather or water conditions.

Yesterday Liam had been able to tell that Billy had wanted to ask him more about the drawings and his time in Afghanistan. They were similar, he thought, but much like him she wasn't that good at talking about the past. He had never wanted to ask too much about her own life story, but he could sense there were sorrows and loneliness that she had bottled up inside. Liam was always respectful of her privacy and although they spent a large amount of the days together, apart from a few occasions, their conversation was usually about day-to-day matters. He could see that yesterday's disclosure had come as a shock to her, not only the fact that he had served in Afghanistan, but also his art.

There was something sensual, yet melancholic in the way he had depicted her in his artwork. His attempts at capturing her feelings, gave an inkling of the wanderings of her memories and hidden emotions, when she had sat for the class that night.

The painting showed her hair, falling in wisps onto her shoulders and waves of flowing crème fabric, draped across her hips. Why had the thoughts in her mind been so easy to interpret? Would others who did not know her, look upon the painting and be able to read the story that was invisible and hidden under the paint?

It was something he had seen before. Sometimes when models sat still for so long their thoughts took over, and it was almost as if they were in a meditative state. Through the stillness of the sitting, their mind often drifted to memories that had previously been pushed to the side.

★ ★ ★

Billy was drying off when Liam emerged from the water. Large drops of rain splattered onto the sand, making indents where they landed, the heavy sky threatening to unload at any minute. Both of them quickly picked up their belongings, making a beeline for the path back up to the house. They had only taken a few steps when the heavens opened, the torrential rain bucketing down on them. Billy took off first with Liam close behind. He chuckled as he watched her run in front of him. The dress she had thrown over her swimmers was already drenched, the rivers of water running down the back of her legs. Casso joined them as they reached the grassy section of the yard, nearly tripping them both as he raced around in excitement trying to catch the raindrops. Sheltering under the roof of the first shed they came to, they both stood looking out at the pounding rain.

'We won't be working in this today and it doesn't look like it's going to be stopping anytime soon,' Liam said, looking up at the heavy clouds that stretched across the sky.

He looked back at Billy who seemed so small beside him. Her dress stretched tight across her breasts and clung to her slim body, the water running down her dark hair before dripping onto the concrete floor of the shed. For a moment he was lost for words and tried to avert his eyes from the vision of her standing in a soaking clinging dress next to him. 'Once you're dry, come up to the house. We can have morning tea up there with Dad before he goes.'

She spoke loudly above the pounding of the rain on the tin roof. 'I'd like that. I'll make a run for it now and see you later when I'm cleaned up and dry.'

He watched as she darted out from under the cover of the shed, long legs and bare feet kicking up the water in the puddles as she raced across the yard to her cabin. He picked up Casso. 'Righto buddy, let's make a run for it.'

★ ★ ★

The main house was warm and dry, the logs and pinecones crackling in the fireplace emitting a heat that permeated the timber clad rooms. Prodding the fire with a metal poker, John rearranged the embers and sticks and soon the flames burned brightly, warming Billy as she stood in front of it.

188

'I thought you'd get drenched down there this morning. The sky came over dark,' John said. He stood up and gave Billy a hug, her smoky-green eyes darker than usual in the dim room. He smiled as she hugged him.

'The rain is amazing,' Billy replied, rubbing her hands together, still cold even after a hot shower and the layering of warm clothes. 'It's great for the garden, everything will grow.'

'How's the herb garden going? I meant to have another look at it before I go, but I won't get to now with this weather.'

'It's all planted out. I just need to get some manure and mulch onto it and soon there'll be herbs for everyone. Yared and Nadir have asked me to grow chillies and other herbs that they use in their cooking. Meron has started teaching the kids at the nearby high school how to cook traditional Eritrean food and she needs some special herbs for her classes.'

'What a fabulous group of people, what with the art class group and then the two families. Who would think that everyone could help each other out so much.'

'It works well and we've all become such good friends. And look at how you met Ruby, all because of the connection between Liam and Matilda.'

John followed Billy as she went to stand in her favourite spot, in front of the print of the family playing cricket. Neither spoke, they had looked at it so many times together and already talked about all the different intricacies that made up the picture.

'She will always be my first love,' John's eyes

189

always misted over when he talked about Liam's mother. 'But now I have met someone who I hope to spend many years with. It is a beautiful thing to fall in love.'

Billy's voice was soft and wistful when she spoke. 'I wish I had a painting like that of my family.'

'One day Billy, you'll have your own kids and then that will be your family.'

'Do you think so?'

He put his arm around her shoulders, her words filled with a sense of longing and the lost memories that made up her life. 'I know so, Billy.'

⋆ ⋆ ⋆

Neither had noticed Liam who stood behind them also looking upwards at the picture. He stepped away silently, moving into the kitchen to get the morning tea ready. There had been an understanding and connection between Billy and John from the first moment they had met. Liam could sense it when he watched them and felt the protectiveness that John had towards her. Billy opened up to John and Liam noticed how she asked John for advice or looked for his approval. There was an unspoken trust and mutual admiration for each other and he knew that Billy was going to miss having his dad to talk to.

He also was going to find it strange not to have his dad around and some more time together would have been great. John though, was the happiest that Liam had seen him in a very long time and everyone agreed that going travelling with Ruby was the start of an exciting new adventure.

Although John had loved getting to know Billy and spending time with both her and Liam, there were others in the family to visit. Now with Ruby by his side, well, he had told them all, it was the start of a beautiful romance and he felt young again and in love.

25

The three of them sat and chatted, the heavy rain-fall on the roof and the crackling of the fire a cosy background noise, complementing the warmth that filled the room. John's bags were already packed and in his car, ready for the drive to Ruby's. When he was ready to leave he hugged both of them. 'It's an exciting new start for me. I'll miss both of you, but there are adventures to be had.'

Liam and Billy waved him off, both standing in the doorway, ducking back in quickly out of the pouring rain once he had driven off.

Billy picked up her umbrella and prepared to leave. 'Thanks for the morning tea. I'll miss your dad.'

'You two hit it off. He gets on like that with my sister-in-law, Kath.'

'He's a gentleman. I'm glad I met him. You're really lucky to have him.' Billy opened her umbrella and stepped onto the small porch, ready to battle the driving rain.

Liam nodded, and she waited for him, knowing him well enough by now to know that he wanted to say more. He looked out across the yard, large puddles forming across the expanse of lawn. 'We won't be working this week. It's supposed to rain for four or five days.'

She shuffled her feet. They stood watching the rain before Liam turned to her. 'Billy, I'd like to ask you something.'

Her eyes squinted suspiciously. 'What?'

'I'm probably going to spend the week in the studio. Would you consider posing for a painting for me?' He added quickly, 'Fully clothed, of course.'

She looked down at the ground. 'I thought you only did naked women.'

'Well I've been thinking, and I have a particular pose in mind. It would be a similar position like you held at the art class that night, but your back would be a bit more visible. Maybe still sitting on your heels, like you did, but your head perhaps to the side a bit more so I can see some of your face, and then the same dress you had on but just undone a little at the back.' The last words came out in a hurry. He wanted to try and explain it all before she said no.

'You've really given this some thought.'

'I have the picture in my mind and I would love it if you would sit for me. Seriously, I see most of your back when we swim at the lake. Really, what's the difference?'

Pushing the mat on the floor around with her foot, she hesitated, and he could tell she was weighing up the options

He continued, talking quickly, his voice nervous. 'If you're happy with that first painting, I do have some other ideas, all fully-clothed poses, but just some different positions that I'd like to paint you in.'

'What sort of positions? If you think I'd pose like some of the women in those other paintings in your studio then you're very mistaken,' she said, drawing herself up taller, her eyes flashing angrily.

Moving quickly, he stood between her and the few steps that led down to the garden. 'I know you better than that. These paintings would be nothing like some of the other ones you saw. I'm prepared to change my style, just so I can paint you.' He looked straight at her. 'Please?'

She stared back hard at him.

'I'll make sure it's comfortable for you and I'll have the fireplace on in there. It'll be warm and you'll make more money than you normally do working for me.' He put on his most charming smile. 'What else are you going to do in this rain?'

She still stared at him and he watched her, intrigued, trying to read her face, wondering what she was thinking.

He used his most persuasive voice. 'It's a job and you've seen my work. I really want to paint you. It will complete the work for my exhibition. You'd be helping me out.' He smiled at her again, his voice soft and cajoling, his eyes big and pleading.

Crossing her arms, she squinted again. 'When?'

'You mean you will?'

'Perhaps.'

'We could start straight away. Are you saying yes?'

'I suppose so, as long as it's just the same as last time.'

'With your back exposed. I need to capture those beautiful curves.'

'Flattery will get you nowhere.'

'No, it's true. The vision in my head is a painting that shows your back, the rest of you can be covered.'

Billy wondered what other visions he had in his head when it came to the topic of painting her. She decided not to ask; perhaps it was better not to know.

Moving around him, she pushed the umbrella open and stepped out into the pouring rain, streams of water running down its covering. She slipped her shoes off, holding them in her hand. 'I will be there in an hour. If you want me to sit still, I will need the room warm.'

She couldn't hear his words for the wind and rain as she ran across the grass, sidestepping the puddles as she made her way back to her cabin. She smiled as she ran, thinking that if she looked back, he would probably still be standing in the doorway, a broad grin stretching across his face.

26

Liam moved quickly, preparing the studio for the sitting, a roaring fire in the fireplace warming the room. Sheets of rain ran down the large windows and even though the light streamed in through the glass he had turned all the lights on in the studio, making the interior a contrast to the cold and dark conditions outside. Casso was already curled up in the lounge chair and only lifted his head for a moment when Billy arrived. She had wrapped a coat around her body and hung on to it tightly as she walked towards where Liam stood, preparing a canvas on the large easel that always took centre stage in the room.

'It's warming up in here. I just need a few minutes to get my things organised here. I've got the low table there in front where I'll get you to sit.'

Billy looked nervous and avoided his eyes instead making her way over to the drawings in the cardboard box. She flicked through them, moving from one to the next without really taking in what she was looking at.

Liam called out to her. 'I'm nearly ready. Come over here and I'll let you know what I want.' He sounded so relaxed about it all, just like how he spoke when he gave her directions on how to cut the lawn or trim a tree.

Stopping what he had been doing Liam looked at her as she stood a distance away from him. 'Come over here, so I can explain.' He frowned when she stayed where she was. 'Christ, you're not nervous, are you?'

She did not reply.

Liam kept his voice patient. 'It's fine, Billy. You've done this before. Once we get started you'll relax. After a while you'll forget where you are. The models tell me it's a great relaxant, they can think about everything they need to while they pose.'

'I do want you to paint me. I like the way you get the feelings in the picture.'

Liam had taken out the last painting he had done of Billy at the art class and now walked over to her with it in his hand. He pointed to the low table he had placed in front of them. 'That table is quite wide and at least there's some light coming in through the window behind it. Now see how you're positioned in this last sitting, well this time I just want you to maybe arch your back, or sit up straighter a bit more and then,' he pointed to her head in the painting, 'can you just tilt your head a bit more this way.' He looked at her hair. 'Perfect your hair is done much the same. We'll keep it that way for this pose.'

Finally she spoke, 'I wore the same dress.'

'It's perfect. Now just go and set yourself up and I'll finish getting the last of these colours ready.'

He pretended to be busying himself with the jars and canvas but instead was watching her as she hesitantly took her coat off.

Soft cream fabric made up the garment that she wore. It was a loose style dress that looked like it was simply a piece of material with armholes and a back opening cut out. It fell in waves around her

197

body, and as she sat back down on her heels the length of it covered to just above her knees. She shuffled a little, finding the comfortable position and waited for him to tell her what to do next.

Liam came around to the front of her. 'Are you okay? You need to find that comfort zone, especially when you're sitting on your feet like that. Let me know if you start getting pins and needles and we'll stop and take a break. Let's leave your arms down to start with, at least that will rest them for a while.'

'Is this okay?' She adjusted the fabric so that it tucked under her, the top of her upper leg and knees showing.

Liam tilted his head to the side. 'You need to just push it up a bit more, show some more of your leg.'

She pushed it up further, tucking it in between her legs, the colour of her legs a warm contrast against the waxy cream material. He walked around her, standing back and then coming forward, moving around to what he would be looking at as he painted her.

'Your back, I need to see your back. All I can see are your shoulders.' He stood in front of her again, a frown on his face, his eyebrows raised.

She reached one of her arms backwards over her shoulders, fiddled for a moment and undid the top button on the back of the dress.

Turning his head so he could see her back, Liam let out a chuckle. 'That does nothing. You need to just undo those buttons so I can see your back. I thought you agreed to that.'

Her green eyes fired up as she looked at him

and she threw him a scornful look. 'I did agree, but you'll need to turn your back because I wasn't thinking, and I've worn a bra. Unless you want a nice bra strap running across my back that you're so bloody intent on painting.'

Liam laughed at her annoyance and watched out the side of his eye as she deftly undid her bra, throwing it angrily onto the sleeping Casso.' He stifled his laughter. The dog hadn't even moved an inch.

He tried to stop grinning before he turned around to face her. 'Are you alright?'

'Of course I am. You'll need to begin before I get sick of sitting here like this.' She sat up straight, her body flexed and upright.

Liam returned to his easel and then walked back to her, standing in front of her again. 'You didn't undo the last two buttons. The best part of your back is under those buttons. It's the curve that shapes down to the top of your lower body. It's my favourite part of the female body to paint.'

This time she glared back at him and he thought how he'd love to capture that look on her face. Her eyes flashed as she spoke to him. 'Undo them then. I can't reach them. You'll have to fix it.' He moved around behind her, his hands soft on her skin as he carefully undid the last two buttons.

'Just let me check,' his voice was husky, 'I'm just going to rearrange the fabric and then I'll get started.'

His fingers moved the soft fabric, pushing it ever so gently to the side, the opening now forming a large V-shape from her shoulder down. He moved it again, flinching as he felt the warmth and softness of her skin, hardly breathing as just those few more inches revealed the scoop and arch of her lower back, running down to where the curve and mound of her bottom began. Resisting the overwhelming desire to run his finger down her entire back he stepped back, the only sound the pattering of rain on the roof.

★ ★ ★

Billy struggled to breathe evenly, the feeling of Liam's hand on her skin sending tingling sensations throughout her entire body. Her nipples were hard against the softness of the fabric and she sat still, not daring to move. Her voice was unsteady when she finally spoke. 'Am I in the correct position?'

Liam answered. 'It's nearly how I imagined. Just push the fabric from your shoulders down, just a bit.' As he stood back she hesitantly moved the fabric, both her arms now up in the air as her fingers played with the material until she had it sitting slightly off her shoulders.

'That's it' His voice was excited and another tingling sensation ran where his fingers had been. 'Keep your arms up there. Can you hold it there, do you think?'

'It's fine, I think I can hold it. I thought you didn't want my arms up.'

'With your arms up like that the muscles in your back are more defined. The lines and curves are ... ' He cleared his throat and she twisted her head around to try and see what he was doing.

'Are you going to start, because this will be

200

more difficult to hold with my arms up, so I suggest you get a move on.'

'Of course, I'm just starting now. The pose is correct.'

Billy held still, the thought of his eyes on parts of her body usually covered up, sending a warm sensation through her body. The sound of his brush on canvas was the only sound in the room and she smiled, knowing how pleased he must be to eventually get her to pose. Her body felt alive, the fabric soft on her skin, the warm air soothing on her bare skin. It was a good feeling, a sense of calm and time to let the outside world roll by. She sunk deeper into the pose, taking care to hold her arms still, her back straight and her head just slightly to the side.

★ ★ ★

Liam worked intently, and after a while a dreamy atmosphere filled the room. He sensed when Billy finally relaxed, sinking deeper into the position, a relaxed pose as the pounding of the rain on the roof continued. Casso snored lightly on the lounge and Liam's paintbrush flew over the canvas. After a while he broke the silence. 'You can put your arms down now if you like. You've done really well holding them there for that long. I've got most of what I need in that area.'

Stretching her arms out first, Billy placed them in front of her, still sitting up straight and holding the pose. She rubbed her hands and watched the rain that continued to run down the window. 'I might need to take a break shortly, I think my legs are starting to need a stretch.'

'You can talk if you like, sometimes that helps to take your mind off sitting for so long.'

'Oh, I wasn't sure if that would disturb you.'

'No, it's fine. My mind still ticks over.'

'Well, what do you think about when you paint?'

'At the moment, nothing except getting as much of this correct while you're in the perfect position.'

'Those drawings you did, of the people in Afghanistan, they're very life-like. Maybe you should paint some of those scenes.'

'I just did them to fill in time and I guess to get some of the issues I was having out of my head.'

'I like the drawing of the boys flying the kite.'

There was no reply from Liam and she repeated what she had said. When there was no reply again she turned her head slightly, just able to see that he was still staring intently at her, the brush moving back and forth from the colours to his canvas.

'I heard you.'

'There's something about that drawing. It reminds me of the print of the cricket game. It's beautiful, there's happiness and fun, but…' her voice wavered, and she stopped talking.

'But what?'

'There's an overwhelming sadness to the scene. I can't explain it, but there are emotions in the drawing that have stayed in my head.' She stopped talking and moved her legs, her back stretching out as she repositioned her body.

Liam realised her discomfort and put his brush down. 'Okay let's have a break.'

Billy moved slowly, unfurling her legs from

underneath her body and stretching them out, her slender feet pointed sharply as she flexed the muscles in her legs. Rubbing her calf muscles, she leaned her head to one side and then the other, trying to get the tightness out of her neck. She stretched her body out further, twisting it from side to side, bending her body backwards and then to the sides, pushing her arms behind her back as she relieved her body of any stiffness that had developed over the last couple of hours. She wrapped her coat around herself and moved over towards the fire, the logs on it burning brightly, the heat pleasant on her body.

'I have lunch ready for us here,' Liam said. He pulled a chair out for her and she sat down next to a large table where he had cleared a corner ready for them to eat. 'The dog's imitating you.' Liam laughed as he pointed over to the couch. Casso had woken from his sleep and stood on the cushions, stretching out one small leg after the other; a final shake, causing the bra that had been resting on top of him to fall onto the ground.

'What a life!' Liam said as Casso did a few circles on the cushion before settling back down again, his legs curled up under him.

'You should paint him. I wonder what he thinks when he lies there, listening to us.'

'All that dog thinks about is food and sleep.' He looked back to Billy, 'What do you think about Billy, when you pose for me?'

She laughed, 'To start with I concentrate on how my body is supposed to be and then once I have that right, I focus on everything else except my body. That is what will allow me to not notice the stiffness in my bones from sitting in the same position.'

Liam passed her a bowl of fruit. 'And after that?'

She took a deep breath, her chest rising and falling. 'After that,' she looked up into Liam's eyes. 'After that, I do not think, I just allow the memories and ideas to come in.'

'Is that a good thing or a bad thing?' He paused. 'I have memories that I would rather not let in.'

A silence hung between them and Liam looked away, watching the rain that continued to fall outside. He turned back as Billy spoke. 'For me it is good thing. There have been many times when I have tried to reconnect with my memories of a previous life. A life when I still had a family. The night I first posed for your class at the studio was the first time that their words and faces came back to me. My brothers' faces, my parent's words.'

Her shoulders sagged and her face saddened. Liam felt an overwhelming desire to place his arms around her, to tell her that he understood, that he wanted to be close to her. But he didn't, he sat still and listened.

'It is because I am blocking everything else out when I pose that I forget where I am and what I am doing.'

Liam leant over the table and took her hand in his. 'That is what I can feel when I paint you. There is sadness.' He went to say more but stopped, his eyes focussed on her hand as his thumb softly caressed her skin.

'I could see that in the painting that you did of me. I am not sure how you read me so well.' She squeezed his hand as they looked at each other. 'I feel like you understand me. We are so different but sometimes I think we have much in common. Perhaps one day I should paint you and then you could sit in stillness and let your mind wander.'

'You would not want to share my memories. I wouldn't want to burden that on anyone. It's good to live in the moment and I try to remember that.'

'I like the moment.' Billy smiled, her eyes looking straight into Liam's.

'You have the most beautiful green eyes,' Liam said. 'One day I will paint a close up of your face and capture the mischief that I often see in them.'

'Ha,' she laughed. 'Perhaps you should first show me the painting that you have been doing of me this morning.'

'I'd rather you didn't see it until I'm finished. Actually talking about finishing, we should get started, the afternoon will slip away from us.' He took his hand away from hers, the smoothness of her skin, gentle against his. For a while they looked at each other and then Liam stood up and started cleaning up the table. The room was warm, and the heavy rain outside wrapped the studio in a blanket of obscurity. Liam reminded himself that Billy had placed her confidence in him and had gone against her earlier decisions and revealed more of her body than what she had originally wanted to. Now was not the time to take advantage of the situation. It was time to get back to the painting and remember that he had told her that she could trust him.

* * *

Billy quickly regained her pose and the rest of the afternoon passed much the same as the morning. This time however her pose was not as relaxed as earlier and Liam struggled finishing off the last part of the portrait.

'You haven't sunk into that comfortable pose that you held this morning,' he said, wondering if she was thinking about the feeling of their hands together.

She sighed. 'Maybe we shouldn't have stopped for lunch.'

Liam took a long time to answer her. 'We can stop now. I think that is a long time for you to sit. I have enough here that I can finish it off.' Billy got down from the table and stretched, keeping her back to Liam and looking out through the window.

'The rain has stopped, I'm happy if you'd like to go. You've done great to hold that pose for so long. Thank you.' Liam stayed behind the easel, pretending to put some finishing touches to the canvas. He tried to keep his voice even but his stomach was churning, his heart thumping hard in his chest. He imagined wrapping his arms around her and looking into those green eyes before kissing her lips. He wanted to stroke her arms, to feel her back that he had been staring at for so many hours.

'I can stay for a while if you want,' Billy said as Casso jumped to his feet and scratched at the door.

'I think it best if you go. Casso needs some fresh air.' Liam concentrated on the painting.

Billy looked confused as she picked up Casso

and made for the door. 'I guess I'll see you later then.'

'Thanks Billy. Now make a run for it. I'll see you the same time tomorrow.'

27

The rainy days provided the perfect opportunity for the painting of Billy's portrait. Liam was always organised, the fire in the corner stoked and lunch for both of them made and ready on the table for when they stopped. He was careful to avoid the intimacy that had caught him unaware on that first day that Billy posed for him. The tenderness of her words and the softness of her hand in his had plagued his thoughts and dreams at night, keeping him awake until the early hours of the morning.

He wondered if she also thought about the moment when they had looked into each other's eyes, or if she too had felt the sensations that ran through his fingers as they touched hers. He reprimanded himself. He had promised her this was a job, just like any other job and that the human body in front of him was just an art form to paint. Nothing more.

The temptation to hold her had been made harder by the fact that as each day passed in the studio they both relaxed more in each other's company. Although there were long periods where they didn't talk, at other times their chatter and laughter caused Casso to lift his head or give a startled yap at the intrusion on his sleep time.

★ ★ ★

Today was to be the last sitting and as the rain began to ease Billy moved into her pose, her eyes drawn to the view outside the window. The morning had changed from being grey, wet and misty to a scene where the sun tried hard to push through the white puffy clouds. Slivers of sunshine filtered through the garden and the trees and bushes came alive as the sunlight bounced off the raindrops that hung from the leaves. A ray of sunshine radiated in through the large window in front of her and Liam worked quickly to capture the moment of the glow of the afternoon sun on her skin.

She looked out onto the garden, careful not to change the position of her head. 'There are ducks in the puddles out there.'

'Lucky Casso is in here because he loves to chase them.'

'Did you ever play in puddles when you were a child?' Billy asked.

Liam smiled when he answered her. 'We always did. My mum used to come out and splash around with us. She loved the rain.' He laughed as he reminisced. 'It usually ended up in a mud fight. When I look back now I realise it was usually Mum who threw the first bit of mud.'

Quietness pervaded the room and he made a couple more strokes on the painting, standing back to check the overall picture. 'Billy, do you remember anything from when you were little?'

It took her a long time to reply and her voice sounded like it was coming from afar as she answered him. 'It's strange, I didn't think I remembered anything before I came to Australia, but lately I've been thinking about some things I do remember. When I sit still here, and when my mind completely relaxes, then surprisingly some things come back to me.'

It was easier to talk about times that had been pushed to the back of her mind when her back was to him. 'If I close my eyes it's easier to hold onto a memory. When I open them, I think it might really be there in front of me.'

'What do you remember? What's something you remember when you were a child?'

She looked out the window. 'It is usually something that triggers my memory. Like the puddles outside the window there. Sometimes, that is all it takes.'

'What is your recollection of that?'

'It is a very clear memory and it only came back to me a short while ago; while I was looking out the window here.' She paused, and her body tensed. 'I fell over in a puddle. It hadn't rained for a long time and the dust had turned to sludge. I can picture my arms and hands, they were covered in dirt and I feel like my hair was in my eyes. I tripped. I was only very little, perhaps four. I fell down and ...'

Liam's voice was quite and gentle. 'Go on, what else do you remember?'

Her voice quivered. 'My father, his big hands, it's as if I can still feel them wrapping around me. He picked me up and held me to him. He brushed the mud from me and pushed the hair back from my face. The skin on his hands was very rough but his touch was soft.' Her head sagged down onto her chest, her eyes closed. 'He had a smell. I loved it. When he held me I felt safe. I think the smell might have been tobacco.'

'Do you remember what he looked like?' Liam stopped painting, his paintbrush now resting on top of the jar of paint.

'No.'

She sat incredibly still, staring through the window as if the scene she was remembering was just outside the glass. Time stood still and even her breathing seemed to no longer exist. Finally she took a deep breath, her back and shoulders moving as she straightened up.

'I think we can finish up,' Liam said, 'You've done well to hold the position.'

He watched as she stretched out, as usual rubbing her legs, pointing her toes to stretch out stiff leg muscles. Casso also stretched and yawned, shaking himself out before jumping down, his tail wagging in anticipation at being let out of the studio. Billy was unusually quiet, picking up her coat quickly and throwing it over her dress.

Liam didn't want her to leave and called out quickly before she opened the studio door.

'Would you like to have a look at the painting?' he asked. 'I just have a couple of parts to do, to finish it off.' She came back to him, gazing at the nearly completed piece of work. 'I just need to finesse some of these sections and it will be as I want it. What do you think?'

Standing in front of the painting, she looked at it for a long time, finally a smile on her face, her voice calm and soft. 'It's beautiful and I can't believe it's me.' They stood together, staring, taking in the different aspects of the painting. 'I like that you can only see a part of my face.'

'It's different from other paintings that I have done recently, but now it's finished I like it more than the other pieces I have in the collection.'

Turning to him she looked straight at him, their eyes locking as they stood next to each other. She was moved by what she saw in his work and her voice shook. 'It shows how I'm feeling. How do you do that? Is it just me who can read the painting? Is it only me who can look at that and know the emotions?'

'Painting is an emotive craft. It's like music or poetry, it's a way to express feelings, to interpret and portray the feelings of others.' His voice was deep, and it was as if he seemed to understand some of the thoughts that had been stirred by their discussions. 'Those who look deeper than the surface and take their time to look into the work, will hopefully see the story. I hope so, because that is the beauty of the art piece that has been created.'

Billy turned to leave, but Liam stood in front of her, blocking her way to the door.

'Are you going to Yared's and Nadir's party in the park on Saturday?' he asked. 'If you are, I thought we could go together.'

Her eyes widened as she stammered a response. 'Um, you want me to come with you?'

'Sure, yes, we could go together. I would like you to come with me.'

She looked down at her feet, feeling his eyes on her as she struggled to get the words to come out properly. 'It would, I mean yes, it, that would be okay.'

'Good. Be ready by ten o'clock. It should be a fun day.'

She nodded as she walked out the door, her heart pounding in her chest.

★ ★ ★

Liam whistled as he packed up his art gear, continually going back to look at the painting from a variety of different angles. It was a good start and he was more than happy with the pose that Billy had held and the way that the painting had turned out. He didn't even mind that he had swayed from his usual style of work and instead, now admired how he had captured the sensual flow of the fabric draped across her skin. He was also happy with the mood of the work, the emotional poise that Billy was so adept at holding and how he had captured what was going through her mind. Strange, he mused, he had felt all along that she was remembering something that she hadn't thought about for a long time.

Pulling his eyes away from the vision of her back on the canvas, he whistled louder to gain Casso's attention, turned off the light and closed the studio door behind him. It had been a very productive and interesting day.

28

A blue sky and warm sunshine looked down upon the gathering of people who had come to join in the celebrations that Yared's and Nadir's families had planned for the day. A corner of the park was filled with colourful rugs laid out, folding chairs positioned to take in the view of the play area. Eskies filled with an assortment of food and drinks were scattered around the designated area. The group from art class sat on chairs, standing up to shake hands and greet those they already knew. There was also much chatter and laughter as Yared introduced other friends, all of them new to the country, one family having only arrived in Australia the week before.

The new family came from Iran, although as they told Liam and Billy, they were originally from Afghanistan, their own parents having fled from there many years before. The head of the family, a young man in his late twenties called Zamir, told Liam that although Iran was a key destination for Afghan refugees, and their families could live there for many years, they would always be considered Afghan. He introduced his wife Ameera, and she smiled shyly, pronouncing her English words carefully and slowly as she greeted them. The young couple's three children, who sat on the picnic rug next to their parents, had all been born in Iran and now spoke four different languages, their identities a mixture of the countries that made up their background.

Billy listened with interest as Zamir talked. 'Generations of our people from Afghanistan live as refugees in Iran but the Iranian laws give them less freedom and opportunity than what they had in Afghanistan,' Zamir said.

'So you still did not live as free people?' Billy asked.

'No, not free at all. I wanted to go to university but because I am not considered Iranian, it was not allowed. Although I am born in Iran, my passport is still Afghani and I am only allowed to work in certain labouring jobs. We are also only allowed to travel short distances away from where we live. It is not a safe place for us to live. Maybe a bit safer than Afghanistan, but still not good. So we are lucky to come here to Australia. My wife and girls will have better opportunities and rights here, more than they would ever have in Iran. I can also now study.'

The two young girls looked up at Billy, their eyes a similar green to her own. She found it hard to draw her gaze away from them.

'They remind me of you,' Liam whispered to her as Billy turned her attention to their younger brother who was dressed in the traditional long pants and vest. The girls also wore long skirts and shirts, their heads covered in shawls, only a small dark fringe of hair peeking out from under the dark blue fabric. She smiled at the children, watching the small boy as he held tightly onto the soccer ball under his arm.

Crouching down, Liam spoke in Farsi to the

small boy. He was rewarded with a cheeky grin as the boy whose name was Asid replied in the same language. The two girls were also smiling, and Billy suddenly found words that she hadn't used in a long time rolling off her tongue as she added into the conversation. When the three children left to go and play, others came over to offer food and the corner of the park was soon filled with loud and joyous conversation as everyone talked and tried to communicate with each other. Sometimes there would be a loud chuckle as those who were new to the English language got their words mixed up or tried to explain something. A variety of delicious food was passed around, along with cans of soft drink to quench their thirst. Laughter filled the area as the collection of young and old, from a variety of places and cultures, came together as one.

As the afternoon wore on, some of the mothers gently rocked small babies, laying them down carefully on the large rugs once they were asleep. Off to the side other children played on the climbing equipment, the bigger ones pushing the smaller ones on the swings or helping them up onto the higher play equipment. Asid, still clutching his soccer ball, came over to where Liam sat talking to Matilda and Meron. He pulled at Liam's arm and then said something to him that Billy couldn't hear. She looked over at him, her face quizzical, wondering what the small boy wanted.

'He wants me to play soccer. It's boys versus the girls.' Liam's face was covered in a wide grin and he stood up, ready to follow the small boy over to the flat area where the kids and some of the others were starting to play.

The girls had already started, and their shrieks filled the air as deft kicks aimed the ball down the grassy area, towards an empty esky that had been set up as the field goal area. Billy watched with interest as five of the girls shared the ball with each other, their quick feet skilfully kicking the ball back and forth to each other, avoiding the equally fast feet of the boys, who ran as hard as they could beside them. Two of the girls wore scarfs that billowed out behind them, like sails flying through the air as they bolted down towards the goal. The girls sprinted faster, the young boys frustrated by their inability to stop their opponents from scoring.

It was a rare sight, a mixture of African and Middle Eastern kids, some with heads, arms and legs covered in long clothing while other wore shorts and colourful T-shirts, running and colliding with each other as they played a game common to them all. A variety of languages were used as they called out to each other, all competitive by nature and focused on the score. Soon the temptation was too much, and the older men joined in, attempting to keep up with the pace of the younger and very nimble children. Liam also threw himself into the game, enjoying the pleasure of running and playing with both the kids and other adults. At one stage Yared's leg extended out as he attempted to push the ball away onto his own side. The two men laughed loudly together as they tackled each other, both of them trying to gain possession of the ball.

Neither noticed the quicker feet that side-stepped in and deftly stole the ball from under their feet. A flash of blue passed by them and Liam yelled out in protest as Billy took the ball, which a second ago had been under his own foot. She ran it up the field, sharing it with the other girls. Back and forth, back and forth, the girls passed it from one to the other, avoiding the now more competitive attempts of the boys and men to regain possession. Billy flicked it over to one of the smaller girls, who kicked it hard and direct, straight past Nadir's hands who was goalkeeping, and into the depths of the esky. The girls huddled together, jumping up and down, the mixture of excited yelling, completely untranslatable due to the variety of languages being used.

Now the boys and men huddled together, preparing their plan of attack, the smaller boys irate that the girls had scored before they had. Asid brought the ball back to the centre, the play beginning again. Others from their group gathered to watch the fiercely contested match, joining in, yelling and cheering loudly from the sidelines. Once again, the ball travelled up and down the field area, one minute the boys having possession, the next moment gasps of desperation as one of the girls steered in from the side to steal it away and pass it quickly down towards their own goal.

Yared and Nadir were both experienced players and flicked the ball around to their team members, making sure the smaller kids all had a go at pushing the ball down the field. A fierce battle took place between two of the smaller girls and two of the boys. They tapped the ball with their feet, running fast as they twisted and jumped in the air. One of the boys used a sliding tackle to successfully stop another goal attempt and loud shouts from his team sounded across the park. Asid, who now had possession, passed the ball to Liam, who although hadn't played for a long time, quickly remembered the skills learned over the years. Liam tapped the ball lightly, manoeuvring and outsmarting a couple of the girls. He passed the ball around and Yared and Nadir made everyone laugh as they bunted it with their heads and did some clever trick passes, moving the ball quickly down the field.

The ball turned out wide to Liam and he looked down towards the esky, seeing instantly the perfect shot to score a goal. He lifted his foot, his eyes focused keenly on the esky, eager to level the score. He heard Asid scream out to him and then the ball was gone. He turned to see Billy, her dark hair streaming out behind her as her long legs strode out, a few small kicks and sidesteps as she passed the ball back and forth to the other girls in her team. She called out to one of the younger girls, Rohna, a thin wiry girl who ran like the wind, her light blue shawl flying out behind her. Expertly passing the ball to her, Billy stopped and watched. Rohna lined up the shot and kicked hard. The ball arched around the goalkeeper and as if in slow motion found its mark, smack bang in the middle of the esky. The girls all screamed wildly and raced to each other again, hugging and jumping up and down in true winning spirit.

Asid shook his head, showing his disbelief that they had let the girls beat them. The rules had been whoever was two points ahead won the game and so now the game was finished. Billy led the girls back to the picnic area, finding them all a drink and then sat down to cool off after the success of winning. The others were all soon sitting around on the blankets, laughing and talking about the girls' victory.

Yared looked at Billy and shook his head. 'You girl, you've been keeping that a secret.'

Billy laughed. 'What?'

'You're a good soccer player.'

Liam still had a look of shock on his face. 'You're all good players. Where the hell did you learn to play like that?'

Nadir joined in the conversation, his skin covered in tiny beads of sweat. 'What do you think we've got to do in those camps? Every kid, whether a boy or girl, learns to play soccer. It's a universal game. It's the only fun thing kids have to do. As long as there's a ball, we will play soccer.'

Asid stepped over Yared who was sprawled out on the ground. 'I'm gonna be Mr Cristiano Ronaldo when I grow up.'

They all laughed at the small boy who was trying to get them to all get up and play another round.

Asid pointed to Billy. 'This time you be on my team,' he said. 'I want to win.'

'Hey,' Liam joked, 'Where's your loyalty? She's on the girls' side, not ours.'

'Maybe we could make some swaps. This girl Billy here, she can run.' Nadir was also grinning, raising his eyebrows and pulling a face at Billy as she sat quietly, her feet bare, her long legs stretching out in front as she sat on the blanket. It had been a long time since she had kicked a soccer ball and she revelled in the feeling of stretched muscles and sweaty clothes. The feeling of running up and down a field, passing the ball to others and tackling the opposition players, had brought back memories. Memories of earlier years spent in the camps. Times when life had been at its lowest and the only pleasurable moments had been those spent playing soccer with the other kids. When she had begun school in Australia, soccer had been the common denominator for all students, no matter their gender or where they had come from. It had been the time she had spent playing soccer at school and the friends she had made through the sport, that had helped her through the difficult teenage years.

When she ran, it was the same feeling as when she swam in the mornings. Her head cleared, and her body felt like it was alive. She was freed from the burdens of lost memories and the loneliness of not having a family to call her own.

Billy turned to Nadir. 'Every kid played in the camp. I used to watch for hours and sometimes if one of the girls could get hold of a ball we'd find a small area to play. Then when I came to Australia and went to school I loved the fact that girls could play just the same as the boys. I was hooked.'

'Well you've got a pretty quick step,' Yared said.

'It brings back a lot of memories.' She looked over at the kids who were re-grouping, getting ready to play again. 'At school all the refugee kids were good players, regardless of where they came from. It seems that every camp had a place to play soccer.'

Yared nodded and grinned broadly as his own

girls ran wildly around the park. 'In the camp it was a dusty ground with flapping tents around the edges. It helped fill in the time. Here,' he held his hand forward, 'it is lush green grass with shady trees.'

'We are very lucky,' Billy said as she jumped up, also eager to get back into the play.

'Now, watch me as I smash Liam's team again.'

Together they walked towards the game that was now in full play; a tall muscular man, his broad smile lighting up his face and a slender dark-haired girl, both with different but similar stories.

29

During the drive home that afternoon, the car had been full of talk and laughter, as one by one Liam dropped Matilda, Lottie and Annika home. Soon it was only Billy and him left in the car.

'You never told me you were good at soccer,' Liam said as he drove past the house and down towards the beach.

'You missed the turn off,' Billy said, looking back to where the driveway of his house was.

'I know. The moon is coming up and it's supposed to be a super moon, so I thought it would be good to watch it come up over the ocean. You don't mind, do you?'

'No, not at all.'

Liam drove the car along a windy track that took them around the back of the lake. He parked the car and they set off on foot, following a narrow path that wound its way through the clumps of grass growing in the sand hills. The thundering roar of waves crashing onto the beach greeted them as they climbed over the crest.

'Here, sit here.' Liam pointed to a spot right on top of the dune.

They sat together, looking towards the east, neither speaking. Right on cue, the tip of the moon pushed its way over the rim of the horizon. As it rose slowly, the colour of its surface darkened and changed, the usual pale yellow morphing into a dark golden hue, perfect in its roundness. Ascending slowly, the moon floated above the surface of the inky ocean, the light slowly creeping over the water, creating a pathway that appeared to reach out and lead straight to where they sat high above the beach. Soon the glow lit up the entire area as the huge ball of golden light rose higher into the sky.

The night air was cool, and a slight breeze rustled the grass beside them. High above them, tiny clouds scudded across the sky, patches that passed quickly across the huge face of the moon.

The night was silent, and Billy whispered when she spoke. 'Why is it so big?'

'It's called a super moon and it's when a new moon is at its closest approach to the earth. It looks a lot bigger and brighter. Our timing's good, because it always looks more impressive when it's nearer the horizon.'

'The colour is incredible.'

For a long while they sat watching the huge circle as it lit up the beach below. Shimmers of light flicked across the white of the breakers, and flashes and lines of brightness lit up the valleys of the waves that rose higher and higher, before curling over and smashing down onto the sand.

Soon the night air became cold, and Billy who was still in shorts and T-shirt, wrapped her arms around her legs.

'Are you cold?' Liam asked, looking at her, mesmerised by the beauty of her face in the moonlight. 'We'll just watch for a bit longer and then we'll head back. We've been here for over two hours.'

Liam looked out across the beach. He could feel her arm next to his and he closed his eyes, the moment wrapped in his memory, the feeling of the cool air and the light of the moon locked away to be taken out at a later time. Neither of them spoke, the only sound the crashing of the waves on the beach.

'You look good when you play soccer.' Liam broke the silence. 'When you run, you float effortlessly.'

She smiled. 'I run better than I swim.'

He laughed, standing up and holding his hands out for her to grab onto. Her hands were cool in his as he pulled her to her feet, for a moment both of them standing there looking straight at one another.

His voice was husky, tingles running through his body as he held her small hands. 'Well, I didn't want to say that.' He looked at her again and then back down to their hands. He wanted to wrap his arms around her and hold her close, but he stood there, looking down at their hands still pressed together, their fingers entwined. 'I guess we'd better get back,' he said transfixed by her dark hair shining in the moonlight, her eyes holding his.

'I guess so.'

'Right, let's go then.' Liam had finally pulled away and walked in front of her leading the way back up the path through the dunes, the golden glow from the moon dancing across the water behind them.

30

The following weeks seemed to fly past and apart from the regular art classes Liam had not had any spare time to paint. Billy had worked with him during the day and at night helped him clean the studio, which was still cluttered but at least in some sort of order. The pieces ready for the exhibition were stacked to one side, and Liam looked at his paints and brushes, all neatly arranged in colour order on the table. The cleaning had kept them both busy but Liam was eager to complete some more paintings. With a long weekend coming up he decided to ask Billy if she would consider posing for him again.

'Thanks so much for helping me clean the studio. It's easier to find everything now.'

'I like being in there. It has a cosy feeling.'

Liam cleared his throat. 'The other night after we cleaned, you rested on the couch with Casso. I'd like to paint you in that pose.'

'I'd probably fall asleep.'

'That's fine. It was just very natural. I'd like you to wear that cream dress you had on. It contrasts perfectly against the darker colours of the couch.'

Billy smiled. 'Could there be flowers in the painting? There're so many plants in flower in the garden at the moment, it would be lovely to bring some of the outside in.'

Liam chuckled, shaking his head, wondering how on earth he would ever say no to her. Her

226

green eyes sparkled as she looked straight at him and he could tell she was excited about a new painting. 'If you want flowers, we will have flowers.'

★ ★ ★

It had taken a while to set up the correct position and Casso had been totally un-cooperative, seeming to know that more was being expected of him than usual. An open book lay next to Billy's head, her face to the side, her body twisted slightly so that one leg was bent and tucked a little under the other. Her body was stretched out, in repose along the length of the couch. One arm rested on her stomach, the other bent, her hand up near her head.

After much manoeuvring and repositioning Liam was satisfied. Casso lay at Billy's feet and had already curled up into a ball, letting them know that this was his position and there was no way he was moving.

'Are you comfortable?' Liam asked, standing back, looking at the pose from the position of his easel.

'Very,' she replied, 'I just hope I don't fall asleep.'

'Okay, hold it there then. I'll make a start.'

As usual in the beginning they both stayed silent and she closed her eyes, Liam's whole attention focused on her body. The dress was loose fitting and she had, as he requested, pulled it up high enough so that some of her upper leg and each of her lower legs were exposed. She lay relaxed, moving into a position that highlighted the different parts of her body. Billy sank deeper into the cushions, her breathing slowing, her body relaxed.

The light coming through the window filled the room with a bright airy atmosphere and the colours of the lounge, purples, deep reds and yellows brightened the background, contrasting with the old green table that was off to one side. Billy had filled some vases with large bunches of red and yellow grevilleas from the garden, filling the gaps with complementary dark green foliage.

Her olive complexion blended exquisitely with the adjacent colours and her dark hair, tied up loosely in a ponytail, lay naturally above her head, a blue ribbon holding it together. The cream dress flowed freely, the contours of her curves visible beneath it. Her breasts rounded down to a tiny waist and Liam inhaled sharply as he painted the outlines of hips flowing down to attractive long legs. Concentrating on her body, he left her face until later, instead focusing on the beautiful shapes that had originally attracted him to her as an art model. He could feel and see the moment when she totally relaxed, and her legs sank deeper into the lounge, her repose simple, but beautiful.

'Are you awake?' he asked, changing his brush, and looking through the colours for what he wanted.

'I am. This pose is so much easier to hold than the last one.'

'It's perfect. I'll try and work fast but it could be a few sittings to get it right.'

Casso snuffled and snuggled into the couch, his wet nose pressed up against Billy's feet.'

Billy giggled and moved her foot slightly, the

dog's nose tickling the bottom of her foot.

Liam smiled and relaxed as he began drawing her legs and feet. 'We will call this painting, *Billy and Casso.*'

She laughed and Casso twitched at the sound of his name.

'What's your real name? Billy, is not exactly an Afghan name.'

'My real name is Belourine. Billy is the name my friends gave me at school and I've always used it since. I think it just made me feel more Australian at the time, so I stuck with it.'

'How did you become so, 'Australian'?'

'It is a long story.'

'Well, we've got plenty of time.'

She giggled again. 'Casso's nose is tickling my feet.' She moved her foot slightly, away from the dog's nose. 'My story has many missing parts.'

'You mean times that you can't remember?'

'Times I can't remember and people and places that I have no knowledge of. There are many gaps in my story, because I was only five when I left Afghanistan. I have my real name written down and the area where I came from, however it is not much to go on. I have only been told my parents' names and that of my four brothers.'

'How did you get to Australia without your family?'

Billy sighed.

Liam was genuinely interested in her story and wasn't going to give up asking. He also knew she wouldn't disturb the pose and walk away, avoiding the difficult questions. She could have asked him not to ask about her family, but he had a personal connection to her home country and after all, as his drawings showed, a better recollection of the land and people than she herself had.

She took a deep breath. 'What I remember is leaving where our home was. Glimpses of the landscape near where we lived and words that my parents spoke, sometimes come to me. Mostly during the night or sometimes a memory will be triggered by a sight or smell. Lately I have noticed that when I am still and,' she paused for a moment, 'actually it is often now, when I sit for you, that the visions come to me.'

'Hmm,' was the only reply from Liam. He had realised from the earlier sittings here in his studio that she was remembering people and places from long ago, as she lay or sat motionless in front of him. He wasn't sure how he knew that, and he didn't know what it was she was remembering, but somehow he knew that she was thinking about her childhood, her family and the countryside where she had played as a small child. He waited for her to continue, intrigued and captured by the words that she shared with him.

Her body was still, the only movement was in her face as she spoke. Sometimes her eyes were open and other times when her words overwhelmed her, she closed her eyes, her long eyelashes rested, dark against her skin. He waited patiently, the paintbrush flying back and forth across the canvas, sometimes a dabbing motion as he worked on a particular section.

Her voice was calm when she continued, eyes wide open, looking towards Liam as he painted. 'Probably my most vivid memory is the day my

230

father planned for us to escape. I can still remember the fear. It's like a smell, I'm not sure what it is, and I can't explain it, but sometimes I can smell it like it's still stuck in my nose. The fear was not so much for me, it was not a fear of where we were going, or what was happening, rather,' she closed her eyes, 'the fear I could feel was coming from my mother and father. I remember them speaking to us calmly and quietly, but I could feel their distress. I could see it in their eyes. Even as a small child I knew that they were scared.'

Liam moved his position in front of the canvas, taking advantage of the sunlight that streamed in through the glass behind where Billy lay on the couch. 'Do you remember what happened?'

'I remember parts. We escaped in a truck, all of us crowded into the back with many other people. My brothers were sitting across from me, they also were quiet, which was unusual.' She blinked as the memories came back. 'I can still see their faces, covered in dirt. They were looking at me.'

She stopped and took a deep breath, her shoulders moving up and down as she tried to hold her composure. 'The others were families we knew, they were all from my village and I remember some other children there also. I don't remember their names, but I was looking at another girl, I think she may have been the same age as me. I think we smiled at each other. When I remember this moment I always know that the girl and I were still looking at each other.' Billy's voice quivered, 'I sometimes see her eyes in my dreams.' She stopped, and Liam continued to work, giving her time to catch her breath, noting that her

231

shoulders were no longer relaxed, and her chest rose and fell quickly with every intake of breath. Neither of them spoke, the heavy silence broken only by nesting birds in a tree outside the window.

His voice was husky when he finally spoke. 'What happened?'

Her shoulders moved up and down again as she struggled to control her voice.

'There was an explosion and the sounds of gunshots. Everything went upside down. I felt very squashed and then there was darkness. I don't remember anything else from that day. I have tried many times to remember if the others were near to me, or what happened, but there is nothing, only dust and darkness.

'So how do you know what happened to your family?'

'The family that took me in, told me years later that there was an attack on the truck and it rolled onto its side. All of my family apart from my mother and I were killed. There were also others in the truck who did not make it.'

'Do you know what happened to the other girl?'

'I think she died. I never saw her after that.'

'How did you survive? What happened to your mother?'

'My mother was injured, and they carried her in a sling that they made from blankets. Those of us who had survived managed to make it out over the border and into neighbouring Pakistan. Some people from our village took me with them and also my mother. Sometimes we walked and then other times we travelled in trucks again. I don't remember that time very well, but I knew we came to somewhere that was near to Peshawar. After that, we went to the camp and that is where we lived. It wasn't long after that my mother died and then there was only me.'

'Do you remember what it was like?'

'I will never forget it. I was only a small child, probably about five, when I arrived. When I left, I think that I was probably ten or eleven. In the camp it was cold and then sometimes very hot. My feet were always cut because we had no shoes.' She stopped as she tried to contain her emotions. 'It is not a time I want to remember.'

'I have heard about the camps and the conditions.' Liam's voice was shaky.

'The family who took me in treated me like their own. There wasn't much to receive, but we survived. We also went to school there and I learned to read. Somehow, we left the camps and travelled on buses across the country. At some stage we got on a boat. It was the middle of the night and I was very frightened because there was water all around us. I could not swim. The family I had been living with took me with them, like I was one of their own.'

'How did they prove that you were part of their family?'

'I guess it wasn't very hard. Once we arrived in the detention camps I just appeared as one of their kids. I don't think they would have had many official documents and probably little or none for their own family. I probably looked very much like their own children.'

Liam had stopped painting, intrigued with her story and the mixture of events that had bought her to Australia. 'What happened that you're not with them now?'

'We were in the detention camps for a while and I don't think it was easy for the family. There was always tension. The mother and father couldn't speak English and there were many arguments between them. They had four children of their own and once we were settled in Australia we all went to the local school. There were many other refugees there, mostly from Africa, Iraq and Afghanistan. When I was sixteen the parents said I could not go to school any longer, but I would have to work to help support the rest of the family. They knew a family who owned a big motel in the city. They said they had arranged for me to work there and the owners would give my wages to them.'

'Could you speak English by then?'

'I did very well at school.' Her voice became shaky. 'By the end of year eleven when I left I was top of the class. My English was so good that I achieved higher scores than the mainstream Australian students. One of the teachers there tried to help me and offered to meet with my carers to try and persuade them to allow me to continue with my schooling. She wanted me to go to university and organised my lessons and tutoring at school to try and get help for me. But the family was adamant, and there was nothing the teacher or I could do. I started working in the motel, changing linen, cleaning rooms and also working in the kitchen. All of my money went back to the family, after all they had been my carers for all of those years and they said I needed to repay them for all they had done for me.'

'So, you never got to finish school.'

'No, I never finished. I always tried to keep reading and practised my English continually, watching television and listening to the radio, always trying to perfect my accent.'

Liam chuckled, 'You mean you wanted an Aussie accent?'

She smiled. 'All I wanted was to fit in and I knew that the more English I had the better chance I would have in life. It was all I dreamed of, just to be like other Australian kids and not have to worry about having somewhere to live, or enough to eat.'

Liam put down his brush, his eyes averted from Billy for a moment as he stared out of the window. 'It's amazing how we take so much for granted here in Australia. Most have never seen war or had to fight for their lives, for survival.'

'That is true, this is what they say it is, the land of opportunity.'

'So, you kept working at the motel?' Liam asked, intrigued by Billy's path in life and amazed at the resilience of someone who had been through so much at such a young age.

'I stayed at the motel for a while, after all I was indebted to the family who had brought me here to Australia and they were fairly persistent about how it was now my turn to help support them and their own children. It was hard work at the motel and I knew I wanted more in regards to my job. Around that time, I also became disillusioned with my faith and the ways of my people. It was my wish to be an Australian, but those ideas separated me from the family who had bought me here. That was very hard as they were my only connection to my childhood. But I needed to get away from them. They were struggling to make money and to support their own children. They started talking to me about marrying one of their single friends who was much older than me.'

Liam could see tears in Billy's eyes and he turned back to the canvas, his brush moving quickly over the painting in front of him. 'Can you hold for a bit longer, I just want to finish this section before we have a break?'

Her voice was so soft it was hard to hear. 'Yes, I can stay in this position for longer.'

Liam painted, watching as her body sank back into the pose, her shoulders relaxed, her legs moving only slightly as Casso squirmed at her feet. 'Did you have anyone else to turn to?'

'I had no one, just myself, to try and work out how to get away from both the work and home situation. I didn't want to get trapped so I stole some money from the motel. It was easy to do, they had come to trust me, and I only took enough for a train fare out of Melbourne and some extra for food. I figured that they owed me for all the extra time I'd often worked and not been paid for. It was difficult to leave my one connection with my family and Afghanistan, but I knew I had to leave. I arrived in Sydney when I was nineteen. For a while I lived in a boarding house and then I got a job at a fruit shop. I even posted the money that I had stolen back to the hotel. Eventually I met a boy, Louie. He also worked at the fruit shop and he was the same age as me. He used to take me out dancing and for the first time I discovered what it was like to go out and just have fun. To be free and not worry about all the serious things in life. We moved in together and,' she sighed, 'I was happy. We were happy, together.'

She sat up and stretched out her arms, bending her body to the side to stretch out her back muscles. 'Those years weren't too bad. We never had much money, mind you. Louie worked at the fruit shop also and we rented a tiny flat. We had some fun times.'

'What happened?'

'Oh, we were too different. He had been born in Australia but had Greek parents. After a while he started telling me how to live my life. By now I was a bit older and there was no way after what I'd been through, I wasn't going to have an equal say in our lives together. We started to argue and soon he was spending more time with other friends. We argued more and more and I knew it was over. So, I packed up what I had. Luckily now I had some money in the bank and I caught the train to Brisbane.'

'Let's have a break.' Liam had been painting without looking down at his work very much. He had been concentrating on her face as she spoke, rather than the canvas. Now as they both stood behind the painting he knew that he had captured the exact expression that had been on her face as she told her story. It was what he strived for: the lines, the mood of the model, the deepness of the thoughts. Never before had he been so driven to capture someone's emotions.

'I think you have my face right, the expressions.'
Billy said.

'I was so engrossed in your story, I forgot I was
painting.' He laughed. 'Well it seemed to work,
because this is a very good start. I'm pleased with
that so far.'

★ ★ ★

Once they had taken a break, Billy made her way
back to the couch. Casso had settled into the centre of the cushions and she carefully lifted him
down to the bottom corner, once again tucked
under her feet. Liam waited until she re-tied her
hair, gathering up the long wavy strands, twirling
it around her fingers and then tying it up with
the blue ribbon. She squirmed around, her body
twisting this way and that until she found the correct position.

Liam looked down at the painting, then back at
Billy, once again an overwhelming tightness in his
chest as he took in the curves of her body, her hip
rising up as she pushed her hand under her head.

This time she didn't wait and started talking as
soon as she was settled. 'I have a piece of paper
and it has my brothers' first names written on it.'

'It's a shame that you don't have that all written
down properly, like where you lived and where
you were born.'

She laughed, a sweet chuckle that made a lump
form in Liam's throat. 'You know, my date of
birth, much like many other refugees, is the first
of January. All the children in the family I lived
with had the same date as me.'

'So you don't really know the year or date you were born?'

'I know I was five when I left Afghanistan. My brother was a year older than me and had his sixth birthday the week before we left. I remember very well because he was given a kite.'

'Is that why you like my drawings of the kites?'

'It's a very special memory I have of my brothers. I have always remembered the kites flying in the air. That is one thing that always stayed with me.'

The noise of the clock ticking echoed in the room, the only noise apart from the sound of Liam's brush on the canvas.

Liam couldn't speak, his throat was tight and his chest hurt. Visions whirled through his mind: kite flyers running through the dust, their shrill cries of delight, their excited words of instructions, the noises echoed in his head.

'I watched you that day at the lake, showing the children how to fly a kite. You threw the sand up in the air to see which way the wind was blowing. It bought back a lot of memories for me.'

'The boys used to kick the dust,' Billy said, her words cut short as if she wanted to say more but couldn't.

'I have seen that and heard their words,' Liam replied, his voice husky with emotion.

★   ★   ★

Billy did not speak again that afternoon. In her mind she could still see the boys flying their kites, running, running faster, yelling out. She had only

239

been a tiny child at the time, but she could vaguely remember sitting on a rock under a tree watching them. It was one of the few memories she had been able to turn to in the years when she had felt so alone. Sometimes it made her happy and other times it threw her into long lapses of sadness.

Now she lay still, the sound of Liam's voice floating in the distance. The memory of the sound of the kids yelling, as they ran faster and faster, trying to get the kite into the air blocked out everything and she squeezed her eyes tight to stop the tears from flowing.

Casso jumped up from the end of the couch and lay up next to her face. He pushed his nose into her neck and gave her a couple of licks on her cheeks. Her hand reached out to stroke him as he put his paws up onto her arm, nestling in closely next to her. She was unaware of Liam continuing to paint. Oblivious to the fact that several hours had gone past and he had changed canvases, beginning and finishing a second piece of work. She did not feel the blanket that he gently placed over her as he lifted Casso off, leaving her alone on the couch, the late afternoon sun streaming in through the window, warming her where she slept.

31

As the date of the exhibition drew closer, Liam spent longer hours working in the studio. One afternoon he spread out the selected works and asked Billy in to have a look at the collection. Wandering up and down, she closely scrutinised each painting, passing quickly over the more risqué nude works that he had completed earlier in the year. Finally, she came to the paintings of herself.

The first and second works were reclining on the couch; the first one had been done the day she had fallen asleep, as she lay relaxed on the lounge. Her favourite was the one where Casso's wet nose was pressed up against her feet, her own head thrown back, giggling as the coldness tickled her skin. A third painting had only been completed the previous week and depicted Billy standing, leaning against the window frame looking out towards the garden. Although a ray of sunshine beamed in through the window, the scene outside the window was of a light shower of rain floating down upon the rambling garden adjacent to the studio. The sun shower threw a mixture of light and shade across both her face and the inside of the studio. Around her the jumble and disarray of Liam's work area added a vibrancy and colour, complementing the hues and patterns that covered the dress she wore.

Billy turned around to Liam who was watching

her responses carefully. 'I really like that one,' she said, standing back a bit further to take in the full effect of the colours and assortment of items that were included in the picture. 'There is so much to it. I think the painting shows more about you than me. I mean look at the array of items on the big table. I even see your box of sketches at the back there.'

'I know. I had so much fun painting all the bottles of paint, and the empty tins. I didn't realise how many empty coffee cups got left on that table until I actually painted the scene.'

She moved closer to the painting again. 'There's so much detail in it. Maybe you could have just left me out of that one. I think it's just as good without me at the window.'

'No. It all fits together. Really, you've spent so much time in here with me lately. It's hard for me to imagine a painting without you in it anymore.'

'Oh, I'm sure once your next model who'll pose in the nude for you comes along, you'll manage to cope.'

'I'm not so sure anymore. I think my style has changed over the last few months working with you. I have different ideas I want to try out now. New thoughts that surprisingly don't always include unclothed models.'

'But you paint that genre so well.' Billy's face scrunched up, perplexed that Liam would decide a change in direction from a field he mastered and was known for.

'Artists change over the years you know. Different times and changes in emotions and life in general, put shifting thoughts into our heads.

Anyway, we'll get this exhibition over with and see what happens. I do have different ideas I want to run with though.'

'Don't change anything because of me. I've always understood that it's your work.' She stopped talking as she moved onto the last painting. It was set aside from the others and was positioned in pride of place on Liam's mother's easel.

Standing in front of it she looked closely at the contours of her back and the sensuality that the viewer could decipher in the mastery of his strokes. It was the way in which the fabric of her dress revealed not only her lower back but also the side of her body, her uplifted arms causing the fabric to move away from the sides of her back. Billy was about to speak when a noise rumbled through the studio and the wind slammed the door shut.

The slamming crash echoed throughout the room, breaking the spell of tranquillity and calm conversation that had filled its space earlier. Casso jumped out of Billy's arms and ran towards the woman who walked through the door; a woman whose shrill loud voice matched the interruption of the slamming door.

'Jesus Christ, it's freezing out there. I've been searching everywhere for you. I could have robbed the place.' The well-dressed woman stopped short when she realised that Liam wasn't alone in the studio. She placed a briefcase onto the ground and attempted to tidy her windswept hair. Squealing with delight as Casso leapt and spun around near her feet, she bent down and picked him up. She ruffled his fluffy coat, rubbing her heavily made-up face into it. 'Shit, Liam. This dog stinks.

What the hell has he been rolling in?' Casso looked up at her, oblivious to her haughty attitude as she dropped him quickly onto the ground. He ran around in circles, obviously excited at the entrance of his usual owner.

'Amanda, this is Billy.' Liam said as he introduced the unexpected guest.

Amanda raised her eyes, her greeting an indifferent nod, as she looked Billy up and down, before she walked between Liam and Billy towards the series of paintings lined up in front of them. She peered closely and then stood back, taking in the full effect of the paintings.

'It looks like you're actually getting your shit together, Liam. Are these for the exhibition?' She walked up and down looking at each painting, nodding her approval at the range of different sizes and subjects. 'I'm impressed. New models, different bodies. It seems that the art classes have provided some interesting subjects for you.'

When she got to the last four paintings of Billy, she stopped, looking back to Liam, before stepping back and then closer again to the paintings. 'These are incredible, oh and I see, this is your little model.' She raised her eyebrows and then scowled as Billy picked Casso up, the dog snuggling into its new favourite person. 'They look like they've been done here in your studio?'

★ ★ ★

'They have.' Liam watched Amanda's face change, knowing that she would be mulling over the fact that he had invited a model to pose in his pri-

244

vate area. Before Billy, Amanda had been the only model that he had painted in his own studio, and that had only been because she had harassed him until he had agreed. Until then he had always kept it formal and professional, preferring to rent out a studio room at the art gallery.

His own studio was full of so many personal and intimate belongings and until Billy came along he had always thought it would stay that way. Amanda had only posed for him once in the studio and then her questions and constant chatter had reinforced his idea that this was his own space. She had been annoyed that subsequent sittings had been in the art gallery rooms, however her desire for him to paint her had overcome her preferences for where the sittings took place.

Now as she looked at the paintings, it was hard to see if she was annoyed or pleased. She looked at his work for a long time, finally coming to the fourth painting that was separated from the others. For a long time, she didn't speak and then she turned to Liam. 'I would say this is your finest piece of work I've ever seen. It has a lot of emotion in it. How much are you going to put on it?'

Liam shuffled the paints and other objects on the messy table, keeping busy sorting everything out. 'It's not for sale. And it's not going in the exhibition.'

'That's ridiculous. It's the best one there. It's a pity your friend here doesn't reveal a bit more though. I think it'd be better if she were nude. Someone will pay a fortune for that last one. How much will you put on it?'

There was anger in Liam's voice and he glanced

245

across as Billy put Casso down, making her way to the door. 'I told you it's not for sale. Now what's the purpose of your visit?' He looked towards the door and gave Billy a wave as she looked back at them both before leaving the studio. Casso followed her diligently and the door shut firmly behind them, leaving Liam and Amanda alone in the studio.

'You're crazy. What's the use of painting if you're not going to display and sell it? I thought that was what this exhibition was for. I've put a lot of work into organising this also, so I think I have a say in it.'

By now Liam's voice was raised. 'You have absolutely no say in this and if you don't let up I'll pull the pin on the entire idea. It was never my idea anyway. For some reason I let you talk me into it. I'm fine with doing it still, but I intend to do it my way and that painting is not part of it.'

Amanda sat on one of the chairs, her legs crossed, her back upright, the look on her face prim and proper.

God, she looks like she's sucked on a lemon, he thought, watching her as she gathered her thoughts.

'I have a new penthouse overlooking the harbour. Of course, it's five bedrooms, three bathrooms, you know, the usual.'

'That's great. I'm really happy for you. What does that have to do with me though?'

'Well, you're not allowed to have animals there.'

'So, you want me to keep Casso here?'

'Well I don't really have a choice. Actually, where is the little darling?'

'He left with Billy.'

'God, that sounds like a boy's name.'

Liam did not answer, instead continuing to glower at her, wishing that she would finish the conversation and leave.

'Can you keep Casso here?'

'Sure, he loves it here anyway. But he's my dog then. There's no coming back for him. He stays here.'

'Well my new flatmate isn't keen on dogs. He's actually allergic to dog hair. So, who is she?'

Amanda's tone changed, and she straightened her clothes, pushing her hair back. 'Surely you haven't taken up with her? Or is it just the modelling you're after? You know I'd always pose for you if you needed. Just because we're no longer together, I mean, I'd have no inhibitions with some suggestive poses. Those last paintings are good, but you need more skin and bare body.'

Liam picked up his coat and walked towards the door. 'Sometimes less is more.'

'You never worried about that before.' Her voice changed and she smiled at Liam. 'I thought perhaps you might ask me up to the house. I have the rest of the day. Perhaps a quick fling for old times sake?'

Liam chuckled, 'God Amanda, I thought we'd both moved on.'

Amanda stood up and came over to Liam. 'We have, but,' she touched him on the arm, 'there's nothing wrong with getting together every now and then. I know you must still have some feelings for me.'

Liam stopped himself from rolling his eyes.

Some of her earlier conversations had alluded to the fact that she would still take the opportunity, if given, to re-connect with him.

'Let's just concentrate on the exhibition. We finalised the other a long time ago. I'm sorry, Amanda.'

He waited impatiently, noting Amanda's surprise at the indifference he showed towards her. Previously she had been able to push him around, usually getting him to do things the way she wanted, but those times were over. He raised his eyebrows, smiling still, as she picked up her bag, a conceited look on her face as she followed him to her car.

He opened the car door for her. 'You know I was only joking about 'a fling',' she said, her eyes narrowing as she looked at him.

'Of course. I'll be in contact before the exhibition.' Liam said.

Her voice returned to its earlier business-like manner. 'I'll ring you shortly to finalise some of the details. Just make sure you have everything ready for the night.'

'Goodbye, Liam.'

'Goodbye, Amanda.'

32

It was as if Casso understood the nature of Amanda's visit and at night he no longer slept up at Liam's house but had settled right in to Billy's cabin. Liam made a small dog door so he could go in and out, but let Casso decide where he wanted to sleep. That place was of course on the bottom of Billy's bed.

At first, she had tried to push him out each night. 'I thought you might not like him being inside,' she said. 'Also his loyalties have become rather fickle.'

'I was thinking the same. You would think that five years of feeding and looking after him would add up to some sort of faithfulness on his behalf.' Liam had resigned himself to the fact that Casso had attached himself to Billy and rarely left her side. Never having owned a dog before, she had also begun to spoil him, and soon there was a small leather collar around his neck and a special crocheted blanket for him to sleep on when they were in the studio. Liam hadn't said anything when he noticed a doggy shampoo and brush resting on the tank stand and had smiled at the new tennis balls that seemed to now be scattered around the yard for Casso to chase.

★ ★ ★

In a few weeks Liam would have to start preparing the paintings, in readiness for the exhibition.

The painting, which he had told Amanda was not for sale, stood, taking pride of place on his mother's old easel.

Art classes were finishing up for a few weeks and on the last night, the artists who sat near Liam had taken in some food and drinks to celebrate the end of the term. Yared and Nadir had brought in African sweets that their wives had made, and as requested had written down the recipe to give to Annika and Lottie. Neither of the men drank alcohol so Matilda had made sure to have some soft drinks, along with a few beers and a bottle of wine for the others. Glasses were filled with the various liquids and they raised them in unison.

'Cheers and best wishes to our good friends,' Matilda said.

Yared added, 'To be without a friend is to be poor indeed.'

Rolande and Pierre raised their glasses high, clinking loudly with the others, all of them toasting the end of a successful round of lessons.

'It's a shame your friend Billy isn't here to join us,' Matilda said, her eyebrows raised high.

'What's that look for Matilda?' Liam wrapped his arm around her bony shoulders, taking care not to hug too hard. She had grown frail in the last couple of months and although she assured them all that she was fine, she had begun to look her age.

'Well, my boy, how long are you going to wait?' Matilda asked, her eyes widening.

'For what?' Liam responded, trying to sound surprised.

They all turned towards him, the men laughing

at the confused look on his face.

Matilda patted his arm fondly, 'I think it's time you let her know how you feel about her. For goodness sake, just ask her out!'

'I don't think she would be interested in me, well not in that way.' He sounded serious and Yared and Nadir sat up straighter, ready to give him some advice.

'Whoa man, are you thinking at all? We see the way she looks at you,' Nadir said.

'She's one fine woman, Liam. If you don't woo her, well, man, someone will win her over before you,' Yared added.

Annika and Lottie listened intently, clinking their glasses together again, pleased at the prospect of a good romance in the making.

'What are you waiting for?' Yared leaned over, looking him in the eye. 'Where there be love there will be no darkness.'

Liam stuttered a little. 'Well . . . um . . . I don't know. I'm not that good with romance. I think she likes it the way it is. We're just really good friends.'

Matilda sat up straighter, everyone as usual silent when she spoke, her words slow and eloquent. 'Can you look me in the eye and tell me that you don't have any feelings more than friendship for her?'

Liam bit his lip, his eyes fixed on Matilda's.

'Can you?'

They all broke into laughter when Liam didn't answer.

Nadir slapped his hand on Liam's leg. 'You're in trouble now. Your face has gone red. All these ladies pushing you along, man, you got no hope.'

The conversation had gone around and around in his head for days and he tried to work out what his first approach would be. The problem had been solved on Friday afternoon when they had finished work just after lunch. It had been a long hot day, and Billy had worked quickly with him to get a large yard mowed, lawns cut and manicured in readiness for a garden wedding to be held there the next day. As they loaded all the gear into his trailer, Billy had surprised him. She talked as she worked, asking him if he would like to come for dinner at her place tonight. 'It's nothing flash, just a nice curry that I started cooking last night. I just thought it would be a nice way to finish off the week. Casso and I would like you to join us.'

He continued packing the trailer, trying to make his answer sound casual and relaxed. 'Sure, that'd be great. I'll bring a bottle of wine.'

'See you about seven,' she said, her eyes focused on the tools she was packing away, neither looking at the other.

★ ★ ★

Casso had barked at the knock on the door, and Billy called out for Liam to come in. Busy in the kitchen with the last of the cooking she had turned around to find him standing on the other side of the kitchen counter. 'I'm just finishing it off, I won't be a moment.'

'It smells good.' He walked over and took the lid off the pot, inhaling the aromas wafting up through the steam. Passing her the bottle of wine, he bent down to pat Casso who was jumping up demanding Liam's attention. 'I'll pour us a drink.'

Billy finished setting the table, looking up as Liam passed her a glass of wine. 'Thank you,' she said, taking the drink from him.

Their eyes met, her eye make-up accentuating the shape and darkness of her eyes. A floral dress clung tightly to her body and even though Liam had spent many hours staring at her body when he painted her, he was struck by her tall slender build and tiny waist.

Liam had also taken extra care to dress for the occasion. His thick wavy dark hair was neatly brushed, his face freshly shaved and even a splash of aftershave had been applied.

As Billy served dinner she relaxed, moving around the kitchen, well used to cooking and looking after herself. Liam complimented her in between mouthfuls of the delicious tasting curry that she piled into his bowl. 'You're a good cook. How did you learn how to cook?'

Now that everything was out and served and Liam was enjoying the food, she relaxed even more. 'I used to cook for the family I worked for. It was out of necessity that I learned. The woman, or the mother, couldn't cook at all, so I bought a lot of second-hand cookbooks and just followed the recipes. Once I found that everyone liked my meals, I got a bit more adventurous. Now I really enjoy cooking. I must admit though, it's nice to prepare a meal for someone else, not just myself and Casso.'

'You haven't been spoiling that dog have you?'

Casso looked up at both of them, as if he was aware they were discussing his daily diet.

Billy laughed as she dished up seconds for Liam who ate as much as she could pile onto his plate.'

★ ★ ★

The night had gone well and as they cleared the plates from the table and washed up they talked, laughing as they recounted some of the work situations that had happened during the week. Liam finished the dishes and looked down at Casso, as if to get his consent. Billy had been reaching up into a cupboard, putting away glasses when Liam came up beside her and took the tea towel from her hand. He placed it down on the counter and turned to her.

They faced each other and their eyes locked.

'What would happen if I kissed you?' Liam asked softly.

There was a slight hesitation and her eyes widened. 'I would kiss you back.'

Liam bent down, his lips brushing softly across hers, his hands gently holding the sides of her face. He stopped for a second. 'You are very beautiful, Billy.' His lips pressed down harder, his passion reciprocated as she kissed him back. Her long slender hands reached up and touched his chest and their eyes locked as their bodies pressed closely together.

33

Liam had been surprised when Billy had asked him to stay the night. Casso was still sulking; Liam had shoved him out of the bedroom with his foot, before shutting the door firmly behind him. This morning he had conceded and given in to Billy's pleas to let the moping dog onto the bed.

'He's a little ratbag,' Liam said as he pushed him out of the way, Casso trying to snuggle into the warmth where Liam's body had been.

Billy picked him up and put him onto the bottom of the bed, before snuggling back under the covers. Her dark hair spread out across the pillow and Liam ran his hands through it, pulling her in towards him. 'You're not so shy about your body when I'm not asking to paint it.'

'I think that's been building up for a while. You shouldn't work so close to me in those tight T-shirts.' She giggled as his hands moved under the covers, both of them disappearing under the blankets, Casso kicked unceremoniously from the covers at the end of the bed.

★ ★ ★

For the next month they were both kept busy, swimming in the mornings and work during the day. Liam spent most evenings finalising his art pieces while Billy tutored Yared's and Nadir's children after she finished work for the day. The children adored her and kept her entertained with their funny sayings and pronunciations. There were always plenty of humorous stories to tell Liam when she came home.

At night when Liam finished in the studio he would arrive at Billy's where he now stayed each night.

'Poor Casso,' Billy said one night as Liam once again pushed him out of the bedroom with his foot, shutting the door firmly in his pouting face. 'He doesn't like the new dog bed you bought him.'

'Poor Casso, nothing. It's not the bed he doesn't like; it's the fact that it's in the kitchen and not in here with you. I swear that dog is jealous. He tries to push in between us when he gets in here.'

Liam and Billy had become inseparable and neither could imagine sleeping or waking up without the other. 'I love waking up with you in the morning,' Billy said as she flung her leg across Liam's naked body, at the same time reaching across to hit the snooze button on the alarm.

Liam pulled her closer to him, his hands tingling with the touch on her skin, his lips pressing down as they clung to each other. 'Forget swimming this morning, butterfly girl,' he said, his hands moving over her as they joined together, the morning swim quickly forgotten.

★　★　★

Both of them had fallen back into a deep sleep that morning, their bodies coiled together as they nestled under the blankets. Casso must have been impatient to start the day and Liam woke to the

256

sound of him scratching at the bedroom door. He ignored the noise and leaned on his elbow, his face above Billy's as he stared down at her. His hand stroked her face, pushing her hair back, his fingers soft and gentle on her smooth skin. Her thick eyelashes were splayed out on her cheeks, her beautiful face, tranquil and rested as she slept. He watched her, reminded of another sleeping face; a smaller face of a child, thick eyelashes, similar olive skin. His heart beat faster. She meant so much to him. Billy was the most important person in his life now and he couldn't imagine life without her. He wanted to protect her, to make sure she was always safe and happy, that she was always by his side. He took her hand as she reached out towards him, Casso's barking stirring her from her sleep.

Liam looked closely. Her fingers were delicate and small, her skin dark against his own. Her hands were small, and he held them firmly, caressing them with his thumb. The colour of the skin on her hand held his gaze and he felt a throbbing in his temples. He stared harder at her fingers. They were perfect, soft and smooth. His head ached, and confusion blurred his thoughts.

Were they hers or did they belong to a child?

He turned her hand over in his. Her hand was small against his own. Was the hand attached to her arm? Perhaps the arm and hand were two different pieces. He blinked quickly, his eyes stinging. The hand and arm were separate. That's what could happen to a child's arm. It could be blown apart. He squeezed her hand hard, her face and body now blurred, the hand the only part that was in focus. If he held it tight his mind would refocus.

Bring him back to where he really was.

His name was called out loudly. 'Liam!'

He bit his lip at the sound. Someone was calling him but if he could hold the hand tightly then maybe it could be put back together.

You could do that.

You could join body parts back together if you kept them all. There were medics who could stitch them back together. The bed tilted, and he sat upright, holding the hand up high. Now he was no longer in the safety of a small cottage on his property, but instead he was sitting in the back of a truck, holding the hand of a small child. Billy's voice faded into the distance and his hands let go of the hand, instead holding his head as he rocked back and forth, transported to another time, another place, another life.

34

Uruzgan Province, Afghanistan 2007

It was the final week of Liam's third tour of duty and earlier that day he'd shared jokes with the boys about the excitement of returning to Australia. Going back to some female companionship and the comfort of a large double bed held appeal. He had contributed to the conversation light-heartedly, at the same time readying himself for the patrol day ahead. It was a dismounted watch and he was fully loaded with his patrol order; a heavy load that did little to alleviate the oppressive heat that weighed down upon the men.

The group had walked in a direction away from the small village where their command post was set up, picking up the pace as they cleared the walled outskirts. Ahead of them lay a small field covered in the subtle shades of pink poppies, the hues of the plants creating a sea of colour in amongst the dryness of the Afghan rubbly soil and the rugged backdrop of the mountains that rose up far to the north.

In the distance Liam spotted a bedraggled group of young boys, their long harem trousers and loose dresses covered in dust, topped by ragged vests that swung down around their knees. The army group slowed and watched as the boys sat down together on the edge of the field, placing their kites in front of them, readying the strings and spools, preparing the sails for flight.

During the rule of the Taliban, kite flying was banned, and it was only in the last six or seven years that Afghans were once again able to partic-ipate in one of the nation's most loved pastimes. Yesterday his group had moved in and around the small village, taking time to sit with the locals, establishing their connections as they talked through an interpreter about the projects about to be put in place.

A few of them were the same kids they had helped yesterday as they put together their kites in readiness for today. Even though Liam knew some of the local language, most of the communi-cating had been done through actions and signals as they compared the best way to make the kite soar high into the air. Today the boys were going to put theory into practice and they waved excit-edly, calling out to the passing Australian soldiers. Liam gave a thumbs-up to the smallest boy. Yes-terday the four-year-old, whose name was Hamid, had climbed onto his lap, intrigued with his sun-glasses and the pockets on his uniform. He had stayed there for the rest of the time, his tiny body leaned back against Liam, just as if he belonged there. When the men were leaving he'd looked up at Liam and Liam stared down into a set of pierc-ing green eyes. A wide smile with deep dimples either side had been Liam's reward as he gave the small boy a cuddle, as well as a biscuit he found in the bottom of his pack.

Now Hamid stood and stared at the passing sol-diers, his scruffy dark hair sticking out from under his tattered cap, his clothes dirty and too big, but a smile that stretched from ear to ear when he recognised Liam. They waved to each other and the sensation that he often experienced when he came into contact with the children caught in the middle of this bloody conflict, pulled at his chest. Looking back a few times he watched as Hamid eventually turned his attention from the group of soldiers and followed the older boys.

Liam's mind turned to more serious matters as the group passed through the green zone and entered the dry dusty areas that flanked the fields surrounding the village. They followed a well-worn trail that led them higher into the hills, eventually stopping at a rocky outcrop where they could survey the dusty desolate plains that stretched out as far as the eye could see. In the distance was the village where they had stopped yesterday, the adjoining green zone fields spreading out to the pegged safety areas, already cleared by previous units. Even from their spot high up in the hills the excited yells of the boys drifted up to them and they stopped to watch the boys running alongside the fields, their kites tucked under their arms, the colours of the sails visible against their dusty clothes.

The kite flyers stopped at a patch of arid rocky ground where the dirt was devoid of moisture, a moonscape that seemed to stretch forever, disappearing eventually into the rippling rays of the rising sun. The men watched with interest as the ancient tradition came into play. The boys stood still, and then turned on the spot slowly, each one of them in turn licking their finger and holding it to the wind. Liam chuckled as Hamid copied the older boys, turning around in circles, nearly falling over, dizzy from spinning and probably unsure of what he was supposed to be checking. The yells of the others were audible now as they began to kick the brown loose dust, calling out together in their own language, 'Kick the dust. See which way the wind blows. Kick the dust.'

The powdery dust flew into the air, rising in a cloud that pushed towards the direction where the soldiers rested.

Soon several kites were high in the sky, spiralling and soaring, fighting for space. Hamid stood close to the tallest boy who occasionally let the small boy help him hold the spool attached to the string.

The men sat for a while, intrigued by the scene as they prepared to move off further into the hills. Liam took one last glance down at the boys. One of the kites had come free, spiralling wildly, zooming out of control across the rocky dusty plains, away from where the boys were set up. The kite eventually speared downwards into the earth, its final resting place, nose down, not far from a clay fenced-off compound.

He wondered if the boys would follow the kite. They were all repeatedly told about the dangers of entering unfenced and often uncleared areas, particularly around abandoned sites. Although the area where they had been flying the kite had been cleared, the pegs of the safety zone did not extend to the distant spot where the kite had landed.

Liam's mate Ben, stood still next to him, shielding his eyes against the glaring sun as he stared across the valley. 'They should be alright. That area would have been cleared.' He watched with Liam as two of the boys took off running in the direction of the grounded kite. Liam stood up as Hamid followed, the small boy's tiny legs moving quickly to keep up.

'Surely not,' Liam muttered, his body stiffening as he leaned forward, his eyes following the direction of their path. He cupped his hands either side of his mouth and yelled loudly, 'Back. Go back. Go back.' His deep voice sounded out across the valley, the wind carrying his words back up into the gullies, echoing off the steep walls and caves in the hills behind them. Liam closed his eyes and held his breath, as did the men around him. Suddenly a flash of light and the loud detonation of a mine resounded across the valley, the sound of the other boys still flying their kites silenced as the explosion rent the air.

* * *

The rest of the day blurred into that one moment and to this day, Liam could not remember descending from where he had stood, rocks and dirt scattering from under his boots as he ran blindly down the mountain path, the others close behind him. He sprinted across the field, following the path already taken by the boys, stopping only when he reached the spot where the bodies of the three boys lay sprawled in the dust. The others were close behind him and he remembered Ben barking orders and instructions, other voices yelling and people moving around quickly to do what they could as quickly as possible. The regimented years of training had kicked in and they worked as a team; their sometimes robotic movements and methodical methods the only sane actions in a scene filled with destruction and horror.

Together they had lifted the broken bodies of the two older boys into the transport truck, treating them with the first aid available, reassuring them that help was on the way.

Not until the injured boys had been settled did Liam take charge of the small lifeless form of Hamid. He had wrapped the body of the small boy securely in a blanket. The shredded, colourful sails that had spiralled bravely when bound for adventure were now draped lifelessly over his blanketed body.

The red of the sails was strangely bright in a landscape of greys and dusty browns, the fluttering colours standing out where everything else now appeared shrouded in a haze of morbid grey. Liam's hands wrapped around the small bundle and he held Hamid's body tightly as he clambered into the back of the truck. Ben jumped up and sat next to him, his words unheard through the fog that was wrapping itself around Liam's mind. The words blurred, the rocking of the truck bounced and smashed, strange and jumbled thoughts filled Liam's head, the smell of death clogged his nostrils and nothing, nothing left in his world made any sense.

★ ★ ★

For Liam it was as if all of his time and experiences in Afghanistan had come to this moment and the small body in his arms signified the misery and suffering that he had witnessed in a country decimated by war. The moaning and crying of the other boys who had been injured filled his ears and mind, and the jolting of the truck speared through every nerve in his body.

Liam floated above all of it, looking down, seeing only the fuzzy shadow of the others in the back of the truck. The only clear picture in his mind was the rounded tiny face of Hamid that appeared below his own. Liam's eyes never left Hamid's face. Transfixed, he stared down into what he thought was the face of an angel. The boy's eyes were closed, dark baby eyelashes, dusty and long against the olive, clear complexion of his peaceful sleeping face. Liam knew however, that the body hidden under the blanket revealed a different story. He kept his eyes on the boy's face, trying to block out the earlier images of a broken child's body, of body parts and clothes ripped apart.

★　★　★

The Australian doctor at the field hospital had let him have some more time with the small boy, but in the end he had gently unwrapped Liam's hand from Hamid's and taken him from his arms.

It was over.

For him, Liam Andrews, the war on foreign soil was finished. He needed to go home.

35

Billy's voice had been a soothing background noise as Liam's mind began to come back into focus. Her hands rested on his arm and she talked slowly to him. 'You're here with me Liam. It's alright. Look at me. Look at me.'

Liam opened his eyes, forcing himself to look straight at her. Her eyes were clear and calm, and she continued to talk to him, guiding him through the turmoil that had once again exploded in his mind.

When he spoke, his voice was barely audible, the words shaky and mumbled. 'I couldn't bear it if anything happened to you, Billy. What if something happens?'

'Nothing will happen to me. I can look after myself and you are by my side now. Nothing will happen, Liam.'

Liam slowly entered back into the reality of the present and what had just happened. 'That came on so fast. I was looking at your hand. It reminded me ...'

'Go on, Liam. Tell me. Tell me what it is.'

Once Liam began talking he couldn't stop. The feelings he had bottled up for so many years, bubbled forth and his words fell out, jumbled at times but mostly clear and concise as he told Billy his story. He told her everything, the details, the smells and the sounds. He left nothing out and when he was finished, although he was emotionally drained there was also a heavy weight lifted from his shoulders.

⋆   ⋆   ⋆

Billy listened and waited, wrapping her arms around Liam when he eventually stopped talking. She held him until he fell into a deep sleep, his breathing even, his mind calmed and at rest. As he slept, the words he had spoken filled her thoughts. The events had been detailed. The small boy he had carried in the truck, the men he had been with and the kites that had flown high in the skies above Afghanistan. There had been and still was, so much misery in her country and it was the sight of the children suffering that had taken the main toll on him.

Liam had talked not only about his time in Afghanistan but also about the difficulties that he'd faced when he returned from that last tour. He had filled Billy in on how his father had gathered the rest of the family together, putting in place the plan of action that would save his sanity and his life. Kath had been the one who had helped the most. Her father had been a Vietnam War veteran and she had recognised the same symptoms in Liam that she had observed with her own father when she was only a young girl. Her entire life had been spent watching the consequences of a foreign and controversial war, on not only her father but also her mother and their marriage. There was no way she was going to let Liam travel down the same path of destruction and fracture that she had observed with her own family.

Now Liam had Billy to help him wade his way through the effects of what he had experienced. She was adamant that she was staying around, that she would help him when the events of the previous years overwhelmed him as had happened this morning. Together they would be okay.

★ ★ ★

Liam had woken after a long sleep, refreshed and with a clear mind. He had searched for Billy who was working in the garden, Casso lying dutifully beside her as she dug in the soil. He waited for her to stand up, her eyes meeting his as they stood facing each other.

She smiled. 'I thought I would let you sleep.'

He reached over and pushed a strand of hair away from her face. 'That has not happened for a long while. Not since I saw you flying the kite with the children at the lake.'

'It's okay, Liam. I understand. It is a good thing to have it all out in the open. You have my story and now I also have yours. We understand each other much better.'

The two of them embraced, their arms wrapped around each other, their bodies calm and peaceful as they stood together.

36

The time had finally arrived for Liam's art exhibition. The invitations had gone out, the artwork packed and picked up, as well as numerous phone calls from Amanda who had co-ordinated the display and made other required arrangements. Although the exhibition had not originally been his idea, he did feel a degree of excitement to think that his paintings would be displayed in the same gallery as other more well-known artists.

Amanda had arranged the settings, the tags with the required information, the selling information and paperwork. All of his friends from art class were attending; Yared and his family ensuring they picked up Matilda so that she didn't miss out on the event. His dad and Ruby had finally re-surfaced from their travels and this morning had arrived at his place in their van, hooking up to the electricity and preparing for a week-long stay.

John looked ten years younger and sported a short beard and a healthy dark tan. Months relaxing with some casual work to supplement his income had done him the world of good and his face was constantly stretched in a wide smile. He had merely grinned when Liam filled him in on the budding romance with Billy.

'You're not saying much, Dad,' Liam had looked quizzically at him.

'Well, anyone could see that one coming a mile away. You're meant for each other.'

Kath and Chris had also arrived and were staying up at his house. Billy had fitted in with the family easily and she and Kath were both out shopping for something to wear to the opening night.

The night before Liam had sat up until after midnight with his brother and sister-in-law and there had been in-depth conversations about both his relationship with Billy, as well as how he was going personally.

'We understand each other,' Liam said. 'We're able to help each other with the times we've had to live through. I've had a couple of bad moments, but with the extra counselling and a few different strategies in place, I really feel like I'm okay. When I go a bit quiet she knows and when she's troubled I can tell. It works well. We come from such different backgrounds and we're very different people, but then we also both have a strong connection to her people and homeland as well as sharing similar interests.'

'You seem to talk a lot together,' Chris said. 'I saw you both last night, you talked for hours.'

Liam chuckled. 'I used to think she was quiet, but now we're so comfortable with each other, Billy will talk and talk and talk.'

'Nothing wrong with that,' Kath interjected. 'We all love a good chat.'

'We know how you can talk.' Liam prodded her playfully in the ribs. 'You'd talk underwater. Kath punched him lightly on the arm, Liam grabbing her and giving her a huge hug.

'I love the fact that she talks to me. I've told her things I've never told anyone and she's the same

270

with me. It's a good combination, plus now she has all of you and Dad. It's an instant family for her.'

'She has no family of her own at all,' Kath said, her eyes filling with tears as she recounted some of the information that Billy had filled her in on. 'She told me how she had looked after herself since she was sixteen.'

'She has us now,' Liam hugged Kath. 'She's had it tough but as she says herself, it has made her a stronger person. I guess even in the worst cases there's hopefully just one person there who you can turn to. Like I had all of you.' Liam hugged Kath again, Chris also putting his arms around them both. It was a tight support team and Liam had never forgotten how Kath had saved him when he was younger. His brother's marriage had always been strong, and he hoped that one day he would have what they had. He wanted that closeness and with Billy he felt sure he would have it.

37

On the day of the exhibition Liam left early by himself, Billy travelling up to the city later with Kath and Chris. Of course Amanda would be there, and he knew that she made Billy nervous. Billy was aware that the relationship had ended a long time ago, but it was difficult sometimes, particularly during the last month, as Liam had been in direct communication with Amanda most days.

Today Billy wore a long, flowing dress, the patterns and colours accentuating the glow of her skin and litheness of her body. Several heads had turned when she entered the exhibition room, and Liam's breath was taken away as he watched her walk towards him. He gave her a kiss on the cheek and placed his arm around her waist, trying to put her at ease. It was obvious that she was nervous, and he wondered if some of that could be attributed to the unfriendly way that Amanda spoke to her. Cutting looks and sharp acidic words were Amanda's specialty. Thank goodness Kath and Chris were there to support Billy. Although Billy was well able to look after herself, Amanda had a way that could intimidate even the most confident person and he had noticed her barbed looks and comments towards Billy the day they had met in the studio.

Liam stayed with Billy and the others for as long as he could, enjoying having the family support. He also had a few nervous flutters as he watched people arrive and start looking at the paintings, large and prominently displayed on the otherwise stark gallery walls. It didn't take long for Amanda to find him. She kissed his cheek and then with only an abrupt hello to the others, stated in her businesslike manner that there were some buyers who wanted to talk to him. She linked her arm through his and led him over to the far side of the room.

★ ★ ★

'Don't worry about her,' Kath whispered in Billy's ear. 'She's an out and out bitch. I don't know what he ever saw in her. You'll find once this exhibition is over she'll be out of his life.'

'Thanks, Kath.' The two women linked arms and started walking around the perimeter of the room, taking their time to gaze up at the displayed works. Each painting hung in isolation, carefully positioned lights shining down, highlighting the expertise and professionalism in the works.

Soon they neared the paintings for which Billy had posed. 'Oh my God,' Billy said. 'They've got stickers on them.' She looked at the stickers on all three of them that signified they had already been sold.

An older man in a business-like suit came up behind them. 'Yes, afraid I was too late. I wanted the three of them also. Apparently, the same person bought all three.' He turned from looking at the painting to face them and held out his hand to Billy. 'If I'm not mistaken you're the beautiful lady in the paintings.'

Billy blushed. The crowd gathered were also gazing up at the paintings and then looking towards where she and Kath stood.

The older man talked almost to himself. 'It's just exquisite how he's captured the emotions in your face, the sensual position of your pose. I just asked the artist if he'd consider doing some more for me, but he said they're unique. Not to be repeated.'

Neither Billy nor Kath responded to the man's conversation, both of them peering up, transfixed at Liam's work.

Billy whispered to Kath. 'They look so different up on the wall, especially with the light on them. It's like you can see every inch of my skin.'

Kath giggled. 'Revel in it for goodness sake. They're absolutely beautiful. God, I'm so glad you didn't give in and pose nude for him.'

'Actually,' Billy whispered, 'I did let him do one, just for fun. Just a small one and it's to be mine. Something to keep and look back on when I'm old and wrinkly.'

They laughed together. 'Oh, that's quite romantic,' Kath said. 'How lovely to have.'

'I know, I actually love it and of course no-one else will ever see it. Liam promised it's just for me.'

Kath looked over to where her husband was standing talking to one of the regular buyers. 'I think we need a champagne to celebrate. Wait here and I'll get you one.'

Billy was absorbed with the paintings and didn't notice Amanda coming up behind her. The perfectly dressed woman stood next to her, also studying the pieces of art, her head tilting to the side as if to get a better view of the painting.

'You know it won't last, don't you,' Amanda said, continuing to look up, her pale hands tipped with bright red fingernail polish wrapped around an empty champagne flute.

Billy looked at her. There was a tightness around the woman's mouth and heavy make-up matched the stiff hairstyle that bobbed perfectly, blonde upon her shoulders. Her lips pursed tighter, bright red lipstick, thin and stretched as she looked down at Billy.

'What are you talking about?' Billy kept her reply short, not wanting to get into conversation.

'He's sleeping with you, isn't he? Do you think you'd be with him if you weren't worth painting? He's groomed you beautifully. Those paintings of you and your bare skin will be hanging in some random man's bedroom. Did he tell you that? I bet he didn't.' She bent over and whispered in Billy's ear, then turned to watch her reaction. 'Yes, I'm right, aren't I? Same for me, I shared his bed same as the others before. You're just a cog in the line-up of past models. Do you realise how much he gets paid for these paintings? He doesn't do it just for love you know. You do hold a lovely pose though, especially when you're naked.'

The colour in Billy's face had drained and she felt nauseous.

Amanda continued 'Oh, I see, so he didn't tell you that he'd shown me the nude one. Nice and small. Ah,' she laughed. 'Oh, you're so young and sweet. He said he'd finally talked you into it. Of course, he said it was because he loved you, and he would never show anyone else, it'd just be between you and him. A special art piece to keep and look back on when you're older.' Amanda smiled, her thinly pencilled eyebrows raised as she watched the changing expression on Billy's face.

'He would never have shown you. You're just making it up.' Billy drew herself up taller, trying not to let the other woman rattle her. 'It's none of your business what Liam or I do.'

Amanda's eyes narrowed, and her lips pursed. 'Wake up to yourself, honey. He's never going to settle for someone like you. He's used you, can't you see?'

Billy took deep breaths. 'It's not true,' she tried to speak evenly. 'We are friends. I trust him.'

Amanda spoke quickly as Kath started moving towards them. 'He will only stay with you until the next one comes along. Believe me there has been a long line of us. Nice to talk to you. Oh and by the way, next time get him to leave the beauty mark on your stomach out; it looks like a dirty smudge on the canvas.' She smiled sweetly before moving away to another group of people.

★ ★ ★

Kath passed Billy a drink. 'Are you okay?'

Billy's hands shook as anger flashed through her.

Tipping the glass up high she quickly drained its contents into her mouth before passing the glass back to Kath. Billy looked over to where Liam was standing, Amanda's arm was now linked firmly through his as they talked to a group who were

276

all laughing loudly and drinking champagne. She looked around for Matilda and her other friends, but they hadn't arrived yet.

She turned to Kath. 'I'm not feeling well. Can you just let them know that I've gone home. I'll be fine, I don't want to spoil anyone's night.'

Kath tried to grab her arm. 'Billy, what's wrong?'

'Nothing I promise. I just don't feel well. Please, I don't want anyone to leave. I'll be fine.'

'Let me come with you, I'll take you home. You're not going by yourself, you're very pale.'

'You need to be here for Liam,' she said. 'Please, I don't want a fuss. I'm okay. I just need to go home. Please, just let me go by myself.'

Billy quickly walked out through the gallery, making her way out of the building and onto the street before hailing a passing taxi.

★ ★ ★

It had taken Kath a while to find Liam who was in deep conversation with some of the guests.

He looked up as she joined the group and came up beside him.

'Billy's gone home. She said she was sick.'

'She was fine when she got here. Was it something she'd eaten?' He ran his hands through his hair, unsure of what was going on. 'Why didn't she come and tell me if she felt sick?'

Chris joined them. 'What the hell is going on? Billy just walked straight past me and out the door. She looked terrible.'

'She's sick,' Kath said. 'I might go back home also.'

277

'Are you sure it's not something Amanda said?' Chris asked. 'She was standing talking to Billy over there, just before you came back with the drinks.'

Liam straightened up. 'God, she's a bitch. That's what it'll be, she's not sick, Amanda has no doubt said something to upset her. Excuse me, you'll have to run the show because I'm going after Billy.' Pushing his way through the heavy glass doors out onto the pavement outside he looked up and down the street for Billy. Yared, Nadir and Matilda were just making their way up the street, their car parked further down. They greeted Liam, the men dressed in their best suits, Matilda colourful in a bright dress, her hair up high in a bun and bright bangles clanging noisily on her arm.

'Liam, we just saw Billy getting into a taxi. What's going on?'

'I think that Amanda has said something to upset her. Look, I'm really sorry, but I'm going back home to find her. I'm not sure what the hell is going on. Go inside and have a look around. Kath and Chris are in there.'

★ ★ ★

By the time he got someone to move the cars that were parked behind his in the loading dock, another half hour had rolled by. It wasn't far back home but the traffic had built up and it seemed like hours had gone past since he had left the gallery. Finally, he drove up the driveway to his property. During the drive home he had phoned Amanda on her mobile and he could tell from her answers to his questions that she had filled Billy in on some of his past relationships. 'It's just the truth, Liam, she needed to know that there have been others before her. I didn't realise it was so serious between the two of you. I thought it was just another fling.'

He had hung up on her and then tried to get the sound of her voice out of his head.

★ ★ ★

Casso barked from inside the cabin and Liam knocked angrily on the locked door. Eventually Billy's voice sounded from inside. 'Go away. You should not have come back here. You belong back with all of them at the gallery.'

'Open the door. You owe me an explanation.'

'I don't owe you anything. I'm leaving. I'll be gone by the morning and then you can look for someone else who'll pose nude for you.'

Liam jiggled the door handle, his strong body pressing against the door until it opened. *So much for the security of a locked door*, he thought. 'What the hell are you on about. I know Amanda said something to you. Surely, you're not going to believe anything she says. She's jealous, and she'll make things up to upset you.'

'Don't yell at me.' Her eyes flashed angrily and he watched as she continued to pack her belongings into a large bag.

'Where the hell do you think you're going?'

'I'm free to go where I want.'

He moved over to her, his hands finding her arms, his hurt eyes looking into her angry ones.

'Billy, what's the matter? What did Amanda say to you?'

'You should know. She said you tell her everything.'

'That's absolute bullshit. She means nothing to me. She never did.'

'Then why did you tell her that I'd do anything for you, including posing nude? Why did you tell her about the other night in the studio when I let you paint me? You said that was between you and me. She told me you had shown her the painting and it was obvious from what she said that she'd seen it.'

'She's lied to you Billy. I never told her or any-one else about the other night. I swear on my mother's life. That was between you and me. The painting is hidden; no one will ever see it except the two of us. She's lied to you.'

'Then how did she know that I'd posed naked?'

'I don't know. She's probably guessed. At the beginning when you used to pose for me I told her that I had asked you to, but you wouldn't. I'd say she knows we're in a relationship and that you may have consented. Please believe me. I would never betray you. You have to trust me.'

'She said that those other paintings of me would be hanging in some random man's bedroom. Why didn't you let me know about that, I never even thought about who'd buy them.'

Liam tried to draw her in closer to him, but her body was rigid and she pulled back from him.

Anger flooded though him as she continued to accuse him of lying to her.

'You're not listening to me.' Liam said. 'I've

told you, I didn't let her see the painting or even tell her about it. If you're not going to trust me, then perhaps there's no point in our relationship. As if I would betray you like that.'

'You can go back to your stupid exhibition. Make all the money out of your paintings, find yourself someone else to pose for you, because tomorrow, I'm going. From the sounds of it it's usual for you to have a progressive string of affairs with your models anyway.'

'That's bullshit. Before Amanda I'd only ever had a few girlfriends when I was younger. She's the only one before you that I've ever had a serious relationship with. If you're going to believe what she's told you, then I can't help you. If you want to leave, then leave.' He had shouted the last words at her and Casso growled as he stood between Billy's legs. 'And you can take the bloody dog with you. I couldn't care less.'

38

Billy stood still, the tears streaming down her cheeks for a long time after Liam had slammed the door shut. She tried to get her breath, her chest heaving from the anger that had built up in the past hour. The words that Amanda had spoken were now jumbled and she tried to think about what Liam had said. Was it possible that Amanda had guessed that Billy would eventually give in? Was she making it all up?

She had described the painting perfectly; it was obvious that she had seen it and that Liam had shown her. But where was the painting now? It was only a small one and they had both laughed as Liam had painted her, sprawled out on the bed, her legs positioned so that nothing was showing below but her arms high above her head, revealing the fullness of her breasts as she stretched out. He had commented on how much he loved the small birthmark on her stomach, her beauty spot he had called it.

It had been fun posing for him, knowing that no one else would ever see the finished work. He had promised it would be hers to keep, that it was a special painting that only the two of them would ever know about. When they were old they could look back on it and remember the fun they'd had during the sitting. It would be a memory of how beautiful and youthful her body had been when he had first met her.

Now perhaps the entire world had seen it. Nausea rose in her throat and her imagination ran wild. Liam and Amanda looking at it together, laughing about the imperfections of her body, Amanda gloating over the fact that he had shown her the painting.

Picking Casso up she headed back to the bedroom, curling up into a ball and pulling the covers over her as she cried into the little dog's matted fur. In the morning she would leave. It was over.

★ ★ ★

By the time Liam walked back into the gallery he had regained his composure, but he was till trying to figure out how Amanda had known about their secret painting. He was also furious that Billy would believe someone else and obviously had no trust in him or his intentions. The gallery was full, the other artists also bringing with them a large number of friends and family to support their exhibitions.

Liam strode over to where his friends were gathered. 'Trouble in paradise?' Matilda asked him.

'Yeah, you could say that. Anyway, we're here to celebrate, let me fill your glasses up. Thank you all for coming.'

It would have been easier not to return to the exhibition and his instincts had been to drive directly down to the beach and walk along the dunes, wallowing in his anger and refusing to face anyone. However, he knew that everyone had made an effort to come and he didn't want to let them down. They had all supported him and helped him with the collection and he wanted to make sure they enjoyed the night. There wasn't much he could do if Billy had no trust in him.

Kath eventually made her way over to him. 'Did you sort that out?' she asked with a frown as she looked around for Billy.

'No, Amanda got to Billy first and it doesn't matter what I tell her, she thinks I've lied to her. She doesn't trust me, and you know, that's so important to me. What sort of relationship can it be if she doesn't trust me?'

'Amanda must have given her a reason to make her react like that. What do you think she said?'

Liam leaned closer and whispered, 'Last week we had a bit of fun and I talked Billy into letting me paint her without any clothes on.'

He scowled when Kath raised her eyebrows. 'I know that, Billy told me she had let you paint her, she sounded happy about it.'

'It was just a bit of fun and I promised I wouldn't show anyone. Anyway, Amanda somehow has guessed what's gone on and has told Billy that I've shown her the picture and shared it with some of the others here at the gallery.

'How the hell did she know? That's a pretty good guess. She wouldn't just be able to make that up. Are you sure she hasn't overheard you and Billy talking about it or somehow seen it?'

'I don't think so, there's no way she could have found out.' He shook his head, still trying to get the events into some sort of order.

His father and Chris walked over to them. 'Where's Billy?'

Liam filled him in on the unfolding events.

284

'I wondered where she'd gone, John said. 'Amanda must have really got under her skin and convinced her that she'd seen the painting. Where did you hide it?' John asked.

'Well, I meant to take it up to my bedroom, but I haven't got around to it yet. It's hidden under a blue scarf in the studio at home.'

'Could Amanda have seen it when she called in last Thursday?' Chris asked. 'Remember last Thursday when you all went out shopping and Liam was helping Yared at work. She called in. I saw her red car pulling out of the driveway as I came back up through the path from the beach. She wouldn't have seen me because she was parked near the studio and then took off in the car before I came up to the end of the track. I'm guessing that she had been in the studio to pick up something for this exhibition. Maybe the pamphlets or the other publicity posters that were in there.'

Liam closed his eyes and shook his head. 'Thank God, this is the last time I have to have anything to do with her.'

At that moment Amanda beckoned for him to take the microphone and make a welcoming speech. He smiled sweetly at her, even though his jaw was tight with tension. This was not the time or place to make a scene and he knew after tonight he would never need to speak to her again.

There was a string of people to thank and Liam did so quickly, making the speech short. 'Oh, and before I finish I just wanted to thank the person who bought the three paintings titled, 'The Butterfly Girl.' The proceeds, plus the commission that would normally go to the organisers here,' he nodded his head towards Amanda, whose mouth dropped open, 'has graciously been donated to a charity that helps refugees with extra educational needs. I'd like to thank Amanda and the buyer for their amazing generosity.' The announcement was met with loud applause. The paintings had sold for five thousand dollars each.

Amanda stood next to him, her whispered words coming out through tight lips. 'You can't do that. I thought you'd share some of the commission with me.'

'I can, and I just did, it's been publicly stated. The proceeds and commission will go to the charity. You've already been paid for the work that you've done.'

John came to stand beside him as Amanda turned and walked away.

Father and son stood together, looking up at the paintings of Billy. 'You bought them, didn't you?' John said.

'I did. I couldn't stand the thought of them hanging on anyone else's wall. Now I'm not sure if I'll be able to hang them on mine either. Billy said she was leaving. We've had a terrible fight and I've probably said things that I shouldn't have.'

'Well, son, you better get your arse into gear and get along home. You have some explaining to do and hopefully you can work everything out. We'll finish up here for you, now get going.'

39

Billy heard Liam's car drive in, however she wasn't quick enough to get up and lock the door. Besides he had just broken it down earlier. She was still huddled up in the bed, her eyes sore from crying, her body exhausted from the emotions that had flooded through her.

Liam sat on the bed beside her. 'I know you're not asleep.' The moon shone in through the window, lighting the room enough that she could see his face.

Billy stayed still, and closed her eyes.

'Talk to me Billy, we can work it out. I can explain what's happened. She came here on Thursday. Chris was coming back up from the beach and saw her leaving the studio. She drove off before he could talk to her. The painting is still down there in the studio where we left it. I know that's my fault, but I'd covered it up with your scarf. I didn't expect anyone to go in there, except you and me. You know I never let anyone else in there. She came to pick up some of the pamphlets for the exhibition. I'm sorry, but I did leave it there and she must have seen it.'

She opened her eyes and looked hard at him, knowing that the doubt and sadness was reflected in her stare.

'I'm not sure what she said that made you realise she'd seen it, but you have to believe me. I would never betray you or show that painting to anyone. You're not just another model and you need to realise her words are lies. You knew I had been with her previously and I have had a few girlfriends many years ago, but they weren't ever women who had posed for me. Those other relationships were never serious.'

Billy narrowed her eyes.

'I've never been in love before. Until now, until I met you. I love you, Billy.'

Her hand came up from under the covers and she tried to wipe the tears that she was trying so hard to stop. Liam pulled her up towards him, holding her body against his own, stroking her arms as she regained her composure, his gaze holding hers.

'She must have seen the painting. She mentioned my birthmark, that's how I knew she was telling the truth. She said that you had shown it to her and that you'd looked at it together.'

She started to cry again, and Liam held her close.

'We need to put this behind us. You need to know I would never lie to you or betray you. We are one.'

He touched her hair and ran his fingers over her lips, holding her gently as he leaned forward and softly kissed her. Their faces were close to each other, and a feeling of calm washed over her as they looked at each other.

'Do you understand, Billy? I will never lie to you.' Liam's voice was soft but firm.

Billy took deep breaths and closed her eyes. When she re-opened them, she looked directly into Liam's searching eyes. 'I will trust you. You have always been truthful to me.'

Liam smiled and kissed her face. He stroked her hair, his voice husky as he pulled back and looked steadily into her eyes. 'I love you Billy. Nobody can come between us.'

Billy reached out and ran her finger along his lips. 'I love you too, Liam.'

★ ★ ★

Liam sat upright, pulling Billy up to a sitting position next to him. 'I want to ask you something Billy. I need to know.' He waited for a while before continuing. 'Will you marry me?'

He had never seen her eyes so wide, the look on her face one of shock. She opened her mouth, but no words came out.

He smiled, his hands grabbing hers, her small fingers closing around his.

His words were loud and clear. 'Billy, will you marry me? Will you be my wife?'

There was no hesitation as she answered him. 'I will. I will marry you.'

Casso barked excitedly as Liam pulled Billy to him, his voice loud and excited. 'You will? Oh my God, I just asked you to marry me and I don't even have a ring.'

She smiled and then laughed loudly as she wrapped her arms around him. 'I don't need a ring. I just need you.'

Liam drew her body in close to his and they pressed up against each other as he folded her into his arms. Her lips were warm and soft beneath his, her hands smooth as they stroked his face. Casso bounded excitedly over the two of them, only jumping down from the bed when Liam finally got up and opened the bedroom door. Casso obediently jumped off the bed and trotted out of the room. Billy giggled as Liam shut the bedroom door behind the dog, wrapping her arms around him as he lay back down beside her.

40

Their wedding took place six months later and Liam's brothers had arrived with their wives, girl-friends and families. The house was full to capacity and guests had been accommodated in both cab-ins, the main house, as well as John's van which was parked down the side of the yard. Annika and Lottie had helped with the planning and this morning everyone had helped position the white chairs on the newly mowed grass.

Billy and Liam had spent the months prepar-ing the garden to look its best and today the blue sky provided a perfect backdrop to the colour-ful blooms that filled the garden. Purple wisteria dripped down from the beams of the pergola, reminding Liam of the first time when Billy had sat and talked to him under the flowering vine.

Today he stood nervously, fidgeting with his tie as Kath tried to pin the spray of baby's breath to his shirt. 'You don't scrub up too bad,' she said, her eyes misty with unshed happy tears.

Liam stopped fixing his tie and held her close to him. 'Hey, Kath, don't lose it on me. You'll set me off.' He wiped his own eyes, looking at her intently. 'You know I wouldn't be here today if it wasn't for you lot and Dad. You never gave up on me, you were always there.'

'I like to think I'm the sister you never had.'

'You are my sister, and for a long time you were also my mother. Mum would thank you for that.'

'Your mum would be proud of you and she would love Billy,' Kath whispered as she wiped away her tears. 'I never thought this day would come. We're all so happy for you.'

'You two were my role models, you and Chris. I always wanted to be like you were, in love and happy and kind to each other.' As they hugged, Liam's emotions threatened to bubble over.

'Right,' Kath said, 'No more tears, we have a wedding to get through yet. I think somehow I'm going to need more tissues.'

★ ★ ★

The guests started filling up the seats and Yared and Nadir, dressed in matching suits, came to stand beside Chris, completing the party of groomsmen. Both men were unusually quiet, and Liam could see they were nervous and unsure about the run of events.

'You two look like you're going to a funeral,' Chris said as he positioned the two men in their place. 'Smile, relax, enjoy, garden weddings are casual and you both look great. This will be your first Aussie wedding. You will remember this day.'

Nadir and Yared nodded nervously, standing upright and tall, smiling at Chris as he took his place beside them. Everyone was now in their positions and the guests stood as a light melody drifted across the backyard, signalling the arrival of the bride.

★ ★ ★

Billy had chosen her favourite song to accompany her, as she walked down the paved aisle. Liam turned around, watching as his father walked slowly from around the back of the house, standing and waiting for the signal to begin the ceremony. Billy appeared next to John, their arms linking as they smiled at each other.

Only last week they had laid a path of pavers that stretched from the back of the house to where he now stood. As the music filled the air, Kath and Meron walked slowly up the path, followed by two of Nadir's daughters. Liam held back a chuckle as he watched the serious faces of the two young girls, their steps timed like marching soldiers, their hands tightly clutching their bouquets of flowers. The wedding party walked along the aisle created between the white chairs until they were standing up the front near Liam and the groomsmen. Once they were in position, everyone turned around and Liam held his breath in awe, as Billy, holding tightly to John's arm, began the slow walk towards him.

Her dress was ivory and contrasted exquisitely with her skin. She looked nervous and focused her eyes on Liam, smiling back at him as his face broke into a wide grin. Her hair was tied up loosely with tendrils falling onto her bare shoulders. Tiny white and purple flowers poked out from the cluster of hair atop her head and in her hands she held a matching bouquet, a mixture of delicate white baby's breath flowers, broken up by fine strands of purple wisteria. The fitted long dress accentuated her slender figure, and Liam couldn't take his eyes off her as she came to stand next to him.

John kissed Billy softly on the cheek before passing her hand into Liam's, signalling the celebrant to begin the ceremony. As Billy turned to pass her bouquet to the flower girl, Liam caught a glimpse of the back of her dress. A V-shaped cut-out, lined by exquisite pearl buttons ran down to the centre of her back, showing off the beautiful lines that had originally drawn him to her.

He took her hands in his and they looked at each other, both smiling as they relaxed in the familiarity of each other's gaze. Billy pressed her fingers into Liam's hand and he wrapped his hand around hers, giving it a reassuring squeeze back.

★ ★ ★

The service was personal and heartfelt and there wasn't a dry eye between the guests or bridal party as it drew to a close. It was, as the celebrant said, a coming together of two people who were not only deeply in love but who were also soul mates and would be there for each other through the good times and the bad.

Both Liam and Billy spoke the words that they had so carefully written to each other in the weeks leading up to the wedding; their vows of matrimony, confirming their devotion and love for each other. When it came to the time for the groom to kiss his new bride, an ache filled Liam's chest; an overriding love for Billy who he knew he wanted to spend the rest of his life with.

Billy was also surrounded by love, not only from Liam, who she had declared she would follow to the end of the earth, but also the warmth of a family she was now a part of. As he bent down to kiss her she looked up into his eyes, the look of love between the two obvious to all who watched. The mesmerising long kiss was only broken by the raucous calls of the guests, cheering and popping confetti containers high into the air, the tiny colourful pieces of paper floating down onto the new bride and groom.

Casso leapt from his front seat position on Ruby's lap and twirled excitedly, yapping noisily at the bride and groom's feet. A blue ribbon collar twisted with flowers stayed intact around his neck as the photographer captured the perfect moment; a photo that would be treasured for a lifetime by the new couple.

The reception was full of laughter, love and dancing, the music continuing long into the night. There had been speeches from family members as well as Atifa and Matilda who both spoke about the friendship and love that Billy and Liam had brought into their lives. John and Liam made speeches and there had not been a dry eye left between any of them.

Everyone had danced and the children all joined in, keeping the others entertained with their fabulous dance moves. Liam and Billy waltzed around the dance floor as though they had done it a hundred times before and Casso, who had eventually been let out to run around, yapped at their heels, his blue ribbon now flowerless and covered in mud.

A contented John looked on, overjoyed with the events. His dance instructions had been worth it. Not once had Liam stood on her toes. He also took the opportunity to dance with Billy, holding her firmly as he waltzed her around the floor, the two of them hugging for a long time at the end of the dance.

Liam had found the right moment halfway through the night to whisper in Billy's ear. Tomorrow they would be leaving on their honeymoon, but before they went he had a surprise for her. He waited until she gathered up her long dress, helping her hold it up so she could walk over the grass towards the house.

Over the last week they had moved most of her belongings across and when they returned she would be living with Liam in the main house. Finally, a place he said, that she could call her own home. Liam led her through the kitchen where Kath and some of the other guests were standing, laughing and talking with John as they waited for food that was heating in the oven. Kath looked up in surprise at them. 'What are you two up to? You look like you're sneaking away?'

Liam stopped for a moment. 'I have a wedding present for Billy. I just want to show her. It's in the lounge. Can you just give us a moment? We'll show you once I've given it to her.'

Billy closed her eyes when he asked her to, taking tiny steps as he led her into the lounge. He stood behind her, positioning her and reminding her not to open her eyes until he said. He whispered in her ear and she slowly opened her eyes.

He had faced her towards the wall, towards the print that she had always admired; the family playing cricket in the backyard.

She looked immediately as she always did, to

the figure of Liam's mother, sitting to the side watching her beloved family, together, happy and having fun. The painting had been moved a little to the side and now her eyes were drawn to another framed picture that was the same size as the cricket print. This one was a painting and she instantly recognised that the work was done by Liam.

Her hands come up over her mouth and she gasped as she looked up at the present he was giving her on their wedding day. Tears streamed down her face and his arms wrapped around her from behind, his chin resting on the top of her head. 'Do you like it?'

'Oh my God. I can't believe it. It's my memory.'

The painting had been done in the same style as the cricket print, and although the landscape was very different, it was as if they went together as a pair. The new painting was set in a dusty dry area, only a few tufts of grass growing on a slope to the side. In the distance, steep mountains rose up, the sky a dusty blue above them.

Two young boys, both dressed in cream loose pants and long dress-style shirts ran barefoot across the rocks and dirt, their hands held out as they grasped the strings of their kites. The kites were colourful and flew high, their fluttering sails standing out against the blue sky.

Another boy stood nearby, his hands shielding his eyes as he watched the kites soaring high in the sky. He was older than the others and wore grey trousers and a long-sleeved shirt with a sleeveless tunic over the top. Next to where he stood, sat a tiny girl, her head covered in an olive-green shawl with white dots on it.

A tiny piece of dark hair poked out on the top of her forehead and even though she was only young, her face was Billy's. She wore a burgundy-coloured long dress and her feet were covered in tiny delicate Afghan slippers, their colours vibrant against the dust. Her petite face was pointed up towards the sky, happy and delighted as she watched the kite soaring above her.

A fourth boy stood off to the side, his clothes similar but more colourful than the others. He looked a bit older than the little girl and his hair stuck out wildly, his face intent on what he was doing. One bare foot was standing solid in the dirt, but the other leg was kicked up, a cloud of dust rising into the air, showing the way of the wind, the direction in which the kite flew.

The picture was full of life and although there were only glimpses of the boys' faces, their features were similar to Billy's and their ages were staggered.

Liam unwrapped his arms from her, watching her intently as she moved towards the painting. Her delicate fingers ran gently over the figures, one by one, her voice just audible as she whispered. 'Ismail, Basir, Abdul...' Her hand finally moved onto the last figure and she took a deep breath, 'and Haji.' A lingering touch, her hand resting on the boy. 'Of course, he would be next to me,' she said as she turned to Liam. 'He always looked after me. He used to carry me high on his shoulders. I remember his face. I have it in my memory.'

She reached for Liam's hand, her other hand

running lightly over the title of the painting, *Kick the Dust*. 'You have brought my family back to me. Now I can look at them every day.'

Liam leaned down and kissed her, pulling her body towards him. 'You have brought love and peace back to me.'

Epilogue

High on a sand dune a group of small boys licked their fingers, held them in the air and tested the wind. One of them picked some sand up, tossing it skywards. Waves crashed noisily onto the beach, the sky a vivid blue, the sand white and pure. Soon, four colourful kites rose steadily in the sky, their tails weaving and twirling as the wind turned them in every different direction. They lifted higher as the boys ran faster, their backs now turning in the direction of the wind.

The kites ascended quickly, rising above a lake that backed onto the dunes. They twirled freely in the air, the only obstacles a few seagulls that swooped and called out as they weaved in between the kites. The wind picked up and one of the kites lifted abruptly then spiralled downwards toward the dunes. The young boy who held the string for the kite jerked it to clear the kite in the air again. But the wind was stronger and the colourful kite, its tail streaming out behind it, plummeted to the ground, its nose plunging into the sand.

The boys yelled and laughed loudly as the youngest boy chased the track of the downed kite. He gathered it up in his arms and stopped for a moment to breathe in the fresh air, the invigorating feeling of sea spray and salt, cool on his skin.

In the lake below the dunes, a man with a strong muscled build swam with a woman, her dark hair knotted up in a bun, her arms thrashing the water, in an attempt at the butterfly stroke. The couple stopped swimming to watch the boy rescue the downed kite from its pinned position in the dunes, then floated on their backs, their eyes following the kites flying above them.

The boy re-joined the others and the man tossed back his head and laughed as the woman splashed water at him as he jokingly imitated her unusual style of swimming. They waved at the four boys who waved back, laughing and calling out, their voices carried away with the wind. The youngest boy held onto the string of his kite with one hand, so he could blow the couple a kiss with his other. They both blew one back, watching the kites, smiling at the cries of enjoyment and the colours of the bright kites against the clear Queensland sky. They laughed as all the boys blew them kisses.

'Mum, Dad, watch us!'

The kites flew high in the sky again and the man and woman watched as their sons scrambled up the sand hills, one stopping to help the other, all of them laughing loudly as they fell over each other before disappearing over the top of the dunes.

Inspiration for *Kick the Dust*

In 2015 I took time off from my regular teaching job. I was lucky enough to teach English as a second language at a school in Logan, that had over 400 newly arrived refugees. It was to be a decisive moment in my life and I have never forgotten the amazing resilience and commitment of the students and the dedication and professionalism of the teachers who worked there.

One day I taught the students about the weather and the wind. Two young boys who had only recently arrived in Australia became very excited and jumped up and down, waving their arms in the air. Their bright green eyes were wide and their voices animated, because now they could teach me something they knew about. Using very limited English and enthusiastic actions, they described how they tested the direction of the wind when they flew their kites in Afghanistan.

'We fly kites, Miss. We fly kites in Afghanistan and we kick the dust, Miss. We kick the dust to see which way the wind blows.'

We do hope that you have enjoyed
reading this large print book.

Did you know that all of our titles
are available for purchase?

We publish a wide range of high
quality large print books including:
Romances, Mysteries, Classics
General Fiction
Non Fiction and Westerns

Special interest titles available in
large print are:
The Little Oxford Dictionary
Music Book, Song Book
Hymn Book, Service Book

Also available from us courtesy of
Oxford University Press:
Young Readers' Dictionary
(large print edition)
Young Readers' Thesaurus
(large print edition)

For further information or a free
brochure, please contact us at:
Ulverscroft Large Print Books Ltd.,
The Green, Bradgate Road, Anstey,
Leicester, LE7 7FU, England.
Tel: (00 44) 0116 236 4325
Fax: (00 44) 0116 234 0205

Other titles published by Ulverscroft:

TWO HEARTBEATS

Rhonda Forrest

When Jess heads west for a fresh start in a small mining town, she soon learns that the dusty outback plains are a far cry from her former life in the city – but she finds herself loving the isolation and local people she lives with. All she has to do is keep her head down and work hard to create a better life for herself and Johnno, the only person she has ever truly cared about. As relationships develop and change, Jess discovers the warmth of a welcoming family and a circle of friends who look out for her. However, problems arise when she collides with her new boss Daniel, who is suspicious of her background story. Has Jess told him everything, or is there a hidden secret to justify his earlier distrust of her?